THE COUNSELOR'S

Heart

Decision

JEANIE CLAYTON

Publishing Coordinator & Book Designer – Sharon Kizziah-Holmes

Indie Pub Press
Springfield, Missouri

ISBN -13: 978-1-970560-09-1

Acknowledgments

A huge thank you to Kathy Garnsey and Sharon Kizzian-Holmes for their much-needed guidance.

Another thanks to Chris for his tutoring on the computer.

And always much gratitude to my family and friends for their support.

i

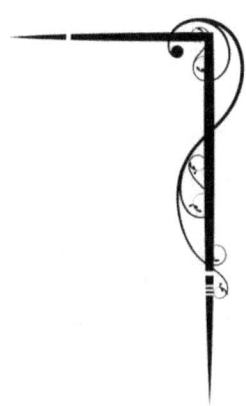

Chapter 1

April Palmer didn't dare move. The teenager's heart pounded against her chest after the stream of light from the opening of her bedroom door awakened her. At the very moment she saw Mrs. Green and a stranger walk in, she quickly shut her eyes and pretended to be asleep. A few seconds passed before she got brave and opened her eyelids wide enough to see, then held her breath. The tall man and her foster mom walked over to where her friend Sandy slept. They woke her up, pulled her from the bed and led the girl out of the room and then shut the bedroom door.

A thousand questions raced through April's mind. What did they plan to do to her roommate? Where were they taking her? A scarier thought raced through her mind. What if they came back for her? She heard whispers in the hallway but couldn't understand anything they said. Terrified, April shook uncontrollably. Did she follow them downstairs now and ask Mrs. Green what was going on, or remain in her bed until morning? The woman's strict rules for the children to behave, follow instructions, and not ask questions, shouted in her head. Hatefulness oozed from her, and none of them ever saw her being nice. Not one of them possessed the guts to defy her.

April had lived in a few horrible temporary homes growing up, yet this place terrified her. Some homes on the surface were good until they weren't. A few places let you play outside with other kids and, once in a while, a foster parent hugged you. This substitute mom didn't care about a kid's welfare, only provided a bed and two meals a day, if you called dry cereal and canned spaghetti dinner meals. She made up her mind to stay in the bedroom.

April realized children disappeared at intervals from the system, just usually not without notice. Marsha never came back from school one afternoon. The pretty blond tried to be a friend and followed the other kids around, which aggravated them. Since Marsha left, April kind of missed her. Sandy, a shy, quiet, blond and the first girl to leave the foster home in the middle of the night, caused no trouble. From what April observed, it didn't seem she left of her own free will.

With the bedroom door closed again, she rushed out of bed and over to the window. She heard the front door squeak open and then shut. A car's engine started up in the driveway, and she saw a car pull away from the curb through the dim moonlight. The sole sound left in the room—silence. She got back in bed, pulled the covers over her head, and tried to sleep.

Sunlight peeked through the faded curtains and woke her the next morning. April sat up and glanced at the empty bed beside her in despair. She put on her thrift-store clothes and went downstairs, ready to push Mrs. Green for answers about last night. She rushed into the outdated kitchen and took a seat at the rickety old table with the other kids, picked up the box of cornflakes to pour a bowl full of the cereal and asked, "Where did Sandy go?"

Before the woman answered her, one of the other girls spoke up. "Yeah, where is Sandy? She went to bed last night with us."

"Stop asking if you know what's good for you."

April lifted her chin and looked directly at the foster mom. "We have a right to know. She's our friend."

"Sandy went to a different home."

The severity in Mrs. Green's voice didn't surprise April when the woman claimed Sandy left voluntarily. They took no one in the middle of the night.

Answers wouldn't change if she kept pressing. Instead, April walked on to school with a heavy heart. In the halls between classes, whispers about Sandy's disappearance circulated among the students. She paid little attention to the rumors until she heard Mrs. Green and the foster home she lived in mentioned and curiously asked some of the other kids what they were talking about. They told her how some foster girls were being forced to become prostitutes, then their pimps got them hooked on drugs. This information worried her.

A couple of days later, April stopped at the local market on her way home from school. She liked to look at the magazine covers and fantasize about being rich enough one day to buy pretty clothes similar to what the celebrities wore. Her daydream would become a reality someday. It just wasn't clear yet how.

The second the bell above the door rang, April automatically looked up from the shelves full of pretty dreams in surprise. Marsha stood in a too-short skirt and an out of style blouse, which left most of her breasts exposed. The former roommate looked nervous, thinner, and her pale face appeared to have bruises. She walked over to the girl she hadn't seen in weeks. "Hey Marsha, do you remember me?"

"Hi April! Of course, I remember you."

She couldn't help herself and bombarded Marsha with questions. "What happened? We asked about you. Did you go to another home like Mrs. Green said? Because now Sandy is gone too. Do you know anything about what's going on in our house? I'm scared something will happen to me next."

Marsha moved closer. "Get out of the place while you can. I don't want you to end up like me."

Even in a murmur, her friend's warning became impossible to ignore. The girl looked over her shoulder and appeared to be afraid of something. Then, an older guy walked up to them, grabbed Marsha's arm, and dragged her away before April asked anything else.

She walked back to the rundown foster home and entered her cramped room with the worn-out carpet and musty scents lingering from the locked windows' lack of fresh air, even more concerned and also confused. First, from the disappearances of roommates and then the rumors at school of drugs. She wondered if this was what Marsha had warned her about. She sat on the lumpy twin-sized bed, frightened more than the other night, scared enough to understand, danger grew closer. If Mrs. Green helped the stranger take Sandy from her bed, then she might not be safe either for long. Did she dare risk staying, or should she leave, like Marsha suggested?

She wasn't about to let her many dreams get stolen. Finding a plan was the problem she faced. What to do when she left, where to go to be safe, and how to survive on the streets? Using the threadbare blanket she wrapped around herself for comfort, she came up with an idea that had to succeed. Go to her classes the next day and then simply disappear. She figured they wouldn't look for a seventeen-year-old. She pulled the mattress up enough to reach in and grab her stash of money. The forty dollars she had earned from babysitting at other foster homes wouldn't last long, but there were always shelters she could rely on. With determination, she stuffed a change of clothes in her secondhand denim backpack along with a jacket and a couple of keepsakes dear to her, then finished her homework before going down for dinner.

April left school the next afternoon and didn't look back. The sheer size of Oklahoma City allowed her to disappear and start over. She needed to make it work. She wanted to survive, though not by being a prostitute in a stranger's bed or on the arm of someone like Marsha was forced to do.

The foster home April escaped from hadn't been in the best area. Living in this older part of the city, though, might prove to be another matter. She looked around and saw most people dressed in ratty clothes. Others clutched shopping bags with all their possessions. She feared her new lifestyle. For now, anyway.

Traffic noise, horns honking, engines idling, and people everywhere surrounded her, which made her wonder if she could fit in somewhere. She watched people enter the brick-faced building down the sidewalk. Surprise and relief swept over her when she read the sign on the front door, which welcomed anyone who needed food or help.

April wrinkled her nose at the smell of stale sweat and the stickiness of dirty floors. From inside, she took in her new surroundings. She didn't want to stand out like a newbie, but people shoved her into a line before she adjusted. As she grabbed a tray, she moved along the serving line, where others stood filling dishes behind a counter. With a plate of food, she found a chair at one end of the wobbly table and sat. People scarcely glanced at her when she picked up her spoon and started eating the chicken pie. A volunteer came around and stopped beside her. "Do you need anything?"

"By chance, are there empty beds tonight? This is my first night here, and I don't really know what to do."

The woman nodded her head, patted April on the shoulder. "Yes, we have one for you here, and you'll be safe. Don't worry."

April, relieved, smiled at the woman. "Thank you."

Fear of the unknown kept her awake most of the first night with the crowded room full of people who snored and made other noises once the lights dimmed. Positioned against the wall, the small army cot left her no space to turn over. She stared at the stained yellow ceiling and realized that this new world she had walked into would likely take some getting used to. Being on her own, had she traded one danger for another? Possibly. Then vowed it wouldn't be forever.

She knew better than to cry or to feel sorry for herself. Despite life's difficulties, the choice to flee was hers. She had been a frightened five-year-old with shaggy red hair – a little girl left behind by her own mother, the last time she shed tears.. She put that little girl in the past. Unquestionably, her exact recourse, stubbornness.

Street life proved harder than she imagined. It didn't take long either for her to learn most people left you alone if you kept your head down and your mouth shut. Businesses practically threw you out the door, not wanting your type around. Some paranoid owners even followed you up and down the aisles to make sure nothing jumped into your hands or your backpack.

Out here, you became invisible, simply another kid on the sidewalk. Occasionally, a group attempted to persuade her to join them and abandon the streets. April couldn't and didn't trust anyone except herself. No one had asked her where she came from after living on the streets for an entire month. A good sign, right?

While she drank coffee in the shelter's lobby, where she had stayed the night before, she couldn't shake the sadness of a stark revelation. Everyone stood in line for the basics, from food to a bed, and this seemed to be her new norm. Forced to use locker room style showers from a place down the street, April missed her privacy. She brushed her clean hair, grateful for the smell of fresh soap and for the old unsoiled clothes they provided. A baggy, worn pair of jeans and a too-tight T-shirt. Thankfully, at least the underwear fit. She grabbed a few sandwiches and cookies—free for the taking—on her way out.

People crowded the sidewalk, waiting to get in the door, the instant she tried to leave. She nodded and then veered away from the few familiar faces. She considered the street people isolated, not dangerous, although she observed other homeless people stealing from each other. This showed her the need to be vigilant about her meager possessions: a small necklace one nice foster mom had given her, and the stuffed bear she carried when her mother left her, valuable merely to herself.

Because she felt safe there, she visited the nearby library. They usually let you read a book with little hassle. On other occasions, it became less complicated to go to a park and hang out. You quickly learned which places welcomed you and which ones to avoid, especially since she appeared older than her actual age. Or possibly because no one really cared. The latter choice possibly became the right answer.

Later, April left the library and went to one of her favorite parks in the city. The older place, almost neglected, provided comfortable places to relax. Hidden benches sprinkled throughout the paths beckoned her to sit. The sky clouded over with the threat of a shower. She really enjoyed clean, dry clothes and hoped the rain held off until nightfall. The day sped by for her, having visited the shelter, then the library and now the park. She left her seat and walked along the path, minding her own business, and munched on a free cookie. It wouldn't be long until darkness settled in, making the area unsafe for her.

Before April roamed beyond the tree-lined borders, a man stumbled on the walkway ahead of her. Two youths whom she saw in the area before followed him. If she didn't intervene, this unaware guy faced trouble. Passing by the two teenagers, she caught up to him before they stole from him or did something worse. Putting her arm through the crook of his elbow, she quietly said, "Keep walking with me," then turned back towards the boys with a grin. They recognized her from the shelter and presumed she scored a John. A sigh of relief escaped her chest as the two juveniles veered away.

Once the boys stayed out of sight, she paused and looked closer at the man she rescued and found herself unable to look away. Her pulse sped up, and a tingle of excitement moved through her. His clothing looked expensive, which added to his appeal. She smelled the alcohol on his breath and knew why he hadn't noticed anyone behind him.

Many people on the streets were cautious, but an introduction seemed necessary before she continued walking with him. She had no plans to share her real name and instead opted to use her middle one. "Hi, my name is Maria. If you stay by my side, I'll keep you safe and help get you home if you tell me where you live?"

"My name is Brock, and I live in a dorm room at the university," he said with slurred words.

April thought he looked sad and vulnerable and wondered what had happened to him. She knew deep down it wasn't safe or wise to offer him help. Some uncontrollable instinct inside her took over, and she didn't have the heart to rescind her offer.

The uneven sidewalk through the park made moving alongside him difficult. The shelters always gave homeless bus tokens. She placed two at the ticket counter and got them seated, and once more tried to make conversation. "What are you doing in this part of town? I don't know if you can tell, but this isn't really a suitable area of the city."

He rested his head in his hands. Getting closer to the college, she looked out the bus window and watched the transition from older buildings to newer ones. Well, so much for her help, especially after she'd saved him from harm. He seemed oblivious of his surroundings and of her. He could have at least acknowledged the situation. Most of the guys she had been around who drank became obnoxious and mouthy. This guy sat with his head down in silence.

She ought to have let him get off the bus by himself when they reached the college, except the overpowering force kicked into play again. Drawn by his looks, she stared at him for guidance on which way to go. He pointed to a specific building, took her hand and headed towards it.

No sooner than they entered the lobby, a woman with a briefcase nodded at the man and called him by his name, then walked past them. April noticed the surprised look on the woman's face passing them. Not wanting to get into trouble for being in the dorm, she asked him, "Is it alright for me to be here?"

"Oh, Miss Burton. Don't worry about her. She's a professor here, and yes, it is okay if you're here with me," he said.

They got in the elevator, and the doors shut behind them; she smiled at the subtle slur in his words. Her heart thumped wildly while they rode up to his floor. At least she hoped it was his floor. April nearly laughed. She should have left him in the lobby, but she ignored the logical voice in her head, which yelled, leave. He totally captivated her and she listened to the unfamiliar, exploratory voice that begged her to stay. He captivated her.

The elevator stopped, and he led the way out. With her eyes stealing quick glimpses of his body, she followed him down the hall, his hand still holding hers. She couldn't stop watching him walk, wondering about his quiet demeanor. She remained beside him like a lost puppy who just found its owner.

April swallowed hard, unable to resist blatantly staring at him and his prominent dimples when he stopped in front of a door. His brown eyes made her want to touch his face and run her fingers through his longish blonde hair. A sexy tuft of hair peeked out of his shirt and drew her eyes to his chest. She experienced sensations she'd never encountered around boys before. No one ever completely fascinated her the way he did.

He retrieved a keyring from his pocket. His hands shook, and it made finding the right key difficult for him, but he finally managed to open the doorway in front of them. He then stood back like a gentleman, looked at her and grinned. Her heart soared.

"Come in." He swept his arm inside the open entrance. "Please."

"I really shouldn't." She stuttered and tried to back away, her actions fading fast. Would she be foolish or rash if she entered his room? Probably both. At the moment, she didn't care. She really wanted to stay with him a bit longer. Oh my, how she wanted...

"You want to, don't you?"

"Yes," she whispered.

He took her hand and gently pulled her inside. He shut the door behind her, then bent his head towards her. His soft lips kissed hers. Her breath caught in her throat, and an unfamiliar heat sizzled from inside her. She wondered if he heard her heart pounding loudly when she moved into the circle of his arms and he pulled her tight against his chest.

The emotions he stirred inside her were far more than pleasant. They ripped her innocent body into pieces. She lacked the power to halt them even if she wanted to.

Immediately, her mouth opened for him, and his tongue began exploring hers. A deep moan escaped her the instant his hands ran down the length of her back to her hips. He groaned and drew her even closer until she grasped his shoulders with a force she didn't know she possessed. She had kissed boys before, even fooled around a little with them. Despite her lack of experience, she could still recognize these actions came from a man.

They backed up to the edge of his bed. He sat her down at the end and finished the kiss. He stared at her with his deep brown, solemn eyes, and it appeared as though he asked an unspoken question. She shook her muddled head. "I'm not sure what I want..."

He pulled her shirt up and unclasped her bra, exposing her. His eyes looked at her face, and then his hand caressed one breast and then the other. Twirling the dusty colored nipples between his fingers while waves of pleasure washed over her.

Subsequently, he moved to her jeans, undoing the button first, then the zipper. The precise moment his fingers reached for the red, curly area between her legs, her breath caught in eagerness and her eyes drifted shut to savor the new feeling. Absolutely nothing ever felt this good. She noticed how the slickness of her skin allowed his fingers to glide through her folds. Her rapid breathing silently pled for him to continue his wonderful onslaught, not leaving one place on her body untouched and causing her to whimper.

Then she unbuttoned his shirt and slid it off his shoulders, exposing the light brown hair her eyes saw earlier, and ran her fingers down his chest hair until she found his hardened nipples. She teased with her hands, then her tongue, the same way he'd done to her. The sensual emotion it caused overwhelmed her. To have this much pleasure made her want more.

He put his hands on her shoulders and placed her back on the bed, then he finished undressing himself. She lay captivated, her wide eyes focused directly on him. She'd seen pictures of naked men in magazines other girls left hidden under the beds in the foster home. However, nothing compared to seeing the magnificent body in front of her. Her gaze traveled from his muscular chest down to his waiting erection. April found herself hypnotized once again and swallowed hard.

He stepped closer, got on the bed and kissed her again before he parted her legs with his knee. At the very moment he probed her core, she gasped and bit his shoulder hard. He pushed his body up and away from her.

"Are you sure you're good with this? We can stop if you've changed your mind."

"No, don't stop. This is what I want."

His body took over, and April forgot he was a complete stranger making love to her. She admitted to herself that the touch of his hands on her hips gave her immense pleasure. A shiver of anticipation coursed down to her toes, with her core throbbing for what came next.

She opened her eyes wide and locked onto his face until she got over the initial pain, then lust and desire consumed her body. Her hips arched up to meet the intensity and fire his body gave her. She gasped, and stars burst the moment the climax shuttered around her. He groaned before collapsing onto her.

April lay still for a few minutes and allowed her body and mind to take stock of what had just happened. Tears fell as she mourned her innocence, despite the unforgettable encounter with a stranger. His gentleness was all she could have wanted. He kissed her forehead and then fell asleep next to her.

She gathered her garments and looked across the floor for the pants he'd taken off. She retrieved his wallet from the pocket of his pants, took the money, and did not look at anything else.

Before April dressed, she found a pen and a piece of paper. She tried to control tears, on the verge of falling, which made it difficult for her to scribble a brief note. The concise note said:

Brock, I borrowed
twenty dollars from
your wallet, and I will pay you
back someday.
Thanks for the night.
Maria.

She placed the note on his pillow, then left the dorm room. Still dazed, she attempted to make her way back to her side of town. Having spent her last two bus tokens on the trip to the college, and with no other choice, she walked down the sidewalks quickly. A couple of cars slowed down, and she held her breath before they passed her by. The situation she found herself in pointed her to the ever-present need to be on the lookout for danger because it wasn't safe to be out in the dark alone.

She breathed a sigh of relief when the familiar sights of her neighborhood appeared. The few streetlights, which weren't broken, beamed a comforting ray of light on her. A few people wandered around the doorways and in the alleys, probably making drug deals. Not wanting to be near any part of an illegal scene, she hurried on down the sidewalk.

With her late-night fun, she missed dinner. Now, her stomach churned with hunger. April walked to the counter, which held a coffee urn and bottles of water. She grabbed a water and spied a few large bits of cookies left over from the evening meal, then searched for an available bed in the shelter. She sat on the cot and nibbled on the meager amount of crumbs and drank the water, having been hungry before.

Afterwards, she tucked herself under the worn-out blanket and let the tears fall in solitude. With the sobs muffled, she shuddered, recalling the unforgettable new experience and remembering the passion he awakened in her. Every kiss, every caress, every quickening of her pulse replayed through her mind. She closed her eyes, touched herself, and felt the lingering fiery sensation from his skin. She didn't regret making love for one minute.

The noise of volunteers getting breakfast ready to serve brought her out of a restless night of sleep. She got up and walked into the bathroom. Looking in the tarnished mirror, she determined the dark shadows under her red and puffy eyes weren't overly noticeable. One woman in the bathroom area disregarded her. A couple more asked if she needed anything.

April's hunger pains smacked her squarely in the stomach the minute she smelled the food. She got in line and picked up a tray. The volunteers piled the biscuits and a bowl of gravy on her plate along with a couple of sausage links and some scrambled eggs. A carton of milk and coffee awaited her at the end of the serving line. Perhaps she craved food and the caffeine for a jolt of energy to continue with her mental, if not physical, recovery from the previous night. She needed to forget and simply chalk it up to experience.

Following breakfast, April approached the woman in charge. "May I take a shower this late?"

"Yes, you can. Do you have any fresh clothes?"

"No, just the ones I have on."

"Then come with me and I'll get you some before you clean up."

"Thank you very much."

April stood under the warm water, letting it wash away the tension from the night before. Afterwards, her outlook on life seemed a little better.

She left the shelter and walked to the library. It provided privacy and quiet, which always grounded her. The books helped her escape into a world all her own with imagination. The knowledge of words also opened a direction for her to escape from the harshness by helping her find her own way. "One day," she vowed. "I'll find my path."

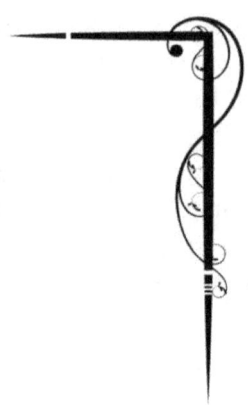

Chapter 2

A week passed since April's encounter with the sexy stranger. Her mind wandered as she walked through the city park filled with brilliant sunshine. She didn't even see the gorgeous flowers in bloom or hear the birds singing. Bees buzzed around her head, only she seemed oblivious to all the sounds.

She wasn't able to concentrate on anything except Brock and still wrestled with the guilt of going to bed with him. It included being rash on her part, and she really knew better, but wow! A chill ran down her back once she remembered his long, lean fingers stroking her back. She vibrated with another wave of desire. Usually shy around guys, the unlikelihood of their paths crossing again had given her the freedom to throw restraint to the wind. She needed to put it behind her and go on with life.

Dusk hovered, with the sun sinking in the western sky. It signaled to find a shelter serving food, and if she got lucky, an available extra bed. She scanned the street in front of her and headed down the sidewalk to the same refuge where she had spent the previous night.

Crowded as usual, the building housed one of the few havens she felt safe in. It didn't mean letting her guard down. Her experience of getting close to anyone made it very difficult to trust or make new friends. It seemed all the people who mattered, even a small amount, left her for one reason or another.

April sniffed the aroma of food and walked in the door and got in line, grabbing a tray from the stack at the front. At the serving counter, the volunteers dished up and handed over the beef stew. The minute she raised her head to take her bowl; she almost dropped it on the floor. The noise of everyday sounds faded away. Her breath caught, and she knew her face turned red.

The man she had assumed to never see again stood in front of her. "What are you doing here?" She squeaked.

"I volunteer. Why are you here?"

"Um, I'm getting my dinner," she answered shyly.

"I have a break in a few minutes. Can we talk?"

"I suppose," she stuttered.

"Okay, here's your food. Find a seat and I'll join you."

April took her dinner tray and sat at a table far from the serving line. Hungry before, her appetite vanished, replaced by nerves. She put the spoon in the bowl of stew and pushed it around, hoping somehow it made its way into her mouth.

The impulse to take off almost overwhelmed her, not knowing what Brock probably thought of her, or what he wanted to talk about seeing her through sober eyes. Invisible strings kept her there.

Brock walked up to the table with a cup of coffee in his hand and sat down. "Hi again. I need to apologize for the other night. I'm sorry for taking advantage of you."

April glanced around the shelter, spotting a small group of women, and blushed. Sally, who witnessed her the morning after sleeping with the sexy stranger, sat close by. The woman had been the one to remark about her pale face, and the vague answer she gave did nothing except confirm what surely happened. One other woman even offered to let her talk about it if she needed to. She declined even though they made her feel not alone. She knew they watched and whispered as Brock sat down at the table with her. Sally grinned and gave her the thumbs-up.

"I am alright. Besides, you didn't take advantage of me. I wanted what happened. Don't feel bad."

"Only if you're sure."

"I'm positive."

"I do have a question for you. Where did you go afterwards? I woke up, and you weren't there. I didn't know where to find you or that you ..." he hesitated.

April finished the statement somberly. "Lived on the streets? Yeah, I do."

"Why?"

"I have no other options." April waited for him to stand and go away. He stayed at the table, though. Her heart skipped a beat. The sudden surge of hope made her feel vulnerable, especially because she knew the world, with its heavy foot on her back, kept her in its appointed place, all alone.

He surprised her and reached across the table, touching her cheek. Drawing back, she looked up at him and drowned once again in those brown eyes, gorgeous enough to gaze in for hours.

"Will you allow me to take you to dinner someplace other than here? It seems the stew isn't what you want. I'd really like to get to know you better."

April pushed her bowl away and laughed softly at the statement. "I think we know each other pretty well, considering the other night, don't you?"

"No, sleeping together wasn't what I meant. I want to know more about you."

Her eyes looked at him in absolute disbelief. This type of man didn't exist in her world. Like the previous time, his clothes undoubtedly cost more than the average person wore. She wondered what he saw in her, an invisible homeless girl going nowhere. Her fascination with him roared like a forest fire once again. The heat and sizzle rekindled, hotter than ever.

She watched him walk over to the woman in charge and say something to her before he grabbed his jacket. He came back and held out his hand; she willingly placed hers in it. They walked out onto the sidewalk and around the building to the parking lot. A cherry-red sports car made her eyes light up with excitement, and the thrill of riding in the fancy car raced through her.

The drive through the streets of the city passed too quickly. She wasn't familiar with the area he went to. The classier buildings displayed a more affluent atmosphere. He parked, and they went into the pizza café he'd chosen and ordered a pie and drinks. The warmth of the environment, along with the delicious aroma of pizza, made April's mouth water.

Once they left the shelter, away from its prying eyes, she felt a little more relaxed. She overcame her initial shyness and discovered simple conversation flowed easily. "Why do you volunteer at the shelter?"

"My family has always helped. I guess it's normal for me. You said you had no other option besides going to the shelter. Don't you have any family to count on?"

"No, no one." She twisted the talk of family back onto him. "Do you have siblings?"

"Yes, I have a sister. Her name is Julie, and she's in college, too."

"What are you studying?"

"The law. My family owns a firm downtown, and I'll join them soon." He said with a hint of hesitation.

A heart-wrenching sigh escaped her. If he came from a family of lawyers, then he looked upon her in the manner of a charity case. She didn't want, nor need, his pity. She pushed her chair back to get up from the table to leave before she made a complete fool of herself.

"Wait, Maria, where are you going? Please stay and finish your food and then, if you want, I will take you back to the shelter. No more questions, I promise." He motioned back to the chair.

Tears threatened to escape her eyes at the gentle tone of his voice. She sat back down and sighed. "I don't belong in your world. Why do you want me to see more of it?"

"Don't you have dreams of your own, Maria?"

"No, I don't have any," she said with resignation. Did she dare expose herself to him? A stranger in many ways. If she told him, he might possibly laugh and humiliate her because they weren't dreams, but merely fantasies.

"Find one and I will help you make it come true," he offered.

She sat with her gaze fixed on his sincere expression. Then while they ate, she stole glimpses of his handsome face and caught him watching her several times. They finished their pizza and walked back to his car. He pushed her up against the passenger door and leaned in for a kiss. The heat once more exploded within her. She couldn't get enough of his taste. A mixture of Italian spices and the mint from the restaurant. She knew her eyes betrayed her excitement to him. "Will you come back to my room? I want you," he asked.

"Yes, even though I know I shouldn't," April confessed.

"Think of it as an adventure."

He placed her in his car, and they drove back to the college. They strolled back to his dorm room, where he undressed her again and slipped on a condom before spending another night making love. The difference is that instantly they were no longer total strangers. April trusted him, which helped her believe maybe life could change for the better.

The next morning, she woke up wrapped in the warmth of his arms. She gently kissed his jaw before getting out of bed. She looked around at his expensive clothing scattered on the floor and the nice furnishings of the college room in amazement. It appeared he took all of this wealth for granted. If she ever owned half of what he did, she wouldn't throw it on the floor.

By the time Brock stirred, she had dressed and sat at the foot of the bed, waiting to tell him goodbye. He didn't appear to be in a hurry for her to go anywhere, as he pushed his back against the headboard.

They talked about his future of becoming a lawyer and what it meant to him. Then he suggested ways for her to make her own wishes a reality. He advised her to go to the community college and ask for help in furthering her education. "I'm sure they'd enroll you in their GED program if you applied. You know, since you are…"

"Homeless. Just say it out loud. I'm aware of my circumstances and thought this conversation became the point of changing for the better." Hurt at the sudden frankness of his revelation, she walked out the door. He didn't stop her.

She spent the rest of the day in the library, her failsafe place to think. Did she dare risk baring her soul? Maybe with his help and a little faith. His mention of her past homelessness led her to wonder if he considered her a charity case. Her instincts screamed yes. He urged her to visit those places. No mention of his coming along, though.

Rather than dwelling on her pain, she left the library and strolled through the park before she walked back towards the shelter for the nightly meal and a place to rest. Lying in a cot, sleepless, she remembered her years at foster homes. They trained her to face the reality of life. It sucked because so many people left; she stopped forming relationships. He wouldn't be any different, she admitted to herself before she finally drifted off to sleep.

April snagged one more cup of coffee before finishing breakfast the next morning. Leaving the building, she searched the storefronts looking for help-wanted signs that allowed her to work. Few places existed where she could get a job, considering her lifestyle and lack of education. Employers wanted proof of a high school diploma and a permanent address. Being reminded of being homeless made her touchy. Brock didn't understand her way of life. She struggled with trust issues, which was why she walked away from him.

Not finding any job prospects, she strolled through the common area. She brought a borrowed paperback book from the local neighborhood library stand to read until evening arrived. At twilight she bounced into the lobby of the refuge, eager to see Brock again and explain her behavior. H wasn't in sight. Disappointment seeped in. She ate dinner, claimed a bed, and settled in for the night. His return conceivably offered her a second chance.

April took a different route the next day. Seeing the help-wanted sign at the newly opened coffee shop, she breathed a sigh of relief. She approached the business owner with a candid request. She asked him to let her work for one day without wages and prove her reliability. The older man consented, and the next night he allowed her to work a few hours cleaning up the place following business hours. The money wasn't much, barely the minimum wage. However, it gave her hope and some cash.

The first evening off in a week, she rushed to the shelter. She missed dinner because of her job and couldn't wait to see Brock. Near the back, she spotted him standing beside an attractive young woman. She stopped and slid back behind the coat rack. April watched the stranger reach her arms up and around his neck, pulling his head down. Before the woman kissed him, he moved his head around to allow her access to his cheek and a hug. Instinct told her the woman wanted more.

April stepped out from behind her hiding place and stared at the couple. Brock's eyes met hers for a brief second before he turned back to the pretty girl. Was he going to kiss her? She couldn't watch this and backed up closer to the door. He made a fool of her, and it didn't seem to bother him one bit. She'd been a plaything to him. The rich, successful lawyer-to-be feigned concern for her future. She wanted to live in the fantasy a little longer, then reality kicked back in with a vengeance. Brock really didn't care.

April ran out the door and down the sidewalk. Tears streamed down her face. Blinded to the beauty of flowers at her favorite place, she hid behind the buffer of bushes around the small lake, just in case he followed. She sat taking deep breaths to steady her heart and didn't see the soft, wispy clouds in the sky overhead. A heavy gray blanket shielded her eyes. She had been foolish to think about escaping this life and to trust anyone. He had come into her world and given her false hope — to be confident and to imagine someone actually cared.

Thrown back into the actuality, she became the invisible street urchin once more, the girl the rich guy used and didn't want. Hurt stabbed her until anger replaced the pain. She vowed to overcome hardship somehow, someway, in the future. Justified, his unspoken words spurred her to succeed.

After being on the streets for months, she knew all the right zones to be in. With the night approaching, April knew she couldn't stay out all evening and needed to find lodgings other than the one where Brock volunteered. She made her way two streets over and found food along with an available bed to sleep in.

Much like the first night with Brock, she cried herself to sleep again, hiding under a used blanket. The tears washed away some of the pain and embarrassment of falling for someone not in her realm. Her rash decision to sleep with him, reckless, yet this betrayal left her feeling stupid.

———————

Meanwhile, the heartache ultimately subsided. April found another way to remind herself not to be gullible, seeing the beautiful artwork on both arms of a woman who owned and operated a tattoo shop down the street. They met at the coffee shop close to her place of business and began chatting.

April begged her to trade cleaning the shop for a small ink. Laws existed, making it illegal for a minor to receive one in Oklahoma. She could have lied about her age, but in swearing secrecy, the woman conceded. The tattoo of a butterfly in flight appeared to rest on a flower petal. In her mind, it signified not trusting anyone except yourself to land where you wanted. Eventually, she would find the courage to ask about the community college. For now, she needed to heal.

When finished at the tattoo studio, April peered through the windows of her regular hangout and looked around the building's interior before she entered. She made sure the tall figure she really didn't want to run into wasn't around and got in line for the evening meal.

A few familiar faces greeted her from the serving line. "Hey April, where have you been keeping yourself?" Sarah, an older woman in the building, asked. Sally glanced at her and remained silent once again.

"Oh, you know, trying to earn a little pocket change, Sarah."

"I hope you got rich," the woman said, then laughed.

"Sure, you know it. Why do you think I'm here tonight? I see new volunteers working tonight. What happened to the old ones?"

"You know they merely come around to make themselves feel better."

"Believe me, I know firsthand. We don't need their kind of help anyhow," April told her. Maybe the experience of having a different lifestyle within her reach once upon a time and then snatched away, left her with a new wisdom. Broken hearts healed eventually.

She slipped back into her usual places of sleeping and eating. The library continued to be where she spent most occasions reading books. Some stimulated her to look past the cruel world and strive for something different again. Once in a while, someone left an unusual paperback book or two at the shelter. She took them and walked to the park and sat on a secluded bench and savored the words. Before leaving the foster home, she escaped by losing herself in daydreams. Regardless of your wishes, the world continued to spin.

In due course, the scent of flowers and the smell of cut grass returned to her senses. Much like April watched over her shoulder escaping the foster home, now she watched and ran from reminders of her gullibility. Not wanting to fall into the trap again, she distanced herself from all strangers. Some tried to make conversation as they served her food or handed her a clean pair of jeans. She always refused, then kept her eyes turned down not to bring attention to herself. One heartbreak proved enough for a lifetime, she decided. Someday, she'd start looking up at the world again once her confidence resumed. For now, all she wanted to do was forget about the tall, sexy guy.

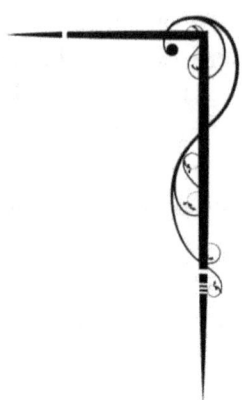

Chapter 3

Brock Andrew Ruggle eventually returned to his volunteer work. He'd been busy with his final exams at law school and hadn't been back for days. To assure Maria that his offer to help her still stood, he hurried into the building. He knew he'd hurt her feelings and honestly had not meant for his words to come out the way they did.

He searched the room full of people and saw a familiar face. Just not the one he wanted to see. The moment the tall, attractive girl strolled over towards him, he asked, "Cindy, what are you doing here?" He dreaded the answer.

"I'm here to see you, of course," she said, resting her hand on his forearm before she slid both of her arms around his neck. "This place is a little beneath you, isn't it?" She turned her nose up and glanced around at the dismal building.

"No, there's nothing wrong with this place. Besides, you know my family encourages serving the community." He defended the shelter.

"Help me instead if you want to assist someone," the spoiled girl replied.

"I don't have the energy for this," and pushed her away from him. "Why don't you leave or pick up a tray and help feed these people?"

Cindy scrunched up her nose again. "Call me right before you finish, and I'll take you out to dinner at an actual restaurant," then walked out the door giving him another one-sided hug and a kiss on his cheek.

Brock spotted Maria coming in at the door before he got rid of Cindy, and then he couldn't find her. His gut told him she'd witnessed the display of affection. He needed to find her and explain the old girlfriend wouldn't take no for an answer.

Brock wasn't used to feeling such powerful emotions for anyone. His desire to be a playboy was less important than helping Maria. He thought he had truly convinced her to search for a better future for herself and worried if he didn't find her, she theoretically would go back to not dreaming.

Although sure to join his family's law firm when he graduated, the run-in with Professor Boden, despite being unfortunate, became the motive for going to the bar, and Brock wouldn't have met Maria if he hadn't gone. Brock remembered he had smirked with arrogance before his teacher handed him the test paper and demanded an explanation. The score must have been flawless until he glanced downward and noticed the huge letter B written across the top in red ink. A perfect GPA ruined. His stomach fell. Not a single coherent word came out of his mouth for a few moments. "I don't understand what happened," he said once his voice returned.

Mr. Boden scoffed, "Yes, you do, Brock. You believed you were too clever, and I'd overlook your shortcomings, didn't you?"

He stayed upset with the professor until he figured out the failure rested on him.

Anxiously, he combed the sidewalks and different shelters for the pretty redhead, and had even hired a friend to look. No one knew Maria. She vanished, similar to Cinderella, except she hadn't left a slipper, and it wasn't midnight. It became apparent that she must have moved somewhere else and didn't want his help. Therefore, he resigned himself to the memories of soft silken skin and passionate kisses.

From the time he met Maria, he appreciated just how lucky his childhood and lifestyle had been. A powerful network of community support surrounded him where he grew up. He never stayed in his bedroom, did not play video games like a lot of his friends, and needed to be outside in the fresh air. The family home, a pristine white two-story colonial in Nichols Hills, a suburb of Oklahoma City where he and Julie grew up, became the meeting place for all the area kids. The entire neighborhood contributed to molding his youth. Whether a barbecue, a picnic in the park or an art festival, his parents made sure he and his sister went to these events despite being busy lawyers to ensure they felt loved and like they belonged to a normal family.

Rather than return to his sparsely decorated dorm room, not having had any luck finding Maria, he picked up his phone to call Rob. The guys always made him laugh and forget about his problems. After he enrolled in college and lived in the dormitory, he occasionally invited Rob and Cliff, two of his buddies, to go with him to visit his parents at his childhood home, where they played football in the backyard like they did when younger. He laughed and recalled how his mom screamed as they tackled each other. "Don't hurt each other too badly."

"Mom, we're having fun."

"Be careful anyhow."

"Yes, Mother."

Rob and Cliff chimed in also, "Yes, Mom."

Predictably, Brock snickered the minute Cliff answered Rob's phone. He knew they hung together. "Hey, what are you guys doing?"

"Oh, you know, hanging out at the local getaway."

"Are you going to be there for a while?"

"We can be. Are you joining us because you're tired of playing nice guy at the shelter?"

He told them about volunteering, not about Maria. He didn't want the extra ribbing he knew they'd dish out. "Yeah, I'll be over in a few minutes. Let's party."

Brock joined the boys at the bar and ordered a beer. These lifelong friends loved to party. Crowded with college students, the bar welcomed him back. Noisy people who yelled at each other across the room, and the smells of beer along with stale peanuts happened to be the exact thing he needed. It didn't take long for him to get back into the full swing of things, of being the popular playboy on campus. The three of them made the rounds, laughed and drank too much. Hey, life being the nice guy hadn't worked too well, and besides, wasn't having fun with good friends and beer one main purpose for college?

Of course, enjoyment also meant girls. A constant stream of dates flowed in and out of his dorm room. He made one rule. Absolutely no redheads.

On the last visit home before graduation, his parents suggested he take a part-time job at the firm to get his foot in the door. "Son, this way you can have most of the summer off before you start a steady position." He shook his head. They even suggested for him to go back to being a volunteer. That he definitely declined.

To justify his sudden shift from playboy to volunteer and back again to playboy, he concocted an excuse for his parents about his behavior. He told them carelessly, "I want to finish out the last summer of my college days hanging out with close friends." He wasn't sure they bought the excuse or his reasoning.

Brock graduated law school with honors, despite not having a perfect GPA like he wanted. His proud parents told him he hadn't disappointed them. The legacy of the family firm would pass down to both him and Julie.

Carefree, Brock moved back home with graduation over. True to his word, he partied all summer with Rob and Cliff. He didn't want to give up his playboy antics, being a hot-blooded man who liked women. He just wanted to have fun, with no serious relationships. Julie caught him in the kitchen coming home one afternoon and asked, "Who are you going out with tonight?"

"Whitney, Brittany, or something sounding similar. I'm not sure. Does it really matter what her name is?"

"I don't guess if you don't care," Julie shrugged her shoulders.

"Not especially. She's someone to have fun with." He raised his eyebrows and wiggled them. The action showed he wasn't too concerned about her opinion. Well, maybe a little. He finished eating his sandwich and went to his bedroom, dressed, and left for his date.

The confrontation with Julie showed him he needed to move before another interrogation arose from his sister. A place he came and went without repercussions and where his little sister didn't judge his choices.

Brock convinced his parents to help pay for a place until he started earning money of his own. He found a furnished condo not too far from the nightlife scene. Colors of muted black and gray in the furniture created a casual yet smart bachelor pad. The entire condo building, much to his surprise and delight, also turned into a hotbed for new dates. He settled into the familiar role of a sexy playboy without a care in the world. He believed the excuse if he repeated it enough.

———————

Fall meant the end of Brock's days of non-stop partying. Pleased, he arrived at his parents' office on Monday morning on the first day of his career and knocked on his father's door. "Come in, son. This has been a long journey for you, and I am very proud to have you join the firm with your family."

"Dad, thank you for the opportunity. I promise not to disappoint you."

"I'm sure you won't."

"Becoming a junior member will be my way of learning about the ins and outs of practicing law," he admitted. "I've made the right decision."

Brock's parents never pushed him to become a lawyer. They showed him the good they accomplished by doing the right things. He started at the bottom, moved up the firm fast, and handled cases no one else wanted.

A twinge of guilt washed over him sporadically. It reminded him how he'd cared for a certain young woman a little too much, or maybe not enough. At their last meeting, he wanted to pull her close but watched her walk out the door, deciding more moments existed later to apologize. Later never came.

Maybe this attitude reflected his love of defending the underdog who stood up to the system. He hadn't supported Maria. Others still needed help, despite this. He preferred cases representing injustices placed on people who tried to get ahead not by breaking the law. Driven by the simple need to survive and thrive, he stuck with them. Many of his clients fought the system for money, and some fought for their own rights against the local and state governments.

Brock's mother called him into her office one morning at work. Since his move to the condo, he rarely saw her except at the workplace. "Hi, Mom. What do you need?"

"Son, you're aware the firm takes on a certain number of nonpaying clients a year?"

"Yeah, I know about them. Has one come up?" His family's firm searched for ways to help the needy and made it mandatory for all the lawyers to take on two or three unpaid cases a year. Pro bono cases became an accepted part of the legal system to allow justice to be served for all.

"You have been handling litigations similar to these and shouldn't have any problems with this one. Usually, it is a modest matter to deal with. I'm afraid this one may make the news headlines."

"Why do you think this one is different? What's special about? Does it have the potential to be high profile?"

"Yes, although not in the way you think. It is about a man accused of stealing a blanket from a store."

"Okay, why didn't he pay for it? I don't understand what the big deal is."

"The store owners are pressing charges. They say they want to send a message, so it won't happen again," his mom explained.

Still confused, Brock asked, "Who do they want to send a message to?"

"The homeless community. The alleged thief is destitute."

"Seriously, they're going to press charges in this weather." The day before, an unexpected cold snap moved in, causing temperatures to plunge.

"That's my point, son, and why I said it may make the news. We have to help this man. Because you volunteered at the shelter this past summer, you have a better understanding of what took place. You are in charge, and I know you will do your best to see to a fair outcome."

His heart dropped into his stomach. How did he go back to the poor community and not think about Maria? He really hoped she'd escape poverty. Her expression before he turned away to hide his intense shame stayed in his memory.

Brock kept quiet about Maria to his mother because he didn't want to say no if she told him to look for the girl again. When he quit the shelter, he stopped his search. "Alright, you've got it. I will get right on it."

Brock pushed the memories back to meet with the store owner. He pulled into the parking lot of the big-box store and saw several people milling around. Some carried signs advertising their services for cash, and others, well, they looked lost. Given their circumstances, he saw both sides of the issue. On the one hand, the people didn't have any choice, and on the flip side, the store owners didn't want their customers to feel unsafe. He tried to reason with the man who pressed charges to drop the case to no avail.

His next meeting took place with the prosecutor handling the case, who told Brock that the accused man remained in jail because he couldn't afford bail. The prosecuting attorney, limited in his ability to assist, sympathized with the old fellow. Restricted by his job, he recommended Brock meet up with an organization that specialized in posting bail for the homeless. The group accommodated the elder man and located a local shelter, which provided care.

Before Brock walked into the refuge, he told himself to stay focused. The stuffy smells, dishes clinking, and the wary eyes that lingered on him threatened to distract him from his mission. He stifled his reaction crashing to the forefront once again. Here in the same shelter where he once volunteered, Brock questioned the man sitting in the dining hall, where a decent meal awaited him. "Why did you steal the blanket, sir?"

"My dog would have frozen. They wouldn't let me bring him into the shelter. I had to stay outside with him. I couldn't let him freeze being inside and warm myself," the old man explained.

Humbled by the simple explanation, "I see, well we will go to the judge and explain the circumstances. If he won't help us, then I'm sure the public will want to hear about this, and then the charges should disappear, and you and the shelter will get a lot of support."

When he appeared in court with the man, and explained the situation, the judge dismissed the charges. Risking his freedom, the homeless man kept his pet warm. The man's compassion for his dog touched him and exhibited how the people on the streets really possessed hearts. The story covered on the evening news, anyhow, started an outcry from the public about the cruel treatment of the older man. Brock gave a brief statement, thanking them for their support. He implored the citizens of the city to help. "Don't allow this to happen again, please."

With the incident behind him, Brock returned to his playboy lifestyle, carefree and being the life of the party. The women he dated never measured up to his expectations and seemed to leave an ache deep in his soul. He met Rob and Cliff at a restaurant down the street from his office for dinner. With his court cases and many dates, they hadn't been together very often, and he missed his friends. "Hey, how have you guys been?"

"We have been busy trying to get our new business up and running." The two men were launching a computer programming consultant company.

"How's it going?"

"Almost done. What about you? Are you enjoying practicing law? We saw you on television about the homeless man and his dog. You looked pleased with the outcome. Did you call the press?"

"Who me? I wouldn't do anything underhanded." Brock winked. "The store owner's future business prospects don't look good."

"Always trying to help, aren't you?" Both friends looked at each other and smirked.

"What can I say? It's in my DNA."

Rather than think about the case and subsequently Maria, he returned from dinner and put them both out of his mind. Well, he tried to. No sooner than he laid his head down and closed his eyes, he slid into a dream where he searched the sidewalks of the city for Maria and couldn't find her anywhere and the cravings for her left him sweaty. He woke up; dull pain throbbed in his body. A cold shower helped erase the gloom produced by the night's lack of peaceful sleep.

Brock knew he should be proud of the previous day's very open outpouring of support for the homeless community; however, the shadows hung on. Julie stopped by his office later in the morning and asked. "How are you doing?"

"I think I'm fine. Though I'm not really sure," he admitted without explanation.

"Are you still burning both ends of the candle, so to speak?"

"If you mean partying, dating several women and working, then yeah, I guess I am."

"Can I ask you something, brother? What are you searching for? You are reckless and unsettled."

The conversation with Julie opened Brock's eyes. Then he questioned the decisions he'd made in life. The never-ending parties and casual dates seemed to have lost their appeal. Exhaustion sneaked in and replaced the fun. Perhaps the occasion for something different neared.

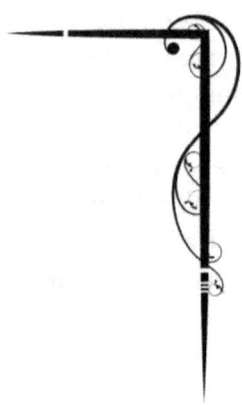

Chapter 4

Bonnie Burton sat at her desk and listened to the hushed voices coming from the waiting area of the maternity center. She found it hard to believe she'd been here for over fifteen years helping young women and their babies. Sure, some things changed — clothing styles, hair colors, and other fads. There always seemed to be a need to help the defenseless. Her journey began with the need to put enormous pain behind her. If she let it go now, it ripped open the scars on her heart.

Her phone rang and pulled her out of old memories — powerful enough to cripple her. "This is Bonnie. May I help you?"

"Hi, Bonnie, this is Gwen from the clinic down the street. A few minutes ago, I talked with a young girl following her examination, and she needs your help. I recommended your center."

"Thank you for letting me know."

"Hopefully, she makes the right decision and shows up."

"Let's hope so," Bonnie said with a heavy heart. Many of the stories she observed of girls without guidance about birth control or abuse from a boyfriend or a stranger occurred too often with similar results. She learned to keep an open mind towards the girls. Don't judge them. They just needed someone to trust.

About thirty minutes later, a gentle knock tapped at her door. Bonnie looked through the doorway. What stroke of fate brought this girl here? Listen to the circumstances, don't jump to conclusions and stay calm, she told herself, as she motioned the young woman towards a chair. If correct in her assumptions, Brock Ruggle, her best friend's son, fathered a baby.

"Hi, I'm Bonnie Burton. What is your name?"

"My name is April Palmer. I just found out I'm pregnant, and I don't know what to do. Do you offer help here?"

Bonnie heard the hidden panic and answered with compassion in her eyes. Rather than mince any words, she started talking. "First, what do you want for your baby? I can help you if want to give her or him a fighting chance?"

"This baby deserves a better life than the one I experienced. A better future, which I am incapable of providing. Any help you offer, I'll gladly accept," replied April.

Bonnie walked around her desk and took the other chair. "I'll do whatever I can. Several options are available. However, the choice will be yours alone. My job is to advise you on these. Then I will explain the outcome of any decision made." Bonnie told April. "You stay in the unwed mother's home and receive medical help, or if you continue to live on the streets and shelters, then the clinic provides medical help. Of course, adoption is also a solution. We even offer to teach skills, which will empower you to raise the baby by yourself."

After more tears, April sat straighter in the seat and whispered, "I want to put my baby up for adoption. Someone has to want to give him or her a better life."

Bonnie owed Kayla so much. Maybe the chance to repay her for all the love, advice, support, and a shoulder to cry on in the past fell into her lap.

Years ago, Bonnie Burton graduated from law school and took a job at a prestigious firm in Chicago. Soon the bustle of big-city pressures finally got to her. She moved to Oklahoma City and started her own firm. This entitled her to pick her clients, and along the way she opted for another couple to partner with her. Steven and Kayla Ruggle proved the perfect fit. They became lifelong friends. Being around the Ruggles children cracked open a hole in her heart.

When the longing wouldn't go away, she called Kayla into her office. "I have something to discuss with you, if you don't mind?"

"Sure, what do you need, my friend?"

"I want a baby. Am I crazy?"

Kayla, with compassion in her eyes, said. "Why give up the chance of being a mother?"

"I'm too old to have a baby, aren't I?"

"Maybe. Your doctor can decide. Look at how you are with Brock and Julie. You'd be an excellent mother."

"It's not the same. I know how to babysit. Besides, they are good kids."

"If the medical situation doesn't work, why not adopt? You know there are plenty of little ones available to love."

The intensity of love she underwent holding Erin in her arms for the first time became the most satisfying and yet the scariest feelings of her life. Erin became her purpose in life and the piece of love she had been missing. Motherhood made her entire life complete.

Perhaps with a little more of the fate which led April to her, Bonnie could give the girl and her baby the future they both deserved.

"If you are confident of your decision, then I have a proposition for you."

"What kind of proposition are you talking about?"

"Keep an open mind and listen. Why don't you come and live with me while the baby grows? I have a big house where you can rest and take care of yourself until the baby arrives. Then I will make the arrangements to place him or her in a loving home. You'll have the peace of mind knowing the family will shower the baby with all the love they have."

April stared, mouth wide open, then spoke. "Yes."

"Are you positive?" Bonnie asked.

"I'm sure. I can't raise a baby. It would be impossible."

"Alright. Do you have anything at the shelter to pick up?"

"No." The girl hugged her backpack closer.

Bonnie knew it held all of her possessions. "Okay, then let me wrap up my paperwork and we will leave."

Suddenly, the light returned to Bonnie's world. Providing a home for April gave her a warm feeling of satisfaction. She had purchased the two-story house, which sat on a dead-end street, shortly before Erin came into her life. She envisioned it filled with many happy, laughing, and well cared for children. The dream didn't work out, and she made peace with her life. She took the young girl home, and they settled into a comfortable arrangement. The changes in April's body amazed her. She brought books home for them to study at night. They focused on her pregnancy to ensure a healthy baby. The young girl listened to everything about preparing for the baby.

One evening the two walked out onto the front porch and sat on the swing Bonnie had installed when she purchased the house. April turned and asked, "Bonnie, why do you help girls like me?"

The question caught her off guard. Bonnie blinked suddenly, unable to look at the young woman for a minute. Instead, she glanced out onto the manicured green lawn. She swallowed the thick lump in her throat and took a deep breath. Clasped her hands together, and remembered the love, then the agony. "Having bought the house, I dreamed of having a big family here."

"Bonnie, I'm sorry. I didn't mean to bring up hurtful memories."

"No problem. Let me continue with the story. This way, you will know where I get my incentive to help."

"Only if you are sure?"

Bonnie nodded. "I adopted and brought Erin home. I loved her with every fiber of my being. She filled an empty space in my heart. Eight weeks later, I went back to work part-time at the college. I sold my share of the law firm I held to the other owners. To teach and take care of Erin became enough for me." Tears ran down Bonnie's face uncontrollably. She knew the difficulty in telling her story. The once callused surface broke open again. The pain she endured while she wandered the big house, sleepless at night with the inability to breathe without crying, crashed back, raw once more.

April reached across the seat. Bonnie grabbed for a lifeline and squeezed the girl's fingers. "What happened to Erin? Did the birth mother come back?"

"No," Bonnie said sadly. "I came home earlier than usual from college one evening to relieve the nanny, fed and played with Erin, then put her to bed and finished eating my dinner. I checked on her. She looked like an angel until I realized she wasn't asleep. My precious redheaded baby was gone."

April gasped.

"I'm guessing you're about her age." Bonnie whispered softly. "Eventually, with the help of Kayla, a wonderful friend, I started breathing again, and the despair lifted. The city threatened to shut down the maternity center where she worked. She enlisted my help, and we won the battle. Then she told me I needed to find a purpose. My calling became the shelter."

Because Bonnie agreed to defend the maternity center, she also vowed to her friend and the community to update the shelter and to better the lives of the girls. Whether with medical care, counseling to make the right choices or with the chances to further their education. True to her word, she expanded the homeless shelter to include financial advice and job opportunities in the city. She instructed fellow volunteers to paint and clean the buildings. Their homelessness didn't excuse inhumane treatment. The city took notice and rewarded her with extra financial help.

"I also returned to practicing law and took on the cases of people who frequented the shelters. They needed my help. Lost with my heart broken by grief, this place became my salvation. It gave me a function and eventually tranquility. I focused on helping young girls like yourself and dedicated my life to the cause. I remain grateful for Erin's birth mother's choice. She gave me the opportunity to love another human being, yet it made me wonder what might have happened if she had received better help. Would my baby have lived? I do this in memory of my sweet baby girl."

"Thank you for sharing your story and for being here to give me a chance to bring a healthy baby into the world."

Bonnie stood up and grinned at the swell of April's belly, then pulled the girl into her arms and hugged her tightly, knowing she gave the Ruggles' grandchild a future. She didn't dare mention Brock's name, causing the girl to possibly bolt, or worse. Not to trust. They respected each other, and neither wanted to cross the invisible boundary holding their secret.

The promise to April and, mentally, to the Ruggles replaced the helplessness of a night long ago. Somehow, the pain lessened, no longer a burning anger, and Bonnie slept better.

As the time for April to give birth neared, Bonnie realized she didn't want the girl to leave. They shared a comfortable bond, similar to a mother-daughter relationship, and acknowledged the lonely house without the teen. Although they hadn't discussed the girl's living arrangements after the baby arrived, she didn't know how to approach the subject without embarrassing either of them.

Bonnie returned home exhausted from a tough day at the shelter. The world constantly tested her patience. Two different girls turned down her offer of help. It frustrated her. Sometimes, despite solutions, they shut down and wouldn't listen to the advice given by the other counselors and became unreachable. The girls' obvious ignorance dismayed her, and she realized the urgency to ask her houseguest about her future.

If she helped April, provided the girl allowed it, the purpose of the center would come full circle and fulfill a promise she made to Kayla years ago. The opportunity to see one girl's tragedy and then successful journey seemed gratifying.

Bonnie sighed with relief to be home, away from the burdens of the day, stepped into her office and put her briefcase down on the large oak desk. She planned a talk with April later. Startled, she saw the girl with a book on the couch, which faced a bank of windows. "What are you reading?"

"Oh, I'm sorry. I didn't think you'd mind my being here."

"No, I don't mind. In fact, I want to talk to you about something. This is the perfect opening for what I have in mind."

"How does reading a book begin a conversation?"

She joined April and turned to face her. "Have you planned anything following childbirth?"

"I haven't considered it. I figured you'd want me to leave."

"Why would I insist you leave? I believed we were growing close."

"I am grateful for all your help, and yes, we have gotten close. Nonetheless, you wouldn't want a teenage girl living here free from any responsibility. Since I don't have any other options, I suppose I'll go back to the streets," the teen said.

"What if I told you education held the key to making something of yourself? I know you've suffered, maybe more than I realize. I'm here for you always. Please allow me to make a difference in your life choices and help you get an education." Bonnie pled with the tenderness of a loving mother.

April looked at her with wide eyes. "Where did you go to school?"

"I went to Yale."

"Wow."

"You see, education put me on a path to work for a major law firm. Then, I wanted a change of pace, so I moved to Oklahoma City and started my law firm. You may not want to be a lawyer. There are many choices."

April found her voice. "No offense, but I don't want to be a lawyer. I'll let you know my decision in the morning?"

"Yes, that'll be fine. We have another month until the little one is born. I don't want to rush you into making the wrong choice." April's insistence on not wanting to be a lawyer didn't surprise her.

Although Bonnie wanted to discuss more possibilities, she resisted. She didn't push further and allowed April to make up her own mind. Her mood improved by bedtime. More hopeful. Optimism replaced the sudden despair that overcame her at the center. Her new mission: to stick with and help the girl make the right change for a better life.

The next morning, April took a seat at the kitchen table where Bonnie sat, eating her breakfast. "I will take you up on the generous offer and, with your help, finish my education."

With tears in her eyes, Bonnie beamed. "Okay, we will get a tutor for you, and then I will help you get into college wherever you want. I have an extra desk in the office you can use. A few students at the college would love to tutor you for the chance to get extra credit in my classes." She laughed; aware she held the power to persuade them to help April. "Talk to me and let's get started, shall we? What level of school did you complete, and how about your grades?"

"I didn't want to ditch school; I didn't have any alternatives and left between my junior and senior year. My grades ranged from A's to B's."

"Alright, I have someone in mind to help you finish high school."

Bonnie discovered the secret to gaining homeless people's trust. To treat them with respect, and April proved no different. Elated with joy and satisfaction, Bonnie felt alive with the possibility of a wonderful future for April. She called Kayla to tell her the good news. Of course, she couldn't tell her everything.

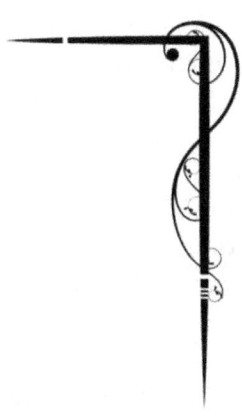

Chapter 5

April placed her hand on her swollen belly, where the baby she carried kicked and kicked often. She rubbed her stomach while sitting on the swing on Bonnie's front porch. In awe of the life inside her, she beamed at the speed this little one grew.

Something hadn't been right. Not wrong. Instinctively, she had just known it would never be the same. The free clinic visit confirmed what she already suspected. She and Brock made love without considering the repercussions. Besides her naivety, she recalled afterwards he hadn't used a condom the first time. What a huge mistake!

The sympathetic nurse suggested the maternity center for answers. Her bleak future, and chosen path, couldn't be a decent place to have, much less raise a baby. Terror strong enough to steal her breath raced to the pit of her stomach. A different nausea from the kind she experienced earlier in the day slammed into her body, and the fear almost overtook her. Why did this have to happen to her?

Panic gripped her throat like chains being tightened the moment reality set in.

No sooner, April entered the brick building and walked into the pristine white, spotless and well-organized atmosphere, a calmness settled in her stomach. An older woman sat at a desk and looked up at her with kind eyes. Bonnie Burton became her savior, having explained all the options she had to choose from. Granted, the instant Bonnie offered to let her move in and help with the baby, she became speechless. "Do I know you?" she had asked the woman later on the first day.

The answer sealed a trust. "No, I've never seen you before."

The sincerity of the generous offer filled her throat with choked tears. Bonnie became a great counselor who took her under her wing and gave her hope for the future of the baby, along with hope for her own future. She moved into the woman's home, a large, old, two-story home close to Edmond, where she felt welcomed and safe in her modest bedroom.

Now sitting here on the front porch, she looked down at her belly once again. The baby kicked again and reminded her that everything would be alright

She choked out the words. "You are my precious baby, and I love you. I'm doing this because you deserve a better future. When I leave you behind, it will tear me apart, still I have to do it for you."

April reassured herself often about the baby; it didn't make it any easier. She'd have a better life without her. She told herself not to get attached. The choice to just stop breathing, a simpler task. This little one already captured her heartstrings, even though she must cut the ties from her at birth, but never emotionally.

Many more heart to heart conversations took place between her and the unborn baby in the days ahead. She told the infant about her own hopes and ideas. Specific ones she never shared with anyone, not even Brock, until meeting Bonnie. Dreams of someday making something better of her life. With affection and tenderness in her voice, she sang the lullaby she once overheard a new mother singing to her baby at one shelter.

One month later, the baby came into the world with no complications. A healthy girl with red hair and blue eyes and all ten fingers and toes. The newborn cried out as if to announce to the world, "I'm here."

April held her briefly afterwards. She gazed at her and whispered with tears on her cheeks. "I have always loved you. You will understand someday you stood a better chance in a new home." Her heart tore into pieces, regardless of how much she convinced herself of the right reasons. She carried her safely in her womb, nurtured her, felt her move, and understood she was already providing a better life for a child. She loved her with all her heart. The ultimate gift to her daughter, a gift of a better life. A love she never experienced herself.

Right before April put the baby in Bonnie's arms, she buried her nose in the pink blanket, which the nurses had wrapped her daughter in, and inhaled the scent of baby powder, the smell forever a reminder.

"You are doing the right thing," Bonnie said.

"I know. It doesn't stop the pain." April murmured while painful tears streamed uncontrollably down her face.

Bonnie put her arm around April's shoulder and hugged her. "The gift you are giving her is priceless. Please understand, it is also selfless."

April bent her head to the little bundle and placed one last kiss on the baby's forehead. "I loved you. Never forget." A warmth of peace glowed softly in her broken heart as she watched Bonnie walk out of the room with the baby. She wiped the tears spilling down her face with the edge of the sheet that covered her body, still sore from labor.

Signing the birth certificate using her middle name, thanks to Bonnie's suggestion, and writing 'father unknown' also became another one of the toughest things she'd ever done.

April received assurances that her baby would go to a wonderful family. Also, her own life held the promise of a future ahead. She healed physically soon enough, although an undying ache never left. Tears remained close and surfaced unexpectedly often. She simply let them fall until she breathed normally again.

———

April finished high school and enrolled in college in Oklahoma City with help. In the evenings, she read the cases Bonnie brought home and discovered she wanted to focus on the language form of writing speeches and to show her students how to examine cases from more than one perspective. Once she entered college, the harder classes became a welcome distraction, one she needed. With success in her grasp, she focused solely on her studies and excelled in her classes. And made the dean's list almost every semester.

Coming home from classes one day before graduation, the two women finished their meal and went to sit on the porch swing. It became the perfect place where they often discussed their daily activities and current events. The counselor, now a friend and mentor, asked, "How are studies coming along?"

"Other students have constantly asked for my help. I don't feel comfortable advising them."

"You're training to be a teacher, right?" Bonnie questioned.

"Yes."

"Then what is the problem? Help them if they ask."

"Okay, thanks. I think I'll go to my room and read a book. Good night."

"Alright dear. Good night."

Bonnie knocked on the door the moment April got into bed. "Come in"

"I forgot to ask you about something."

"What is it?"

"I need some extra hands at the shelter tomorrow. Do you think you're up to it?"

April let the idea float into her head. She felt indebted both to the place and to Bonnie and hated refusing the woman. Apprehension tightened her throat with the weighty request.

Bonnie saw the look of anxiety on April's face and assured her. "You won't have to be around the children. Staying in the kitchen will be a safe spot for you."

"Good, I don't mind helping, but I can't be around babies just yet."

The next afternoon in the kitchen, April helped prepare the evening meal. It proved to be easier than she thought. The insight of a debt being repaid by giving back pleased her immensely. She volunteered regularly, which Bonnie accepted with a warm heart.

Julie, another volunteer who worked alongside her, asked, "Why do you work at the shelter?"

"I owe it and Bonnie an enormous debt. After my classes are over for the day, I come here to help."

"What are you studying?"

"I'm going to be an English teacher. I have one more year before I graduate," she declared with enthusiasm and pride.

"Congratulations. I'm sure you'll make an excellent teacher." Julie inquired, "Do you have any family nearby?"

"Only Bonnie. The woman is like a mother to me." April didn't make a habit of advertising the fact she and Bonnie lived together..

Regardless of their differences, the two new friends talked about the needy and how they improved lives here. Julie talked about her adopted little girl and relayed stories of some pranks the child played on the family. Little kids' antics often sent shivers down her spine. Funny thing — this story of adoption made April catch her breath for a second, though it didn't bring tragic regrets to the surface.

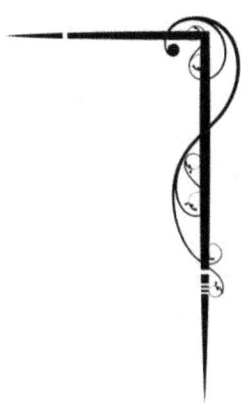

Chapter 6

After Brock defended the homeless man accused of stealing a blanket and being back in the underprivileged community, awareness slapped him squarely in the face of why Maria disappeared. She wanted someone to believe in her, although she hadn't asked. Perhaps with his own immaturity, he hadn't been ready to take the next step to actually help her realize her own dreams. Then he turned his back on her instead of pushing Cindy aside. He lost her, and along the way, lost his true self.

He sat in his office with his head in his hands, then took a deep breath. The harsh, well-meaning words from Julie struck home. His present lifestyle no longer worked. He needed to step out on his own, not in his parents' shadow. He knew they never questioned his behavior, aside from their disapproval sometimes. Confident because independence sounded great, he wanted to be on his own two feet. Granted, being a little afraid of failure scared him.

Brock would have to be assertive rather than reactive in telling his family about his plans. By not being too far away, it made it less upsetting, especially for his mother. He walked onto the front porch and opened the door of the family home. "Hey, where is everyone?" he called out.

"We are in the dining room," his mom responded. Kayla Ruggle, a petite woman, possessed a sharpness not to be ignored, who won cases challenged in court with an appeal of dignity. He kissed her cheek before he sat down at the table, then greeted his sister Julie and Cash Dryer, her fiancé and co-worker. Following dinner, Brock stood, smiled lovingly at his family, and announced his intentions. "Family, I need to change my life. I'm moving to Tulsa to start my law firm." He looked directly at Julie and grinned. He couldn't forget their intense office conversation.

"Son, we will miss you and understand your need to be on your own. You know we'll always be here for you," his dad stated. Steven, like him, turned a jury's head and swayed them into making moral decisions.

Brock's mom wiped tears from her eyes and sniffled. "Tulsa's not too far away."

Julie told him, "We'll take care of Mom and Dad and the firm. Start your own future. Anytime you want to come back to the firm, it is your legacy the same way it is mine."

━━ ▬▬ ▬▬ ━

Brock moved to Tulsa, found an apartment, and started his law firm in a small office space in the downtown area. With the business open, he called a real estate office and inquired about any ranches for sale in the area. The company found a small spread near Broken Arrow. The town within commuting distance of Tulsa enabled him to keep his office and oversee his new home's construction and management. He stood apprehensively, scanning the area. The land and old house weren't much to look at, and there'd be a lot of work to make the place livable again.

A lot of his clients, rural people, didn't always have money to pay his fees, so he accepted their help with the ranch. Carpenters and others who knew how to build fences or how to fill the fields with excellent stock helped him rebuild the ranch, along with the barns and stables. At a rapid pace, they remodeled the ranch-style home with modern appliances and furnishings and restored the outside to its past style.

Brock stayed busy in his law office in Tulsa and hired a manager to help him on the ranch in Broken Arrow. He possessed the best of both worlds, content with his choices. Since he moved away from the bigger city and his family, his actions pushed him to mature into a well-respected man and changed his life.

Brock seldom stayed away for extended periods, and it felt odd to go back for a visit. Occasionally, work made it inevitable. Broken Arrow and Tulsa had become home. He remained away for a longer period than usual. Brock arrived back in Oklahoma City for the weekend wedding between Julie and Cash. Witnessing Julie happy with Cash made it worth the trip.

He walked out of the church with his parents to go to the restaurant where the couple were having the reception. Julie called out. "Brock, wait up. I need to talk to you in private, if you don't mind?" She pulled her brother back into the church with a strained look on her face.

He asked cautiously, "What's wrong?"

"I need to ask you about something before I talk to Cash."

Brock feigned being shocked and teased, "What, have you changed your mind? It's a little too late."

Julie laughed, then huffed, "No, I haven't. Do you have any opinions about adoption?"

"Adoption, sis, really. Come on, you just got married. Isn't it a little soon to be worrying about kids?" he asked with a puzzled look on his face.

She sat down on a bench in the family room of the church and invited him to join her. She took a deep breath and then explained her situation. "Bonnie Burton brought a little girl to my attention. She needs a home and someone to love her. I have been with her three and four days a week for over two months now. I love her. Don't ask me to explain because I can't," Julie cried. She described the little girl to him. "She is smart and lovable. Not shy either. You will fall in love with her completely, like I have."

"Well, all kids need love and a home. I think you would give her both if this is what you wanted and if Cash is fine with it. However?"

"I understand. Something is pulling me to her, and I can't stop it." Julie exclaimed.

"Then you have my blessing, if this is what you want." Brock hoped she wouldn't regret it. Their parents raised them to have compassion for other people and to help them in any way possible, though he strayed occasionally. Even now, the memory of what he did left a bitter taste in his mouth.

Brock called to find out what kind of present he could bring on his first visit to meet Riley. Julie told him she liked butterflies. The new uncle found a small butterfly necklace, the perfect size for a child. Cash opened the door to greet Brock. He hadn't seen him since their wedding. "How's family life?" he asked his new brother-in-law and added mischievously, "I don't see any gray hairs yet."

Cash stood with a look of pride. "Honestly, I initially dismissed her desire for a child as insane."

Brock followed the other man into their living room. His head lifted the moment his sister and a little girl came into the room. Seeing the child in person instead of the pictures Julie sent often caught him off guard.

While Brock watched the little girl with red hair and blue eyes, she pointed to him, then looked up at Julie. "This is your uncle Brock."

She flew into his legs, grinning with dimples that matched his. He lowered himself to her eye level, and she clasped her little arms around his neck. "Hi, Unca Bock."

He picked her up and swung her around. She giggled and giggled. A bond forged between them quickly. He understood Cash's words of how he compared Riley to a gift from God.

They all moved into the living room. Brock sat on the edge of the sofa and watched in amazement as the beautiful child danced around the room, carefree. He reached into his pocket and brought out a gift-wrapped box. Riley stopped and jumped onto his lap in a flash. He passed her the box. "This is for my favorite niece."

She fumbled, trying to rip the paper off until he helped her. "Oh, but fly," she exclaimed.

"Yes, butterfly for you." Brock placed the necklace around her little neck and fastened it.

The child kept her tiny little hand on it and spun towards Brock's face and kissed each of his dimples with a wonderful wet mouth. "Did you come to play with me?"

"If your name is Riley, then yes, I came to play," he teased and winked at his sister.

"I'm Riley, and my dolly's name is Maria."

Brock's heart jolted, and he felt his face pale. Between the red hair of his new niece and the mention of the name Maria, it took a minute for him to regain his composure. She had existed in the past. Now this beautiful little girl and her doll were in his present.

───────────

Riley visited Brock's ranch every chance she got. He taught her how to ride horses, and they enjoyed camping out under the stars. She always told him, "You are my favorite uncle." They laughed. She touched the butterfly necklace again and declared, "I am your only niece, Uncle Brock."

His parents passed, and he found more time for Riley. They spent most of the weekends together at the ranch. Sometimes she invited her best friend Kadina to come with her. They rode horses, fished or camped out. He bought the land next door and made his ranch bigger. A creek on his newly gained land flowed to a small lake. The perfect spot for camping overnight trips.

Brock noticed changes once Riley began visiting regularly. As she aged, her red hair became a richer shade, and her blue eyes brightened. Cash would have his hands full later fending off boys. Amused at the thought, he chuckled.

Over the years, he shortened his long blond hair, and a trimmed beard enhanced his jawline. Work on the ranch seemed to be the only exercise he needed to keep his body honed.

Brock appeared to have a busy social life with charity events, dinners in Tulsa, and benefits. "If you constantly have me attending galas with random women, what's the point of a proper date?" He teased his sister about them every time she brought up the subject of him settling down with one of those women on a recent visit.

"Brother, you understand they are not random. Most of them you have already met at another function. Despite what you think, I don't have a list to go by," she rebuffed him.

"Are you sure one's not in the wings waiting for me? I don't need a woman beside me. The ranch and law office keep me occupied."

Later in the day, Riley teased him about not having a special someone. "Uncle Brock, why don't you have a wife?"

"Why did you also decide I need someone special? You sound like your mom. Did she put you up to asking this?" Brock pretended to be irritated, letting Riley assume her mom was in trouble with him. Despite the tease, he reflected on his future and not having a family.

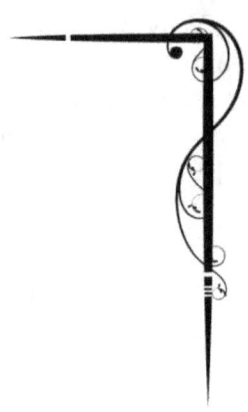

Chapter 7

A new chapter in April's life awaited. Having passed all the exams, graduation day finally came. She regarded the accomplishment as superb for a former foster kid and then a homeless person to be named valedictorian. Her memory of the vow returned. To be better than the invisible street person Brock knew.

April started her career being an English teacher at one of Oklahoma City's middle schools in session for four days, then she helped at the shelter in the evenings or on weekends. Grading and prep taking up her evening didn't bother her. She chose to enjoy it all and made teaching her number one priority. Ultimately, she found her niche and began instructing high school classes. Older kids who required to be reached sooner. Because she loved her job, time flew by quickly, and before she knew it, years passed unnoticed.

While attending college, she rarely dated. The need to go out with a man wasn't on the agenda. Usually, she simply tagged along beside a group of girls. She had only been with one man in her life, and it cost her dearly. One mistake she wouldn't repeat. If she spent the rest of her life alone, so be it.

During her career, April turned down several requests for dates. The current teaching semester brought a new face to the school. Scott — persistent, handsome, and a history teacher with black hair, brown eyes and a slim build — always seemed to be in the hall outside of her classroom. She made many attempts to ignore him. He wouldn't give up and begged her. "Please go out with me?"

A week later, she conceded. "I'll go to dinner with you."

Scott grinned. "Dinner works!"

The other single teachers good-naturedly teased April because he asked none of them. With the first two dates going fine, she gave in to a third one for dinner and a movie. Everything went well until he walked her to the Bonnie's front door. Scott's lips brushed against hers, then he deepened the caress. She didn't respond and broke the kiss. Shaken, he attempted to go farther than she wanted. He had never tried to push himself on her before.

"Why are you cold towards me? You pulled back."

"I'm sorry, Scott. You don't deserve this kind of treatment. I just don't feel any sparks between us."

Stunned, he said, "You didn't feel a thing? Are you heartless or just cold?"

"I wanted to. I really did." Anger flashed in her eyes at the harsh words, then relief washed over her not to have to pretend any sort of emotion for the guy. She wasn't certain if the leftover feeling of rejection from Brock played a part. Something in her heart remained frozen. One thing she knew for sure, no fires of passion burned for him..

Gossip from the other teachers started immediately because she rejected the school's best-looking single teacher. One of her co-workers even caught up to her before she got into her car one afternoon and angrily asked,

"Why did Scott call it quits with you? Is something wrong with you? He is one of the nicest guys around here?"

"There's nothing wrong with me. I didn't want to be pressured into a relationship, and what he wanted I couldn't give."

She hadn't wanted to string him along and give false hope. The honest conversation didn't stop the whispers in the teachers' lounge. Because of the hurtful gossip, she avoided dating and close friendships.

Despite being shunned by her fellow teachers, she became one of the most popular teachers with the students. She made English a fun subject for them. Her years of observing Bonnie prepare for court cases helped her know how to manipulate language, making her students hang on all the stories. Her lessons revolved around using certain perspectives to communicate theories and tell the different outcomes. Writing speeches, similar to debating, except on paper.

An argument stemmed over a tough case in class one afternoon, causing one of her students to ask. "Why do you teach to write speeches about real people?"

"Sue, they are real people with their own stories. I explain this way to help you recognize there are always two sides and different ways to resolve problems." She gained the respect of her students through her honesty.

With the cold treatment from her co-workers, an unsettledness settled in April's spirit. She ought to have been happy in her new life. This wasn't the case. Unaware of how to find out why, she asked Bonnie. "What is wrong with me? Why am I not satisfied?"

"Perhaps you need to get out on your own. Why don't you think about a smaller school in a different town? The city keeps expanding."

"My students deserve better, and class sizes are becoming unmanageable. It makes it hard to focus individually," the seasoned teacher stated. "I'm not sure how to feel if you're not around."

"Think about it some more and don't worry about me. I'll be fine, and so will you."

"Maybe you are right. I'll look into jobs in a smaller city." Freedom to stand on her own. Support from Bonnie being simply a phone call away.

April woke the following morning to the local news of the tragedy. Julie, her friend and her husband died in a car accident the previous afternoon. She stopped at the shelter before she went to school and comforted the other volunteers. Everyone, including some of the homeless, shared stories about how Julie made their lives a little better. Bonnie made a statement from the heart about the tragic loss the woman would be to all of them. Meanwhile, she couldn't do anything more except grieve in private.

Though saddened by memories of Julie, she hurried to her classroom, trying to put Julie's death out of her mind. She sympathized with the daughter for finishing growing up without her parents. Loss strengthened you if you allowed it. She discovered this early in life.

Instead of eating lunch, April sat at her desk, turned her laptop on, and took Bonnie's advice. Rather than take a job in a suburb of Oklahoma City, she searched for one in nearby Tulsa and found a position teaching basic English available. It sounded like a good place to start over. Once she decided for sure, she contacted the school. With a couple of weeks left of the school year remaining, she made the step to move by looking over the contract with Tulsa. She wanted to be certain. Doubts plagued her if she allowed them to take hold. A strange city with new coworkers — scary.

April arrived home and met Bonnie in the living room, where they discussed her job search and the offer from Tulsa. She related the skepticism before they ate dinner.

"I'm afraid to begin at the bottom. This opening is a little different from my regular teaching methods."

Afterward, the two of them retired to the front porch swing. "You don't have any ground to be worried. Your reputation is impeccable. The only apprehensions are coming from you."

With careful consideration two days later, April tentatively accepted the offer from Tulsa. With the hesitations mostly resolved, she began preparing for change and dragged a suitcase out of the closet. Bonnie approached her bedroom before she started packing. "Have you completed the plans to teach in Tulsa next year?"

"Not entirely. I haven't signed the contract yet. Why?"

"Well, would you consider going to an even smaller school?"

"Where is it?" she asked cautiously.

"It is in Broken Arrow, a suburb of Tulsa. They contacted the college and asked for a teacher who specialized in language, with debate and speeches as their primary emphasis. Your students here learned a lot from you."

"This sounds more like my work here. I'll contact them tomorrow if you have their number?"

"Yes, I have the number right here. Perhaps we can go together on whatever day they want to interview you. If you like the job offer, we'll look for a place for you to live while we're there."

"Sounds good." A rural teaching job wouldn't be much different, she assumed. Given her history of overcoming obstacles, she optimistically figured this latest development to be easy. April checked out the town on the computer. The suburb, according to the internet, appeared to be a thriving, family-oriented place to live. She surmised this meant excellent schools.

She and Bonnie completed their plans to spend some extra days in the town, then left for their road trip early

Thursday afternoon. School wasn't in session on Fridays, allowing them three days.

Traffic thinned as they left Tulsa. Country two-lane highways replaced the freeways. The scenery made the twenty-minute drive from the big city enjoyable. Broken Arrow looked greener with more open spaces. From the highway, you saw where old farmhouses used to be. Definitely a slower pace of traffic than the multi-lanes and overpasses she had become accustomed to.

Maybe she needed this change. It occurred to her she hadn't paused since the escape from the foster home all those years ago. With a slower lifestyle, she might, if possible, overcome her restlessness.

April located a parking space and glanced around the smaller school building. It looked clean, not rundown. Her appointment with the principal occurred at nine o'clock in the administrator's office. Down the hall she walked, peeking into the various rooms, impressed with their size. The bigger city held double the number of desks.

She relaxed instead of being apprehensive about the meeting. If the principal approved of her, the next step, a final interview with the school board. She wasn't worried about her qualifications, given her ten years of job experience. Hopefully, her novel and controversial teaching style didn't spark too many valid concerns in the rural school system.

Mrs. Kelley ushered her into an office and invited her to sit. "Why do you want to leave the Oklahoma City schools for a smaller one? It is usually the other way around."

"I decided I need a change. A chance to be more independent. I intended to take a position in Tulsa until someone informed me about this position. I thought it might be a better fit."

"Your qualifications are outstanding. I think the board will like you," Mrs. Kelley told her and scheduled the more extensive teacher interview with the school board for the next day.

They talked for several more minutes. Both discovered they had begun their careers in the Oklahoma City system. April asked, "What brought you to a smaller school?"

"Like you, I needed a break from the hustle and bustle of the city. This place has been a lifesaver for me, and I hope it will be for you too."

"I have felt like I have been missing out on something. This move may be the very thing I need," April disclosed.

"What do you think? Did the principal like you, and do you want the job?" Bonnie asked the minute April returned to the car.

"Yes, Mrs. Kelley is very nice, understands my reasons for change, and has a meeting already in place for tomorrow."

"Good, then I've booked a room at one of the local hotels for the night." They explored the area to search for available rental houses. Some they checked out seemed fine; others lacked the coziness April deemed important.

While they waited for the interview with the school board. Bonnie suggested they go shopping for new clothes. Although pretty dresses were one of April's weaknesses, she said instead. "Why don't we play tourist and go to the area parks? See their walking trails."

"Great idea. You will want a nice place to get exercise."

They spent the rest of the day out in the fresh air with spectacular views of rolling hills and valleys, and prominent features of the parks. The landscapes showed a rich tribal Indian influence, and April's research of the area revealed several lakes, a short drive away.

The following morning, the meetings progressed well. April sat in front of the board members and answered their questions honestly. "Where did you get the inspiration to become a teacher?"

"I understand the need to help young people broaden their horizons and to have empathy for them. Trust me, I'm aware of life's challenges. I witnessed the consequences of teachers and other caregivers not providing guidance since I grew up in foster care. Hopefully, I can make a difference, and the best way to do this is to teach them in school."

April won over the school board members. Her ability to reach even the troubled kids and to get their grades up played a major role. They offered her the job on the spot, and she didn't hesitate to accept. Something about the small hometown pulled her in. If she started over here, it perhaps altered her life.

"The move will be good for you," Bonnie stated. "And it is close enough to Oklahoma City. We can visit often."

The younger woman beamed and said, "Now I need a place to live. The ones we looked at yesterday just seemed okay, not the right fit, if you get what I mean."

Bonnie grinned back. "We passed a small house on the way to the school this morning. I noticed the rent sign. Why don't we check it out?"

"Okay, sounds good. It wasn't very far from the school?"

"Not far at all. If you wanted walking's not out of the question.."

April liked the cute house and the neighborhood immediately. It appeared comfortable from the outside without being old-fashioned, airy with several windows. She called the number on the sign in the yard. "I saw the sign about your house for rent. Is it still available?"

"Yes, it is. I can meet you in ten minutes," the man replied.

The small house held two bedrooms, a small kitchen, and a spacious living area. Someone already decorated the rooms with colors just right for her. Best of all, a swing suspended from hooks on a wide front porch sealed the deal. She wanted to be settled before school started in late

August. April felt relieved immediately once she gave her principal the news she wouldn't be back next year.

April moved into the house with excitement for the chance to start fresh and be totally on her own in a new town and in a new home. Independence. The freedom to pay her own bills, eat her own cooking, may have seemed routine for others, but not for her.

Energized, she looked forward to school the following month, got her class schedules and a list of what the board wanted her to teach per requirement. She hoped her new students were bright and spirited, similar to the ones she had taught before. Sometimes at a smaller school, the parents preferred you to be more sedate. Having already discussed this, the school board supported her. She wouldn't change her methods to pacify a parent without a clue to the real world and to what the kids faced nowadays.

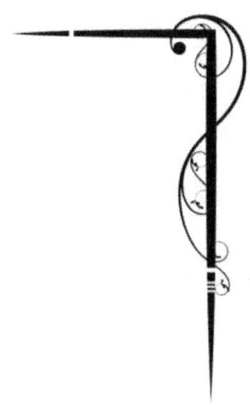

Chapter 8

B rock sat at his stylish African blackwood desk in the law office, where he reviewed notes for an impending trial. Because he dismissed his staff early with the impending storm, the room's quietness allowed him to work uninterrupted. The clouds churned, eerie shades of green and gray turning the skies dark with heavy rain coming down in sheets. An odd electricity loomed in the air. He jerked, startled by the opening of the front door. He rose from his desk and went into the lobby, where a highway patrolman stood waiting. "Can I help you?"

"Are you Brock Ruggle?"

"Yes."

"I am afraid I have some bad news for you." Brock squared his shoulders and braced himself. "Your sister, Julie Dryer, and her husband, Cash, have been involved in a car accident in Oklahoma City."

"Are they hurt? Which hospital?" He reached for his jacket and phone, intending to hurry to their sides.

The officer shook his head, placed his hand on Brock's shoulder and said with remorse, "I am very sorry. They did not survive the crash."

Brock's legs almost buckled as he fully grasped what the man said. "What about their daughter? Don't tell me she's gone too."

"No, she's at school. We wanted to inform you first."

Brock's world suddenly turned black. He sat down on the edge of the desk, took a minute, then asked, "What caused the wreck?"

The officer shook his head. "A drunk driver, speeding and going the wrong way on I-235. They couldn't have known what hit them. It isn't much help, but they didn't suffer."

"I hope you got the SOB?" Rage replaced the darkness.

"Yeah, we got him. He's in serious condition. The guy will go to jail."

"Well, I will make sure of it," he stated with conviction, before the police officer walked out. He followed the man, locked the door and started towards Oklahoma City.

The drive racing to the bigger city passed in a blur. His sole concern now focused on Riley and how he would destroy her world. Almost panicking himself, he paused long enough to take a deep breath and run a hand through his hair and down his face to calm himself before he entered the building where his niece attended school. It wouldn't benefit Riley if he lost it, and she'd need him now more than ever.

He sat on the edge of the chair in the principal's office as his body trembled. She grinned until she looked into his eyes. "Sit down, Riley. I have bad news. It is about your parents."

"Are they hurt or sick?" He saw the tears gathered, waiting to fall from her eyes. His stomach plummeted again. Powerful arms grasped her body before she jumped up. He tightened the hold as she fought against him.

"No, sweetheart, something far more dreadful has happened. There's been a car accident; they're gone." He clutched her even tighter. The reality and fury slammed into him again.

Riley screamed. "No, no, you must be wrong! Please, Uncle Brock, you have misunderstood. This can't be happening. They told me about a vacation in a couple of weeks. How can we go if they aren't here?"

"Baby, I wish it weren't real. I'm so sorry." Brock pulled her onto his lap, and rocked her gently the way he used to when she got hurt on the ranch.

Riley sobbed against his chest, and her shoulders shook with the enormous amount of pain and grief. Finally, the tears slowed, and she asked, "Will you take me home?"

He nodded, and she stood up. Then he led her towards the door.

They walked into his sister's house, where an unnerving quiet waited. He placed her on the couch and sat. Pulling her close, he hugged her while she sobbed more tears for her parents. He knew they needed to come to terms with this heartbreak. After an hour, she calmed enough for him to leave her side and begin making calls.

The doorbell rang the minute Brock finished talking to the funeral home. "I heard about the accident on the news. I came right over to offer you some help."

"Thank you."

Bonnie hugged him before she asked, "Where is Riley?" The woman looked over his shoulders, searching for her surrogate grandchild. Julie always described Riley this way.

"She's in the living room, and I'm afraid she is in shock."

"Don't worry, I can take care of our girl," Bonnie told him. He showed her into the room.

Sobbing, Riley continued to sit on the couch. Brock watched from the doorway. His heart ripped open with pain while his parents' old friend stroked Riley's head with gentle but firm hands. "You loved them, and they knew it. Let the grief out now. Loss will take a lot of healing. Remember, you have your uncle who loves you, and I am just a phone call away if you need me."

Riley choked out between more sobs. "Why did this happen to them? They didn't deserve it. How am I going to survive without them? Please tell me how."

Listening to the conversation, he saw the older woman holding back her own unshed tears. "You are strong, Riley. Your parents raised you to be. It doesn't seem like it now. The pain will ease into wonderful memories you can cherish for the rest of your life."

When the loud weeping subsided, Brock stepped to the doorway and saw Riley asleep on the couch. Bonnie placed a blanket over the girl and met him in the hallway, then said with a firm voice, "You are taking her back to live with you." It was a statement, not a question.

Brock answered sternly. "Of course, I am. She is my family."

The fight started immediately following the funeral. Riley stomped her feet where she stood in the living room of her childhood home in front of Brock and exclaimed, "I thought you could move back to the city? This way, I can go back to my school and my friends."

Mildly aggravated, although understanding her outburst, he told her, "My life is in Broken Arrow and Tulsa, and it will be your home. There are excellent schools, and you will make new friends."

"I don't want to go," she begged. "Please, can't we stay here?"

"No, Riley, we can't. I have already told you. You are my responsibility, and besides, remember you are my only family as well."

Brock hadn't stopped all summer. Handling Julie and Cash's personal affairs, selling the family's law office, and moving Riley into his home drained Brock. His patience wore thin with the grief-stricken young girl at the point she started getting mouthy. He acknowledged the sorrow, only it didn't make life any easier with her. The school year started, and her new hobby grew until she ignored whatever he said. The only response to him, grimaces and eye rolls. He felt frustrated. What did he know about raising a teenager? She used to be so sweet before. The once-loving niece in his custody rebelled, and it killed him to see her act this way. Surely if he went to the school, they might give him advice.

Mrs. Target, the counselor at Riley's school, ushered him into her office. "Mr. Ruggle, how may I help you?"

"Thank you for seeing me so fast. I'm at my wit's end. This is about my niece, Riley. Between the loss of her parents and moving to a new school, she has become sassy with everyone around her. I wondered if there's anything you can suggest because the grief counselors we talked to don't seem to have made any progress."

Mrs. Target opened a file on her computer. "I'm not surprised you're here. I noticed your niece's grades from her previous school and then from this semester here. Except for one class, they have all fallen. Perhaps this teacher holds the answer to connecting with her."

"Who is this teacher?"

"Miss Palmer. She's a new hire and is becoming one of the school's most popular teachers. I can ask her for help if you want me to?"

Brock asked with curiosity, "What does she teach?"

Mrs. Target said, "Language with an unorthodox approach."

"How can language be unorthodox?" he speculated out loud.

"She brings everyday scenarios into play," the woman explained.

Wise enough to seek help, Brock stated, "I don't really care how she does it, as long as she can get through to Riley, unorthodox or not, I will appreciate the help. Thank you." He exhaled and stood to leave.

The counselor replied, "I'll keep you informed of the results."

Brock left the school more optimistic about his niece. He contemplated the prospect of what this teacher could actually do for Riley driving back to the ranch. Time would tell. If his niece returned to her old self, provided he tolerated her current behavior long enough, he owed the mentor his approval.

Rather than arguing with Riley, he made a conscious decision to ignore the sudden outbursts of unacceptable conduct until change came about. He spent countless hours at the barn, eager to come up with fresh ideas to market his horses' bloodlines, which benefited the ranch. Although he didn't see any children of his own in his future, he could pass on a new legacy of a successful ranch to Riley and her children. He rode across the pastures where something about the solitude calmed his ever-present grief for Julie and reassured him things with Riley would eventually be okay.

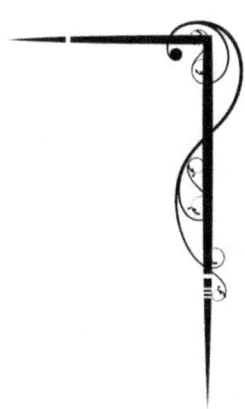

Chapter 9

April settled into her new life. It had taken little effort to get used to the perfect and peaceful home. She sat on the porch swing in the evenings to relax. A cool breeze blew through the trees in her yard, and it felt like heaven. Fireflies floated across the grass like hundreds of little stars kissing the ground. It amazed her how they disappeared and then flickered their lights again a few inches away. In the darkness, with these sights and sounds, she found a world completely different from her youth. They almost made her forget the mean, cruel world they all lived in. *Almost.*

She liked the school with smaller class sizes, which enabled her to give more one-on-one phases to her students. On the first day, she stood at the front of the classroom and scanned the youthful faces. "My rules are simple. You will pay attention to the conversations and take part in the debates. If you think you can fool me, then you are in the wrong class. I have ten years of teaching behind me from the big city and have seen everything life and students can dish out. I refuse to be deceived. And please don't cross any lines you are not willing to explain."

The court records omitted a few gruesome details from the transcripts. She eventually caught their attention with different scenarios of court cases, stories which piqued their curiosity. While they learned to adapt old cases to new ones, if they saw both sides of every story and wrote speeches supporting the latest outcome, she succeeded at her job. Hopefully, before the year's end, they all understood that life choices made or broke someone.

Pretty much all her students paid attention to her expectations, except for her last class of the day. The small group of kids who sat together in the back of the room had been harder to connect with. They barely listened to her instructions, which challenged her work. It took almost two full months to reach them and to make progress, but she did.

At the official end of the first semester, Mrs. Target stopped April in the hallway. "Will you please come to my office in the morning? I need to talk to you."

"Okay," she said cautiously.

Though April hadn't been overly concerned about the meeting the previous night, the teacher found herself unable to avoid worrying. She knocked on the counselor's door the next day, blew out a soothing breath and then entered the room.

"Have a seat. I have a favor to ask you."

The statement relieved her anxiety enough for a genuine smile.

"One of your students' guardians met with me yesterday about his niece. The girl has become hostile to him and his employees. He also raised concerns about her new friends. Do you think you can talk to her?"

April struggled to identify one of her students being this difficult as the reason someone issued a complaint to the school. All of her kids seemed reasonable and eager to learn from her. "Who are we talking about?"

"Riley Dryer. I looked at her grades and noticed they have all slipped except in your class."

"Yes, I have Riley in my class. Some kids in the last hour were too clever for their own good and spoiled. Eventually, they all listened and now take part. You know, friends can be a prominent influence."

"She's striking out at the people who want to help her. This has to be her way of coping with the grief and changes in her life. She moved in with her uncle and started school here since her parents died in a car accident at the end of last year in Oklahoma City."

"You say her parents died last spring in Oklahoma City?" April questioned.

"Yes, a tragedy, from what the papers said. Her mom, Julie, was a big part of the shelters in the city where she volunteered. Wait a minute, didn't you live in the city?"

"Oh wow, Mrs. Target, I knew Julie and didn't realize Riley was her daughter. We volunteered together and got to know each other; except I never met the girl." April shook her head, thinking, what a small world.

"Possibly this is the way you reach out."

"I'll see what I can do, Mrs. Target."

Therefore, April quietly watched Riley in class that afternoon. The girl with a shade of hair similar to hers had caught her eye on the first day of classes. Her heart jumped with pain once more because her own baby, born with red hair, would be in the same grade. Her behavior appeared consistent with her normal actions. It seemed impossible the little girl from Julie's stories could become so hateful. Maybe her uncle misread her students' actions.

She called Bonnie in the evening to catch up on the everyday happenings in their lives. "How did the court rule today in your recent case?"

"I won, of course. How are things with you at school?"

"They are going very well, and I think I needed a change."

"Great, I'm glad to hear you are happy."

"I also called to ask, do you remember Julie from the shelter? She died last spring in a car accident, along with her husband."

Bonnie replied, "Yes, I remember her. I visited her daughter following the awful, unexpected, and sad accident."

"Oh, you know who Riley is, then. She's the reason I'm calling. I have her in one of my classes and don't have any problems with her. Apparently, though, she's having trouble with her other studies and, from what her uncle said, at home, too. He reached out to the school for help. I'm sure it is just grief which has caused her to lash out. Mrs. Target has asked me to talk to her. Should I?"

"You worked with Julie. Connect with the girl. Let her know you knew her mom and see if anything you tell her eases her pain some."

April stood by the door to her classroom at the end of her last class the next day and told her students to have a good evening, like she always did. Once Riley approached the door, she pulled her to the side and asked her, "Can you stay over for a few minutes?"

"I'll miss my bus."

"I will take you home."

"Am I in trouble?"

"No, no, I wanted to talk to you about something."

Riley hollered at Mick and her other friends, who waited in the hallway. "Miss Palmer wants to talk to me. You guys go on."

The room emptied. April closed the door, then sat down at a desk and motioned for Riley to do the same. "I want to be honest with you. Your uncle came to the school." The teenager rolled her eyes. To hide a slight grin, the teacher turned her head and coughed, so the girl wouldn't see.

"Mrs. Target asked me to talk to you. I regretted hearing about your parents' deaths. Your mom was a delightful woman."

Riley's eyes grew wide. "You knew my mom?"

"Yes, we met at the shelter where I volunteered in Oklahoma City. Your mom helped me in the kitchen, where we served the needy."

"I sometimes went along. She said the other kids liked to play while their parents worked or got advice."

"Julie often spoke about you." April understood she got the girl's focus.

"What did she say about me?" Riley whispered.

April noted that the pain of loss lingered in the girl's eyes. "Your mom said you were a gift from God to her family, and you made her proud. She felt blessed to have chosen you."

"You know I am adopted, then?"

"Yes, she never hid it."

"No, she always told me the truth, too." Riley's eyes filled with tears. "It hurts. I never told her how glad I was to have her for my mother."

The restrained sobs from the girl escaped and tore at April's heart. "Your mother knew you loved her and loved you back with her entire soul."

The connection between the teacher and student forged an instant bond. They talked more about Julie's stories. Riley laughed at some of her childish pranks. The girl told her a few stories she hadn't heard.

Those types of memories, April wished for herself. When the ache of loss for both of them became a little less unbearable, she stood. "I need to take you home before they search for you. Tell me how to get to your house."

She followed the directions Riley gave. They talked more on the way. The girl mentioned her Uncle Brock often. "He's a nice-looking single man."

April's mind stuttered. Okay, it wasn't a typical name like Bob or Mike, and without a doubt, others had named men Brock. She chuckled as Riley explained further. "He's single, and so are you."

"Uh, don't concern yourself with me. I'm fine. His singleness is safe from me."

The teacher pulled into the driveway of an attractive sprawling ranch house, which circled around to the front. A big man came down the steps close to where she stopped the car, and Riley opened the door. April's eyes widened, and she literally couldn't breathe. The girl said something else, but it didn't register. She waited until her student got out of the car and quickly said, "Riley, I will see you tomorrow. Goodbye."

April gripped the steering wheel until her knuckles turned white. She didn't draw a good breath until she arrived back in town, thankful there weren't any distractions along the way. She barely remembered turning off the car's engine and stumbled to the porch where she flopped down on the brightly colored cushions of the swing, her haven of peace. Her heart pounded, and her body sweated profusely as she tried to control the anxiety. She dragged more oxygen into her lungs to calm herself.

The darker blond neatly trimmed beard made the familiar dimples she remembered more prominent, and his long blond hair appeared now shorter. If possible, he looked sexier than in the past. The only solution, shut her eyes and let the memories rush back. Ones she tried to keep buried in the dark.

The powerful attraction between the two of them, undeniable and inevitable. With one glance into his chocolate-colored eyes, almost instantaneously the battle with herself disappeared. The second time they met, she thought he was offering help with her future until he abandoned her. The impulsive fascination changed her forever and had caused the biggest regret of her life.

Unable to find any immediate answers, April finally entered the house to analyze her choices. How did she continue to help Riley face her ghosts and not face her own? When she borrowed the money, she hadn't looked at his ID. She absolutely needed to avoid Brock at all costs, even if it meant she lost her connection with the girl. She refused to quit her job. It possibly posed a tricky problem explaining to Mrs. Target why she couldn't help anymore. If she needed to come up with an excuse, then she would. With her decision made, she got ready for bed.

April woke up soaked to the skin. Her nightshirt clung to her back with sweat. Sheets tangled around her hips, and heat stole her breath. She imagined her heart leaping out of her chest as the sensations flooded through her body and drained her. Her dream relived in every kiss, each caress, all the sensual feelings of her experience. He had been confident, but gentle. She tossed and turned and tried to go back to sleep until she couldn't stand the torment any longer.

Despite being the middle of the night, April got out of bed and showered. The cool water relieved some of the tension. She pulled a robe on, went to the kitchen and started coffee, sat down and reflected on her options. Life surprised a person in a flash, and this undoubtedly became one such instance. The coffee machine finished brewing, so she got up and poured herself a cup. The hot liquid she sipped too fast burned her lips.

She knew the shadow winding its way through her past was now in the present, and he lived right here in Broken Arrow. She couldn't risk an encounter between them and wrestled with the uncertainty of the situation, her future here in danger. Brock, a popular lawyer in town, held the power to get her fired. It also jeopardized Riley's finding her path from grief. How could she do both? Avoid Brock yet help Riley. The coffee cup threatened to break from the pressure of her hands.

Just thinking about abandoning her new life here made her nauseous. She didn't want to give up because the entire purpose of her move motive to start fresh in a new place. The house felt like home to her, and the other teachers welcomed her. They gave her something she had never experienced: friends. Sometimes they met in the evenings for dinner or a drink at the local coffee shop. The subject always came back to the lack of single, eligible men. She laughed every time Crissy mentioned rich cowboys. With no interest in them, she always dismissed the conversation.

April realized she couldn't call Bonnie for advice because the woman, without a doubt, knew about Brock. She faced this problem on her own. If she confronted him and he didn't remember her, then she looked like a fool. Her giving reasons for said conduct tied to a secret she wanted to stay hidden would ruin her and him if it came out.

The likelihood of his ever seeing her again seemed unlikely. Really, the resolution shouldn't be too difficult. The key, distance herself from the student except during school hours. She sighed with relief once she figured out what to do about Brock and Riley. She finished her coffee, got dressed, and started another day.

Riley waited in the hallway at the end of class. "Miss Palmer, will you tell more stories about Mom?"

"I'm sorry, not this afternoon. I have to grade extra papers tonight and won't have time. Why don't you come by at lunchtime? We could talk a little then." It hurt her to turn the girl down to stay over, but... April couldn't take the risk and circumvented Riley's effort. Her heart hammered as she rushed out the door to avoid being cornered again and got into her car. The disappointment on her student's face bothered her because the girl craved a connection with her mom. April knew that by becoming the link, she set a pattern. Her lunch hours would now include visits from Riley.

Tortured from her own past, April didn't have the luxury of parents like Riley did. No hugs or cuddles in her childhood memories. Abandonment issues plagued her on more than one occasion. She locked the powerful emotions deep within her soul to survive.

April arrived at school the next morning eager to continue her classes. Enthusiasm tingled in her stomach. She'd found a tough case to present to her students. The results of the debates she strived for played an important role in her method of teaching and made her proud of them and herself when accomplished.

Arguments got heated occasionally, and the one between Riley and Mick wasn't any different. Riley stood her ground with passion and a strong will for justice. The endurance to argue with the outcome of the trial showed her different sides of her students. April couldn't help but be in awe of the girl's spirit. Thankfully, the school bell rang, ending the school day just before the classroom tension escalated. She absolutely didn't want to draw unnecessary attention to herself or her class.

April left work early instead of staying and grading papers. To relax from the potential overshadowing fallout from her students' argument, she sought solace in the one place that never disappointed her. The park she and Bonnie found when they first came here made her think of one in Oklahoma City. A haven in her youth. Nearby, she located a bench close to a stream and sat. Her attention to the lush landscape relaxed her anxiety, and the sound of a gentle trickle of water flowing over the pebbles quietened her tormented mind. She breathed in the scent of wildflowers, which bloomed along the edge, and rolled her shoulders to ease the last of her pressure. With self-confidence restored, she went home.

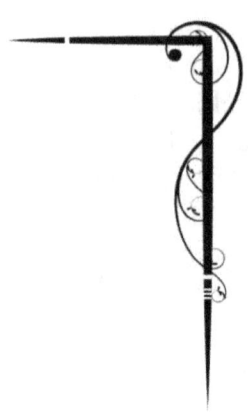

Chapter 10

Brock left work in town early, and with Riley riding home on the school bus, he took advantage of the quietness in the house to get some extra work finished.

Assured the bus always dropped her at the end of the drive, it startled him when he heard a vehicle's tires scrunch on the gravel. He raised his head from the paperwork in front of him, noticing the time. Riley wasn't home from school yet, and the noise he heard sounded too close to the house.

He walked to the front door and out onto the porch and saw a small, dark blue SUV parked with his niece getting out of the car. Starting down the steps, his intention had been to greet the driver and find out who brought Riley home and why. Instead, when his niece got out and shut the door, the driver sped away, and he didn't have any opportunity to see the person behind the wheel.

Riley's ear-to-ear grin deepened his confusion. "Where

have you been? You're late." Brock roared until he saw the spark of light fade from her eyes.

"At school."

His sharp tone softened abruptly. "Why didn't you ride the bus, and who brought you home?"

"Miss Palmer, my teacher. She asked me to stay and talk to her."

"You should have called," he said in frustration. He longed for the uncomplicated little girl again. A teenager stood in her place.

"I'm sorry. Mrs. Target asked her to talk to me, and it took me by surprise. Do you know what?" Before he guessed at the answer, she exclaimed, "She knew Mom."

"How did she know your mom?" His anger simply evaporated.

"They worked together at the shelter in the city, and she told me stories." Her shoulders slumped.

"I'm sorry, Riley. I worried about you." He pulled her to him, hugged her, and kissed the top of her head.

She returned the embrace, then whispered, "I miss them."

"Me too, kid, me too," he quietly answered.

Their moods being in unison for a change, he said, "Let's go for a ride. You can tell me some stories."

———

Brock called Mrs. Target a couple of weeks later, in a better state of mind than the last time they talked. "Thank you for the advice. Riley has stopped being sassy and seems happier. I really appreciate it."

"I'm glad to hear she seems more adjusted at home, too. Her grades have improved. You can thank the teacher I recommended. I had nothing to do with it."

"Maybe I'll drop by one afternoon and show her my appreciation in person. Until then, please give her my thanks."

Miss Palmer, Miss Palmer. Two weeks later, doubts set in about this new influence. Her name came out of Riley's mouth constantly. Everything the woman did appeared to be a clear miracle and the gospel truth to hear his niece talk. It seemed whenever they watched the evening news, or he read a newspaper article, sitting at the kitchen table, the girl always mentioned something the teacher disclosed about the article. He thought the woman taught language /speech, not current events. This must be what Mrs. Target meant about unorthodox ways.

He knew deep in his gut he owed Miss Palmer, but foolishly; he found himself jealous of the relationship between Riley and the woman. He needed to meet her soon and say thank you, because his niece had reverted to her normal self. The two of them sat on the front porch on the swing again like before, where they discussed the day's events. While she told him about her dreams, it always came back to unforgettable emotions for Maria and her red hair, the same shade as his nieces'.

The feelings ran rampant through his thoughts. He didn't have any information about her apart from her first name. His private investigator friend even searched for her, to no avail. She had awakened in him an ache of lust and desire, which surged to be explored more. She cared enough about him to rescue him from the streets, then disappeared without a trace.

Brock walked from the barn, across the driveway, to meet Riley coming home from school two days later. Her behavior alarmed him when the teen kicked dirt and spat venom after she got off the bus. "What's wrong?"

He flinched as she detailed the reason behind her anger. The vivid case the teacher expected them to write a rebuttal about started the argument. Flabbergasted at first, then angrily, he replied, "It's too gruesome for teenagers. You don't need to be exposed to these gory details." Determined to confront her, he remarked. "I will call Mrs. Target or Mrs. Kelley. Who is this teacher?"

"No, Uncle Brock, it isn't her fault. Mick wouldn't listen to my ideas about how to solve the recent case."

"It is her responsibility. She brought the subject into class, didn't she? Now, answer the question. Who is she?"

"Please don't cause her to get into trouble. I like her, and she's a wonderful teacher," Riley begged before she started into the house, then turned and mumbled. "And a good friend."

The comment aroused Brock's suspicions, yet he repeated it. "Riley, tell me."

"Miss Palmer," she muttered, and left him standing alone.

Brock sat down on the porch steps. Certainly, he didn't want to upset Riley considering the progress she made, yet the more he thought about it, the angrier he got. Orthodox or not, if this teacher taught this way, then he needed to stop her. He made plans to pay the woman a visit tomorrow. This type of instruction couldn't happen.

Brock left work early in the afternoon. He wanted to meet the infamous woman. "Hi, Mrs. Kelley. I'm here to see if it's alright for me to observe Miss Palmer's class. Mrs. Target told me she helped reach Riley. I preferred to watch her in action before I said thanks." He didn't dare voice his real reason for the visit to the teacher. An imminent conversation loomed between the two of them privately, for now. Unless she pushed back.

Occasionally, he exploited his position, leveraging his wealth and influence to get his way. Mrs. Kelley led him down the hallway to an open doorway with a classroom full of students. Brock slipped into the room.

Miss Palmer stood with her back to the open door. When Riley spotted him, he winked, and a look of fright crossed her face. He put his fingers to his mouth for her to remain quiet and sat down at an extra desk in the back of the classroom to observe. Then, he looked around and saw a group of law books he recognized from college.

The teacher stood over one of her student's desks looking down. Clearly, the kid found the work difficult and needed help. From what Brock gathered of the conversation between her and the student, it involved a murder in Oklahoma City years ago, where a father who killed his wife and daughter pleaded not guilty. In the end, they found him guilty; the woman wanted them to build a case that proved him innocent. He cringed again when he sat and listened. His chief priority for Riley's welfare remained number one. Rapidly, all the students became his concern.

When Miss Palmer straightened up in front of the entire class, the kids bombarded her with several more questions, asking about the outcome of the trial and what the sentence entailed. She clarified the answer. An automatic smile curved his lips until recognition hit him.

Brock knew his face paled, and then he watched the blood drain from hers. He whispered, 'Maria.' He wasn't sure if the noise he heard signaled the end of class or if the warning bells in his head exploded. Shaking his head, he cleared the haze where the fog in his brain blanketed his rational mind. He rose out of the chair, and his legs turned to rubber for a brief minute before he walked towards the door where she stood telling her students goodbye.

Brock held his body rigid. Riley bounced up to him and beamed wide-eyed. "Miss Palmer, this is my Uncle Brock, and Uncle Brock, this is my favorite teacher, Miss Palmer."

Brock instinctively extended his hand. The electricity of her touch stunned him. "Riley speaks of you often," he stated curtly.

"Well, she is an excellent student and very smart."

Regaining his equilibrium, Brock turned to Riley. "Will you wait in the hall for a minute? I want to talk to Miss Palmer in private."

"Uh, yeah, sure." Riley exited the room and shut the door behind her.

Brock scrutinized April as she moved back to her desk and saw her wipe the palms of her hands on her skirt before she sat in her chair. He had already rubbed his sweaty hands on his slacks, really wanting to mop the bead of wetness from the back of his neck. He followed her and leaned against the edge of a nearby desk instead. "I initially intended to come here to thank her teacher for talking to Riley about her mom. Then, Riley came home upset over an argument about a lesson from the same instructor. Determined to find out why, I now see things are not at all what I expected them to be. Are they Maria?" He asked vehemently, unable to keep his tone of voice neutral.

"The naïve young woman you knew back then is gone. Brock, I hid from you as Maria. She is no more. I am April Palmer, a teacher. Now, can I do something for you regarding my student?"

Outrage poured out of him. How dare she dismiss the fact of who she had been in the past? They would discuss the subject of Maria later. Right now, Brock sighed inwardly before he formally and firmly replied. "Yes, it is about your techniques of teaching. I have issues. We need to talk about them, Miss Palmer."

April sat up straighter and said, "Okay, Mr. Ruggle, what kind of help do you want?" She addressed him in the same stiff tone, which antagonized him further.

Brock stated, "I think you already know."

"Why don't you elaborate, then both of us will be sure of the subject?" She replied with an air of defiance in her manner.

"We will play it your way." He adopted the approach he used in the courtroom. "The discussion between Riley and

Mick the day before upset her, and I want an explanation. These cases that you have brought to your class and want the kids to learn by are too graphic and not appropriate for teenagers. You have exposed them to too much."

She snorted out loud. "Too much exposure. This is not a game. This is real life, and whether or not you like it, they will face reality sooner than later."

"It doesn't justify their need to perceive it now. Wait until they have to confront it," Brock argued back.

April said, "I disagree with you. If I show them a little piece of realism and the consequences of those actions by having them write briefs and speeches, then I can only hope it does them and maybe you, the lawyer, a favor."

"You argue well, Miss Palmer, for a teacher."

"Probably because I lived with a lawyer," she retorted.

"How do we solve this standoff?" Admiring her determination.

"I'm not sure we can," April said with the same defiant stance. "I won't allow anyone to stop me from instructing my students about the facts of real life. The board knew my methods when they hired me."

Brock narrowed his eyes and looked at her. He saw intimidation wouldn't work, and she had reached Riley. "You may proceed, though if I hear your students struggle to cope, then I will intervene."

"I'm sorry you feel this way, Mr. Ruggle. Pressure to alter my teaching methods from those clinging to fairytale solutions won't sway me. I refuse to let my students go through life with blinders on. If there is nothing else, we need to discuss…"

Brock's eyes narrowed once more. Threats and power bounced in the air between them. "Nothing for now." He left the room even more agitated. Fairytale endings, really? He scoffed.

Riley stood in the hall as he left the classroom. "Well, what do you think, Uncle?"

"What do I think about what?" Brock asked bluntly, preoccupied.

Riley smirked. "You know, Miss Palmer, isn't she beautiful?"

Brock stuttered suddenly defeated. "Well, yes, she is very attractive. What does this have to do with your studies?"

"Nothing." She shrugged her shoulders. "I'll go tell Mick and my other friends goodbye. I won't be long."

"Meet me at the truck."

Before Riley returned, Brock needed to get a grip on his emotions. He left the building and got into his vehicle, then pounded the steering wheel in exasperation. The sight of Maria, a beautiful woman now, shocked him; she still aroused him.

Riley jumped in the truck and asked as she put her seat belt on. "Uncle, are you alright?"

"I will be, don't worry."

"You look upset. Did Miss Palmer say something?"

"Nothing to concern yourself with." He started the engine and pulled out onto the street. Once they arrived home, the logic he sought wouldn't come to him. "I'm going for a ride, Riley. Tell Mrs. Shefield not to hold dinner for me."

"Okay, do you want some company?"

"Not now."

He needed to think about the situation, and he couldn't do it with Riley around. Besides, he couldn't let her suspect anything about the history between Maria and him. The girl gave him the impression she wanted to get them together.

First, how did he handle the reawakening awareness of his body for Maria? Did it come about like a new passion or simply sentimentality plaguing him? Body parts other than his heart throbbed just from the sight of her. The heat rose to a fever pitch in a matter of seconds in the classroom. He admired yet wanted to be upset with her.

The way she defended herself made him want to find out more about this version of the woman he never forgot. Obviously, to him she wasn't the old Maria.

Second, she wasn't his Maria, at least not the girl he once held in his arms and made love to. This woman called herself April and was Riley's teacher and, according to the staff and his niece, a damn good one. She intrigued him.

The apparent acquaintance of Julie's helped Riley understand her grief with reactions he couldn't. Memories and stories of antics about his niece, which his sister communicated. This meant April kept in touch with the shelters after escaping her previous lifestyle.

He suddenly felt tremendous pride. Perhaps she listened to him more than he thought. It couldn't have been easy for her to get her GED and then go to college. He wondered how she accomplished becoming a revered teacher and, no less, in his hometown. He replayed the entire conversation with her and abruptly remembered her saying she had lived with a lawyer. This explained the law books in her classroom. And what about this lawyer, a boyfriend, or a husband? No, not a husband. She went by Miss. Whoever assisted her needed to be commended.

———— ▬▬ ▬ ▬ ————

Friday afternoon passed by slowly at Brock's office. With his workload light, and since Riley reverted to her old self, he'd promised her a weekend of horseback riding and camping.

Brock arranged for Kadina's dad to drop the girlfriend off at his office on his way to a job site in Arkansas to surprise Riley with a visit from her best friend. They left for Broken Arrow, the young girl talking non-stop, and he wondered if he'd made a mistake. Hearing constant chatter could be hazardous to his health. Oh well, it felt good to have Riley smile again. Definitely worth it.

Before they entered the school building to pick Riley up early, he saw a familiar face getting out of a car. Brock walked over and asked, "Miss Burton, what are you doing in Broken Arrow, and why are you here at the school?"

"Oh, hi Brock, how are you and Riley doing?"

"We are doing better now. We hit a snag, and one of her instructors helped. Do you have a client here at the school?"

"No, I am here to visit my 'adopted daughter', April Palmer."

"Your daughter is Miss Palmer?" Brock stammered with surprise in his voice.

"My adopted daughter I said. I have helped take care of her," the woman clarified.

"She's Riley's teacher. In fact, she's the one who helped her."

"Yes, she knew Julie from the shelter."

"I need to pick Riley up. We are going to the lake and spend the weekend. Imagine me with two teenagers. Wish me luck; I will probably need it," Brock laughed, and started on into the building.

Bonnie mumbled something under her breath, turned back towards her car, and said out loud, "Oh no, I forgot my phone."

Brock and Kadina strolled into the school and met Riley at the bank of lockers. The two teens jumped up and down, as if they hadn't seen each other in months. "I want you to meet my favorite teacher," Riley said and led Kadina down the hall.

When the girls got to the open doorway, April motioned for them to wait. "Don't worry. I understand we can go later."

Riley asked, "What's wrong? You sound disappointed."

"Oh, everything is fine. My 'mom' and I planned a trip to Tulsa this weekend together. Something came up to change our plans."

Brock had avoided talking to the woman because his phone rang just as the girls entered class, diverting his focus. His manager at the ranch informed him of a minor setback in operations. In the short period on the phone, he must have missed part of the conversation. All he heard was Riley and Kadina both talking loudly, and then April's sharp refusal over the girls' heightened voices drew his attention. "Riley, why are you and Kadina squealing, and why is Miss Palmer saying no out loud?"

Both girls spoke. "We want..."

Brock held up a hand to stop them. Then he pointed to his niece and said, "Explain, please."

"Miss Palmer's plans with her mom changed. Wouldn't it be fantastic if she went with us on our camping trip? She keeps saying no."

Brock looked at the teacher, then back at the girls. He grinned mischievously. "Yeah, the idea sounds good to me." The perfect opportunity just fell into his lap.

April's eyes widened. "I don't know how to ride a horse, and I have never been camping in my whole life."

"Maybe you should learn now?" Brock issued a challenge.

She attempted to change their minds. "I don't want to intrude on your weekend with Riley."

"You won't be. Kadina will be with her. I'll be by myself and have my hands full with two teenage girls. Help. Please." The plan blossomed right before him. For her to go with them so he could observe her in his familiar place.

With excuses falling on deaf ears, she said, "You won't need much help."

"I might surprise you." He should have said, 'You did it once'. With the girls within earshot, he kept his remark to himself. This became an opportunity to give her the chance to expand her horizons. A reward for Riley turned into a prize for him.

Despite her objections, April caved and agreed to go with them. Brock discovered he faced a better outlook for the weekend than expected. This became an opportunity to give her the chance to expand her horizons. Enthusiastic feelings took him back to his childhood days of looking forward to a birthday or Christmas.

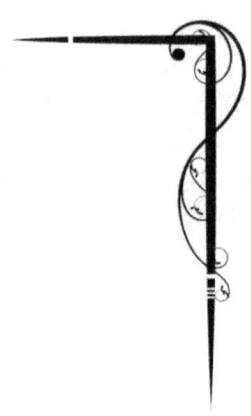

Chapter 11

April hadn't looked at her surroundings the day she gave Riley a ride home, and definitely not on her way back. She paid better attention to the drive now. The smooth road lined with fences held cattle and horses and marked the winding roads to the ranch. A typical country scene with a few trees and green grass. She found the sight irresistible.

Therefore, she pulled into the driveway, and the uncomplicated design of the house utterly stunned her. Stone-covered walls and the porch reminded her of an old farmhouse and the familiar style reminiscent of old Westerns she watched while in the foster homes or shelters. A table with matching chairs sat at one end of the porch, and a massive porch swing hung at the other. She admired the landscape around the porch, full of roses and annuals in all shades of the rainbow, and the flowers lining the walkway softened the ruggedness of the stones.

April pulled alongside a newer black pickup and sat quietly. Breathe deep, she told herself over and over to settle her nerves. Had she been completely crazy in agreeing to go on a camping trip? If she left unnoticed, a quick call to the girls with a fabricated excuse should be easy. She let out a deep breath and straightened her shoulders, then found her strength.

April knew the confrontation between Riley and Mick would cause trouble. Because experts claimed people learn personality traits, that her student's passion resembled Brock's so much shouldn't have surprised her. So much for keeping a low profile. She pledged to keep her head down and not to draw attention from Brock. Her blood pressure increased dramatically when he left her classroom. Pain then shot through her foot when she kicked the metal trash can under her desk, and it made her furious all over again. How dare the man accuse her of being too explicit with her students?

She refused to become an invisible street urchin again, especially in front of the man who had already turned his back on her once. He wouldn't destroy her again. Perhaps if he got to know her and recognized she wasn't a terrible teacher, then she could go back to her happy new life. She accepted the camping trip with this logic in mind.

Someone knocked on her window. She jumped and blinked. He stood tall, rugged, and very attractive in jeans and a button-down western shirt with a black cowboy hat on his head. Her pulse quickened at the image. She fumbled with the handle before she opened the door.

He gazed down at her. "Welcome, Maria, or shall I call you April?"

"April will be fine," she replied rigidly and got out of her SUV. Brock stood back to let her look around the ranch. She stared in awe, suddenly nervous. "This is a beautiful place. Where are the girls?" Maybe their presence became a shield.

"They are at the barn getting their horses saddled."

She laughed tentatively and made the comment, "You heard me say I have never been on a horse?"

"Yeah, I heard you. Don't worry. It won't take you long to catch on." Brock replied.

April reached in and grabbed the small overnight bag in the back seat of her SUV. It held the few items the girls said she needed. Toothbrush, T-shirt, underwear, a sweatshirt and pajamas and gripped it like armor.

Brock glanced at the case and held out his hand. She reluctantly handed it to him. "Come with me and I'll introduce you to your horse."

Much to April's surprise, Riley and Kadina ran out and hugged her. Both girls chattered nonstop. "We're happy you're here. Uncle Brock picked out the gentlest horse for you. We have our own." They all walked towards an enormous barn, where she scanned the area anxiously. They led her to the corral with a black and white animal, and the girls explained, "His name is Pepper."

The horse came over and nudged its nose against her arm. She nervously laughed. "Hello Pepper, be kind to me."

Brock walked up behind her, close enough that she felt his whisper on her neck. "Don't worry, April. He's very gentle. I'll give you a quick lesson while the girls go to the house and get their bags. Are you ready?"

April nodded her head and said, "I think so." Before she exhaled to release the tension in her chest, he reached down and put his hands around her waist. She had barely caught her breath before he picked her up and sat her in the saddle. Despite her apprehension about the ride, she felt the tingling pressure of his hands at her sides.

He shortened the stirrups to fit her legs and handed her the reins. He led Pepper around the corral using a lead rope. This helped her get used to how the horse felt against her.

Next, he showed her how the reins controlled the horse's direction.

The girls returned, and they set off across the field. The lake rose at the far edge of his property. April swiveled her head at the unfamiliar sights and tried to see everywhere. The land opened in front of her. Trees skirted the boundaries, and the tall grasses reached the horses' bellies. The green grass, colored with a tint of gold, swayed in the gentle breeze. Pepper seemed tiny next to Brock's giant white stallion, Pegasus, on the trail. A sweet smell wafted in the breeze. She wiggled her nose, turned and asked, "What weird smell is in the air?"

He grinned. "It is called fresh-cut hay. We grow, cut and bale our own for the cattle to eat."

"I've never been around a ranch, much less fresh-cut hay."

"You can count on getting an education this weekend about country life. You're here; enjoy it."

"Basically, are you saying you are going to teach the teacher?" April uttered with amusement before she caught herself.

"I will be glad to give the teacher a lesson or two," he teased.

"Oh, heaven help me," she silently prayed, overwhelmed by the charged atmosphere. She styled her hair in a high ponytail before leaving her house to make it cooler. Between the nerves of being near Brock and his apparent flirting, her face turned bright red. She hoped the sun beating down on her neck hid the blush spreading over her face. Feeling the heat in the other parts of her body, she moaned. If she wanted to show him she succeeded at her job, this kind of conduct couldn't go on. She needed to keep the conversation neutral and not encourage him. Her mouth locked in silence.

Brock drew her attention from their flippant behavior, pointing out the foothills of the Ozark Mountains. He explained to her that part of the Arkansas River flowed through his ranch. "Take in the museums in town. They focus on the history of the area."

"Bonnie and I visited one or two places the weekend I interviewed for my job. They didn't show everything you just revealed. I'm surprised."

"I told you I could teach the teacher something," he reminded her.

They stopped twice to stretch their legs, and the nearby scenery amazed her. Clouds danced across the blue sky like a ballet set to music. Birds sang songs to lure their mates or to say We're cheery in the sunshine. The music of the plains, she told herself, suddenly happy.

Brock's hands burned like the blazing sun on April's waist whenever he lifted her onto Pepper. Despite her attempts to hide it, her rapid heartbeat betrayed her, affecting her breathing. Maybe he wouldn't notice.

After being on horseback for more than an hour, they came to a small lake at the end of a valley. A creek ran into the lake to feed it with fresh water. Underneath a leafy canopy, a picnic table sat beside a stand of trees. A metal fire ring sat a few feet away from the table. The scene's warmth enveloped April.

With the girls' help, Brock unsaddled, secured the horses and made sure they had plenty of water. "I employed one of my ranch hands to set up camp here earlier this morning for us."

His remark drew her to the area he pointed out. Her eyebrows lifted with curiosity. "Only two tents?"

"Oh, Uncle Brock sleeps under the stars. He said tents are for wimpy girls," Riley explained before she carried their bags to the pad of soft pea gravel.

"One is yours and the other is for the girls. Believe me, you won't get any rest if those two are with you." Brock asserted.

"Okay, thanks then," April said and reached for the bag he untied from her saddle, then placed it in the other shelter.

"My cook prepared sandwiches. Why don't we eat first, then explore the lakeside and the outcrop of rocks over by the creek?"

The fresh air and physical activity made the sandwich taste better, April realized, sitting at the picnic table. The girls shared the bowl of chips and laughed when there wasn't anything left in the bowl to fight over. Growing up with laughter over sharing food between the teens was a rare sight for her. Especially when there never seemed to be enough food to go around. She insisted on helping with the cleanup because she didn't want anyone to find fault.

The girls kept a steady stream of chatter while they explored the area and gave her more information about its origins. Brock studied the range prior to his purchasing the land and found out the rich history of Indians and settlers. The teens searched for arrowheads, ones the Native Indians left behind. The crystal-clear, narrow strip of water made it easy to see the tiny fish by the creek's edge. Footprints of deer and other small animals coming to drink from the water dotted the bank.

When they returned to the campsite from their exploration, April watched the two girls roll their pant legs up to their knees and step into the water. Riley hadn't mentioned wading in the lake. Their joyous reactions motivated her. She sat down on a big rock, rolled her jeans up, and pulled off her shoes and socks. Relieved to see the clear shallow water along the fringe of the lake since she didn't want to slip and fall. To embarrass herself in front of Brock and the girls would have been humiliating. Because he still possessed the power to fascinate her, she sensed coffee-colored eyes on her back, which made her self-conscious. The lake, colder than expected, made her shiver.

Anyhow, she told herself; it had to be the chilly water, not him.

Afterwards, April finished playing in the water, thankfully without falling, and balanced on the water's edge, stepping carefully to get out. She sat down on a rock as radiant heat from the lakeside rocks bathed in the sunlight's warmth dried her water-cooled feet. She pushed the air out of her lungs, sighed and finally relaxed. Peacefulness washed over her, and the stress from the new experiences of the day melted into the background. Aware that the sun began its journey into the western sky, leaving hues of warm color behind, she stared mesmerized at the different shades. Gold, copper and rose. She stood by the lake's edge and marveled at the vision; it reminded her of an artist's brushstrokes across a blank canvas. The city's many tall buildings and air pollution usually prevented sunsets from looking this spectacular.

April left the lake's edge, knowing the unobstructed sight lived forever in her mental book of memories. She went back to the picnic table area, curious to observe Brock's activities. He walked over to the metal ring on the bed of rocks and bent over to pick up wood to start a fire. "Is this how you will fix our supper, whatever it is?"

Both girls said, "Roasted hot dogs and cowboy beans with s'mores for dessert."

April laughed. "Show me what to do. I have never been to a cookout either."

Brock challenged. "One more lesson for the teacher."

They instructed her on how to put a wiener on the roasting stick, place it in the open flames to get hot, and later also how to build the s'mores.

No sooner than she licked the sticky goo of chocolate and marshmallows off her fingers, a picture of having him lick her fingers clean raced to the very core of her body. Firelight danced around the shadows, obscuring her expression, thankfully. Internally, she scolded herself for her longing for him. This shouldn't be happening. Her body said otherwise.

Regaining her sanity, she told Brock, "You are an excellent cook."

He grinned. "I'm glad you enjoyed it."

Once again, April helped the girls with the cleanup process. In the meantime, Brock built up the fire with more wood. During the rest of the evening, she stared into the flames and remained quiet. She listened to the sounds of the night, which filled the air with their musical din. The noise seemed much louder here than in the city and made the trees appear alive. She didn't want to break the silence, which settled over all of them. Words didn't sound necessary.

Brock stood to get more firewood. "You two girls ought to go to bed. Morning will be here soon, and you wanted to take the long way home."

They both yawned, stood up and said, "Yeah, we did. Good night, both of you."

April rose also until his voice halted her. "Why don't you sit a little longer?"

All day, wherever she moved, he stood nearby. The intensity of his smoldering gaze had puzzled her, by the casual way he brushed his hand along her arm, reaching for a chip at lunch, or the way he held out his hand to steady her around the lake. She hadn't wanted to refuse his help outright and risk an accusation of rudeness. And if the girls took note, she didn't want to explain her actions. She ignored the subtle touches and groaned inwardly.

Now he asked her to stay and talk. The sane and sound reasoning burned away, like the flames from the wood in the firepit circled by stones. His voice hypnotized her, making her unable to move. She swallowed the lump in her throat, battled with her conscience, and whispered, "Okay."

The call of a distant owl hooting reminded her they sat alone. Stars twinkled, and the glow of the fire lit the area.

The girls, already in their tents with the doors zipped up, took away her last remaining barrier. She tried to keep the conversation focused on him on a less personal level; meanwhile, the sound of his voice captivated her. "Tell me how you ended up here. I know you lived in Oklahoma City."

"You remember my parents used to be lawyers in the city?" She nodded yes. "Julie and I both followed in their footsteps. I needed to become independent. Therefore, I moved to Tulsa, opened up my law office, and then bought the ranch. I renovated it, acquired more land, and increased its size. Added livestock and now own a successful ranch and am raising Riley." He said the last part with a tinge of sorrow in his voice.

April teased lightly, trying to lighten the mood. "You are more of a cowboy than a lawyer?"

He shrugged his shoulder not denying the observation. "I answered your questions. It's my turn to ask you some. How did you end up in Broken Arrow? We ran into Miss Burton at the school, and she called you her adopted daughter."

"You ran into Bonnie yesterday? Was this the cause of...?" Her voice trailed away.

"For what?" Brock asked.

"Nothing. Never mind. Back to your question. I was born in Oklahoma City." She cleared her throat before she spoke. "I met Bonnie after we, uh, parted. She provided crucial support during a difficult period and helped me get into college. I taught school for ten years and lived with her until I moved here."

April hadn't given details about her tough time, and, to her relief, Brock didn't pry for her to elaborate. Before he asked anything else and the fire died down completely, leaving her in total darkness with him, she stood up. "I should go to bed. Good night."

He told her, "Sleep well."

April zipped the tent up behind her and lay in her sleeping bag. A groan of desire caused her thighs to clench together. She smothered the moans in her sleeping bag, hoping he couldn't hear. He lay right outside her tent, under the canopy of stars, and with him close, alarms blared in her brain. She reflected on the odd day of unfamiliar sights and old, not forgotten feelings. Each place Brock touched her still tingled, reminding her of their past. A matureness in his manner and powerful voice commanded respect. On the day she argued with him about her teaching methods, he appeared inflexible. And she realized the toughness he projected made him tough to cross in a courtroom. Intense enough, she imagined the earth rumbling under her feet. The night sounds eventually drowned out the bells and allowed sleep to claim her.

She woke early in the morning to see frost sprinkled on the grass like diamonds sparkling in the sunlight. They ate granola bars and drank coffee Brock made. Afterward, they saddled their horses and rode away in a different direction from yesterday. She glanced at the lake with sadness at never seeing this magical place again.

The breathtaking views in the early morning, with more wildlife visible, enchanted April. Brock stopped the horses once to point out a mama deer and her baby where they nibbled on grass up ahead of the trail. The girls moved on. She could have spent an hour admiring the view of Mother Nature's secrets. She'd witnessed nothing similar.

When the ranch house and barns came into view, April couldn't believe how fast the morning had flown by. She followed Brock to the corral, where they dismounted the horses. The girls unsaddled their animals, and she moved to unsaddle Pepper. "Go on, Miss Palmer. We will take care of him for you. Thanks again for coming with us. See you at school," Riley told her.

"If you are sure? And thank you for inviting me. Nice to meet you, Kadina."

"Come on, April, I will walk you back to your vehicle."

"Oh, don't bother. I can find my way." She needed to get some space between her and Brock before yearning raced through her body again. She tried to keep her distance this morning, which proved no easier than the day before. Often, she caught herself staring at him. She needed to get to her car and drive away to escape the heat surging in her body.

April moved to the SUV and opened the door. "Thank you, Brock, for a pleasant weekend. We got off on the wrong foot. I want you to know I really am an excellent teacher. Riley is a bright student and a joy to teach."

"No, my pleasure, and I'm glad you enjoyed yourself."

She smiled apprehensively, shut the door, and then pulled the car out of the driveway. What ulterior motive did he have in mind in being extra pleasant to her? He hadn't said anything about their past, which scared her even more. Her response to him over the weekend shocked her. Although going through the greatest pain and heartache in her life, she still couldn't seem to get over the attraction to him, which stunned her. She thought time healed everything, apparently not her heart concerning Brock Ruggle.

While she drove back into town, she tried to come up with a solution to remain friends with Riley and how to avoid Brock. The sight of him again, knowing what transpired and what would happen if he found out, terrified her.

She treasured the happy memories of her weekend adventures with Brock and the girls. Her only consolation.

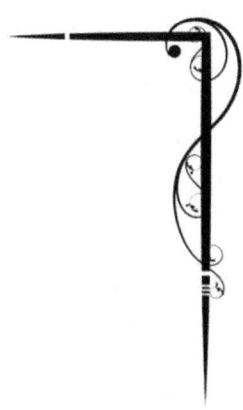

Chapter 12

Well, the trip went better than Brock expected. As he walked back to the barn to make sure the girls took care of the horses, he speculated about his reaction to April. He wanted to connect with this unique version of the woman he once knew, and Riley's offer worked perfectly in his plans.

Anxiety weighed heavily on his shoulders as he stood and watched her pull out of the driveway. He then pondered the prospects of whether she would ever allow him to get closer and to trust him again, although electricity sizzled between them all weekend? She tried to hide it, only he caught her staring at him. The look in her eyes at the shelter had screamed betrayal, which burned the image in his mind. The presence of the two girls prevented any meaningful discussion about their past.

Unsettled, Brock paced around the corral, where he waited impatiently for the girls to finish grooming the horses. They chattered about the excursion until Brock thought he'd explode. Riley strolled over to him and put her arm around his waist. "Uncle, did you have a good time?"

"Yes, I did." His calm, satisfying life suddenly gave the impression of spiraling out of control from being with April.

"I did too. Maybe we can all go again. You know, invite Miss Palmer too."

"Perhaps." If they repeated the weekend, would he flirt again? Why not? It wasn't from lack of experience.

Wide-eyed, she adapted to his world with a good-natured attitude. He knew she battled with the decision to take the trip yet; she yielded. She listened to the girls and their antics and returned some of their playfulness with laughter. They pulled her into arguments over the differences in their musical tastes. She remained faithful to the older types of music, not hip-hop or rap. He laughed during the debate with Kadina over whether James Bond was hotter than Aquaman. He held his breath when Riley asked, "Do you think Uncle Brock is hot?"

April paused a minute and looked at him. "I wouldn't know. I don't have a thermometer to take his temperature." He laughed at her witty and quick response.

The return trip sped by way too fast. Brock didn't recall spending a more enjoyable visit. April listened to the instructions and impressed him with how she held her own.

The girls wanted one more batch of s'mores. Brock built a fire in the pit behind the house. They reminisced and giggled about the camping trip. How Kadina shrieked after she glimpsed a black snake slithering towards the tent. He had shooed it away, although the reptile benefited the ecosystem. Riley would tease her for weeks, he surmised.

The teens' excitement died down, along with the flames. They told him "good night" and left him alone. He welcomed the quiet until the embers smoldered to ashes. Though the fire ebbed, it didn't stop the heat in his lower body. He groaned and looked up at the dark blue night sky. Stars twinkled, along with the brightness of a rising full moon. It left him burning to repeat the previous night with April by the campfire.

As the quiet evening crept on, he couldn't hold his eyes open any longer and rose to go into the house. What his next move brought with his continued reintroduction to the alluring teacher, a mystery. His excitement at the future possibilities with her caused his blood pressure to rise, and he grew hard with desire. He growled with frustration.

The smell of the crisp bacon tantalized Brock's nose, along with the aroma of hot pancakes Mrs. Shefield prepared coming from the kitchen. He waited patiently for his niece to get settled. Her mood seemed antsy this morning, which worried him. It reminded him of her being younger and tried to influence him to her side against her parents over something unsafe. "Uncle Brock, what's your opinion if I said I wanted to be a lawyer, like my parents?"

He gulped, almost spilled coffee, before he replied casually, "You realize I am one also, right?" He didn't want to jeopardize the conversation. Riley sounded like her old self asking for his advice.

She laughed at his comment. "You know what I mean."

"You meant our family's legacy of being lawyers." The newfound idea of her future pleased him.

"I ought to get ahead of the college classes with some help."

"Do you want me to hire a tutor?" He sensed the eagerness in her.

"I have another idea. Miss Palmer. If it is alright with you?"

"Have you said anything to her about it?"

"No, I wanted to ask you first."

Pride surged into his chest. "Let me know what she says. We can plan for her to come out here if she wants." The adage raced through Brock's thoughts. 'When fate tossed an opportunity to achieve your goals your way, you didn't question it.' This chance to be around April, possibly twice a week, made him giddy, and he rubbed his hands together in anticipation. The question of how to approach her had plagued him. Now Riley's quest to get help with her studies benefited him.

Riley came home a week later, beaming from ear to ear. "What are you happy about?" Brock hoped the good mood resulted from April's answer since his niece hadn't given him any clue whether the teacher said yes.

"I asked Miss Palmer last week. She told me she required space to decide, and today she agreed to do it on one condition."

"Oh, what condition?" he asked, with his pulse racing.

"She wants me to come into her first hour of school and study."

"Not here! Don't you know that being around other students will distract you from your studies?"

"Yes, I do. She seemed adamant about it, though."

"I'll drop by and talk to her tomorrow and see if we can come to a compromise."

Riley left to do her chores, leaving Brock wondering why April didn't want to come to his house. It wasn't as if they didn't know each other. Despite his desire to regain her good graces, he couldn't pressure her. He planned to remain cool and collected during the stop at her classroom. Allow her to explain her reasoning and then reassure her he wouldn't be around very often. Well, not much. He grinned roguishly.

Brock pulled his truck into the parking lot of the school, into the slot conveniently beside the dark blue vehicle April drove. Subsequently, school ended soon, so he waited instead of going into the building. Ten minutes later, she exited and walked to her car. He opened his door and stepped around to her car. "Hi. How are you doing?"

She glanced at him in surprise. "What are you doing here, Brock?"

"I'm waiting for you. May we talk for a minute, please?"

"About what?"

"Uh, do you prefer to talk here openly, or shall we go somewhere more private?"

"What do you want to discuss that we can't do it here?"

"For one thing, we haven't discussed our past, and the other matter is about Riley. She asked you to tutor her."

"I don't know what one has to do with the other. Perhaps you would like to explain."

"You really want to do this here, in front of your coworkers?" He repeated.

"Fine, let's go to the coffee shop down the street. People may see us together, but they won't overhear us," she conceded.

He followed her, which gave him more time to plan what he wanted to say. He owed her an explanation about Cindy and why he had stupidly turned his back on her. They parked near each other, both got out and entered the cafe.

They walked to the counter and ordered drinks. He took a breath to calm his suddenly paralyzed nerves before they sat down at a small table. "I need to explain and apologize to you for many things. First thing, why I turned my back on you in the shelter. Cindy always tried to get me to date her. I wasn't interested; however, that never stopped her. Shame swept over me, and I didn't want to expose you to her inappropriate behavior."

"I saw her with her arms around you," April accused.

"If you had only stayed long enough, you would have seen a simple hug, nothing more, before she left. You didn't. You ran." He didn't want to accuse her outright and jeopardize the chances of something growing between them, yet he couldn't rightfully take all the blame. "I frantically searched for you. No one knew a Maria. A few days passed, and I assumed you didn't want to be found, much less allow me to help you with your life. I possessed the means to, you know." He paused in the candid conversation while the server brought their coffee to the table.

"Are you sure? Your actions said otherwise. You wouldn't even say the word homeless when we talked about my dreams."

"What dreams? You said you didn't have any." Outrage bubbled until he got it under control.

"Maybe I didn't trust enough to tell you everything back then. We knew each other for two days."

"I'm truly sorry. I know I'm too late to say the words." Brock's embarrassment at being confronted with the way he acted then haunted him like a ghost gliding through the mist to this very day. "Do you think you can trust me again?"

"I am not sure. Perhaps we both have changed? The jury hasn't reached a decision, Brock."

"Can we get past this for Riley's sake? She needs your help with schoolwork," he asked. He pulled out his ace the moment he detected her resolve fading. "She doesn't have to know anything about our past relationship. Start over and get to know each other better. I really want to discover April. She seems like a friendly woman," he replied, blatantly flirting.

April sat in silence, with her cup of coffee wedged between her hands. Knuckles white.

Brock raised his eyebrows amusedly. "Let's find out where this leads us! Allow the jury to make the right decision."

"Okay, for Riley's education, I will accept your apology and see where this goes."

"Good. One more thing, though." She rolled her eyes. "Come to the house and tutor her. You know during the first hour there will be interruptions."

"What do you call yourself if I'm present and you are at home? Won't you be a distraction?"

"Don't worry, I won't be inside much," he answered. Hopefully, his little white lie wouldn't get him struck by lightning.

They left the cafe in agreement. He scrutinized the new challenge, which took shape in his mind. He hadn't lied when he told her he wanted to get to know her again. If she ran again, the chase wouldn't stop, with the prize being well worth it. All he needed to do, prove himself trustworthy.

The attraction he felt toward her hadn't changed over the years. He wanted her, and if he wasn't mistaken, she reciprocated those same emotions. If he suddenly showed up at the house, who could blame him? He lived there too.

April brought Riley home from school twice a week and stayed to help with lessons. The tutoring sessions didn't last long. Usually, she left before he came home, much to his disappointment. Once in a while, though, he got lucky. Rather than chatting, Brock strolled into the dining room, where Riley spread books out on the table, and paused coolly. He stood near April, looked over her shoulder at the lessons, then heard her breath catch. It gave him satisfaction and hope. His mouth watered at the scent of vanilla coming from her. With his heightened pulse, he exhaled and tried to keep from touching her arm. Did she feel the same intensity of heat? "Carry on with your studies, ladies." He winked at Riley and walked out the door.

The tutoring sessions between Riley and April at the ranch continued into the winter months, with his making an occasional appearance. Colder weather with a forecast of fast and furious snow blared over the radio on his way home. The reporter bragged about how they got it right. Brock grimaced as he rushed home before the storm got too bad. Snow had already begun in town. The closer he drove towards the ranch, the heavier it came down. It became harder to see the road in front of him. He drove his four-wheel-drive truck slowing down anyhow to be safe. A pickup passed him, going too fast. *If they got to their destination safely, it would be a miracle.*

Suddenly, he saw headlights shining dimly at an angle in the heavy snow. Hazard lights blinked on a car in the ditch ahead of him. He stopped to make sure they were okay. More than likely, they were waiting for a tow truck to arrive. He put his emergency flashers on before he got out of the truck, made his way to the car and knocked on the window. No one sat in the vehicle. Panic suddenly bolted into his chest. April's SUV. Where was she? No other cars passed him to pick her up. His throat tightened when he saw footprints going back toward his house.

He trudged through the snow to his truck, put it in gear, and slowly drove down the road with his window open to make the roadside more visible. The footsteps he followed filled with snow rapidly. A quarter of a mile farther, he finally spotted her. He eased over to the ditch without going too far and got out. "Why the hell didn't you stay in your car? You could have slipped and fallen in the ditch, and I wouldn't have seen you," he bellowed angrily and shook her shoulders. His voice became an outlet for his fear until he saw the red splotches on her cheeks and her blue lips. He grabbed her arm and pulled her to the truck. He'd yell at her later. Right now, he knew it became essential to get her warm.

The scared look on her face showed her relief at seeing him. The tone in his voice faltered, and he tried to get hold of his anger. "What are you doing out here this late?" He couldn't completely hide the sound of annoyance.

April took a deep breath and heard the irritation in his tone. "Riley and I had our heads down studying. Before we knew it, snow started falling. And the closer I went towards town; the snowflakes got heavier and then the truck... I wasn't far from the ranch."

"Yeah, the same guy passed me going too fast. Why didn't you listen to the weather forecast? They called for several inches." He explained.

"Well, I thought I might get home," she still challenged him.

Brock said smugly, "Your plan didn't work out too well now, did it?"

She didn't answer. It gave him satisfaction. He helped her into his truck and fastened her seatbelt over her waist. Even now, he attempted to get close to her as he rubbed her hands to thaw them. She tugged them away. He smirked to himself. For the rest of their trek to the ranch, only the soft sounds of his radio and the powerful heater broke the quiet.

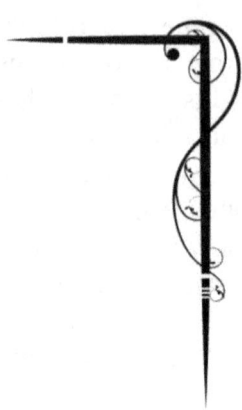

Chapter 13

April sat quietly in Brock's truck, berating herself. If only she had noticed the snow coming down hard sooner and left. She'd been home by now, safe and sound. She shook her head, sighed and tried to clear the cold fog in her mind. He looked over at her and scowled, and the sliver of optimism faded. Her heart sank. She knew he wouldn't go easy on her, and it wouldn't be pleasant. She detected his irritation seething under the surface while they drove back to the ranch in silence.

Before her car slid into the ditch, everything had moved in slow motion. It appeared she stood on the outside, unable to halt the car's movement. When the car stopped, the impact pinned the door against a tree, leaving her stuck. No matter how hard she pressed on the gas, her tires kept spinning. Left with little choice, she put her hazard lights on and crawled over the gearshift. Her anxiety decreased a little the instant she stood free of the wrecked vehicle before the icy wind whipped around, and she shivered violently. Remaining with the car may have been the logical thing to do. However, there hadn't been traffic on the road.

With her stocking hat pulled down over her ears, April headed back towards the ranch. She couldn't recall how far she had driven. Her face, nose, and fingers stung from the cold and snow and felt like icicles. The thin, stylish boots appropriate for school offered little insulation, and her feet were numb before she trekked any distance. Committed by already walking several feet from the car, she thought it senseless to turn back, instead kept her head down and walked slowly with one foot in front of the other. She visualized a hot cup of coffee right before the lights of a vehicle approached. A ray of hope appeared and rapidly disappeared when a certain truck stopped. Of course, it just had to be Brock.

.

They pulled into the garage, and the automatic door opened and then closed, leaving the snowstorm outside. She reached for the truck door clumsily. Her fingers slid off the handle, given how the cold affected them. Brock snapped, "Wait, and I will help you." He rushed around the front of the truck.

She rolled her eyes before stopping herself, then replied softly, "Thank you." April didn't want to appear ungrateful.

He led her into the kitchen and abruptly swung around to face her. "We need to address some things once you are dry and warmed up."

She simply nodded and followed him into the house. And stood poised for the impending scolding to begin.

"Sit down and try to pull off your shoes and socks," he told her before he started the coffee machine.

Her stiff fingers fumbled when she attempted to take her shoes off by herself. Brock noticed, then squatted, pushed her hands aside, exposed each foot, and rubbed. The motion brought tears to her eyes, and she couldn't help crying out until they tingled with returned circulation.

He stood up, poured them both coffee and told her, "Wrap your hands around the cup to warm them. I'll be right back."

April didn't recognize this side of Brock. He differed from the version of years before. He came back with a plush blanket and draped it over her shoulders. The gentle touch of his hands on her neck as he pulled it up against her made her ponder. Did she even know the real man? He sat in the chair next to her and remained quiet, although he had been the one to broach the issue; she saw he wrestled with what to say.

Therefore, she spoke first. "We got off on the wrong foot once again. You need to know more about me, April, not Maria. You don't approve of my teaching method, and I have my reasons. I know you consider me irresponsible for the mental safety of my students. If I tell you, then maybe you will understand my commitment to all of them."

"Fine, April, I will listen."

"I lived in the foster care system from the age of five until I ran away at seventeen. There was never enough to eat or clean clothes, and they didn't care if you went to school or not. I never thought I could do anything better. Much less trust you with my dreams at our chance meeting. Later, Bonnie took me in and showed me a path to a different future. The lifestyle she provided, with its benefits similar to affluent kids like you, I presumed. If I hadn't experienced the other side, I wouldn't have known about real life. By showing these kids reality and its potential consequences, then possibly they grow up and become better human beings. More compassionate. And maybe the most important takeaway for them, understand that people who are less fortunate have feelings. Riley has changed with my help, and I stayed tonight because I didn't want to let her down or make her feel like I didn't care because I truly do." With tears in her eyes from the passion she tried to convey to him, she turned back towards the window and looked away.

He reached over and tugged her face back to him. "I am sorry for yelling. You scared me." His soft lips brushed against her cheek.

April's breath caught. The last of the chill left her body. "What now? Do you take me back to my house?"

"No, spend the night. I'm not getting out in this snowstorm to take you home. We have plenty of room. It will not hurt you to stay here."

April wasn't so sure. The way her pulse rapidly sped up with a simple kiss. Just the thought of him in his own bed, close by, gave her goosebumps. She shivered again. Brock jumped up. "I'll get you another cup of hot coffee. It'll ward off the last of your cold."

As he handed her a second cup of the hot liquid, she thanked him again, because she couldn't reveal to him the reason for her sudden chills

Riley ran into the kitchen. "Uncle Brock, who are you talking to?" The teen then halted. "Miss Palmer, what are you doing back?"

"I tried to make it home, then a truck ran me off the road into a ditch, and I got stuck. Your uncle found me."

"Please make sure the guest room is suitable. She will have to spend the night."

"Yeah, no problem." Riley grinned, then looked back before she left. "Good night, you two."

They finished their coffee in silence. "Come with me and I'll show you to your room. I'm sure Riley has it ready."

Brock put his hand on the lower part of her back, led her down the hall and opened a door. He flipped on the light and stepped back. April turned and looked up, caressed his cheek and softly whispered, "You rescued me this time. We're even."

He moved closer. "No, you will always have the upper hand." Then, he kissed her on the lips. "Good night, sleep well."

"Thank you." She gently shut the door behind her and trembled.

Riley had placed a T-shirt at the end of the bed. April put it on, although it swallowed her. She smelled the material and recognized the scent, Brock. A window seat full of pillows and a fuzzy throw beckoned her. She sat down and wrapped it around her shoulders, warding off another chill. As she looked out the window, the snow continued to swirl around and pile up. At this rate, she wouldn't be able to leave in the morning.

Unless she wanted to compromise her relationship with Riley, who was smart yet considerate and a joy to be around, she wasn't sure how to put the desperately needed distance between her and Brock. He irritated her to no end or spun her into a jumbled mess of desire if she let him.

The latest kiss between them knocked her socks off and became more potent rapidly. Scared, April reflected on the two kisses. One sweet, yet this last one felt like a promise holding the means to destroy all her reserves. No man had ever kissed her in such a way. *Heaven help her.* What *would she do to resist the stunning good looks again?*

The next morning, she woke up and stretched her arms over her head. She glanced towards the window seat, where she had sat the night before, with so many questions. And the answers still evaded her. She got out of bed and looked outside; the snow covered everything. It magically turned the land into a winter wonderland. She lamented the fun she probably missed growing up by never being allowed to play in the snow.

Her nose led her to the kitchen, smelling fresh coffee. Brock sat at the table. She picked up an empty cup from the cabinet and poured herself a cup. "Well, I will call a tow truck and have them pick me up here."

"April, no one is going anywhere today. They are calling for even more snow before it ends tomorrow. Most of the roads are closed."

"Terrific," she grumbled.

"You and Riley can find something to do."

Her student walked into the room and went to the frig for a glass of orange juice. Catching the last comment, the teenager's grin widened. "Oh, goody, you are staying all day with us."

Were all the signs lining up against her? First the snow, then the kisses, and now Riley's enthusiasm. "From what your uncle says, I don't have a choice," she answered regretfully.

"Don't worry, we will have fun. We can do anything you want to do."

A spark of mischief in her thoughts from earlier gave her the courage to speak. Her bravery waned temporarily, glancing at Brock. The playfulness won out. "I want to build a snowman."

Riley shrieked, and the man's expression cracked April up. Pure shock from ear to ear.

"You want to go outside after last evening's adventure?"

She stood her ground and told him, "Yes. I've never played in the snow."

"Do you know how?"

"No. However, I'm almost sure Riley would help, and if she doesn't know how, then you can show us." A smirk met her challenge.

Before they went out the door, Brock stepped in from the utility room. "Here, wear these. They will be big, but you should stay dry and warm." He handed her a pair of boots and heavy socks, along with a thick pair of gloves and a stocking hat.

April stammered. "Thanks."

Riley gathered an old scarf and a carrot stick from the kitchen. "Okay, we're ready."

Pure joy erupted in April when she viewed their work of art. A well-shaped snowman stood near the front porch. To preserve the momentous occasion, she pulled out her phone. Right before she snapped the picture, Brock walked onto the porch and grinned. She captured his image in the background with the snowman before they went back into the warmth of the house.

Following grilled cheese sandwiches and tomato soup for lunch, Riley asked. "Will you help me put up the Christmas decorations? Uncle Brock never wants to."

"Yeah, leave me out of the decorating," he said. "I'll be in my office."

The two of them straightened the kitchen before proceeding to the attic.

Riley asked for more stories about her mom while they got the decorations down. A mixture of emotions — bittersweet, sometimes choked April's throat when she shared more stories from Julie. Painful, vivid memories triggered periods of breathlessness and agony from the absence of her own mother's love coupled with the adoption of her daughter. She shut her eyes tightly because even now, the devastating reactions lingered. Wondered if her little girl owned stories to listen to from her new family? She needed to regroup herself and remember; it hadn't been possible to have raised her baby on the streets without being scared for either of them.

With all the boxes of decorations in the living room, Riley pointed to the usual spot of the tree—next to the fireplace and its large stone mantel. The sheer size wouldn't overwhelm the spacious living room. Two couches faced each other in front of the fireplace, with a coffee table in the middle. The dominant color scheme, of blues and grays with splashes of orange mixed in for highlights. April admired the tastefully decorated room from the first glimpse. The open floor plan with the kitchen and a huge country-style table completed the rustic look. If she speculated on it, a woman's touch helped decorate this house. Did Brock build the place for a special woman and, more important, did she still exist in his life? Jealousy darted through the pit of her stomach, though she had no right to something she couldn't afford to let grow.

Riley explained while putting decorations on the tree that some came from her grandparents, and others from her childhood. The girl hugged one beautiful ornament close. "This was a special gift from my grandparents. Uncle Brock or Grandpa picked me up to place the angel on top of the tree, which started the family tradition." Except for the tree topper, the huge artificial tree looked realistic and exquisite, April admitted, transforming the room into a winter wonderland. Then Riley stepped out into the hallway. "Uncle Brock, we're ready to put the angel on the tree."

Brock entered the living room and scanned the decorations. April stood ready to leave the room, because this ritual felt like a private family affair and she didn't want to intrude. He picked the angel up and started towards Riley. "Hold on, Miss Palmer is our guest and has red hair like both me and the angel, so she gets the honors."

"No, no, it is your family tradition, and I'm not family," April protested intensely.

"It is my angel, and I have the option to select who puts it on the tree. I choose you."

April's eyes darted from her student to Brock. He shrugged his shoulders. "Just give in. It's easier."

He picked her up, and Riley placed the angel in her hands. She carefully placed the topper on the tree and secured it. Instead of lowering her to the floor, though, he held her tight for what seemed like an eternity. Mesmerized, she felt every hard, rigid muscle. She sucked in oxygen to calm the powerful stirrings his body awakened. Their eyes locked and didn't break contact until Riley asked. "Isn't the angel beautiful, Uncle?"

Still staring at her, he said, "Yes, she is."

Later in the evening, since the housekeeper, Mrs. Shefield, couldn't make it to work. April found a container of beef stew in the freezer. They began fixing the meal by warming up the stew along with biscuits she stirred together and baked. A salad completed their dinner.

All the time they worked in the kitchen, her student kept up a torrent of questions. Where did she grow up? Which college had she attended? Not to be rude, April finally admitted she grew up in the foster system before aging out. It came across as a much cleaner version than, to tell the truth.

"Weren't you scared?"

"Sometimes, yeah, terrified, and others …well, happiness existed." At the precise moment she bared a piece of her soul; Brock entered the room. She realized from his fleeting gaze that he'd overheard the statement. Her heart ached with tender memories of their past.

While they ate, April watched Brock interact with Riley. Some antics the girl proposed came across as outlandish or even silly. He took charge with little difficulty. Sadly, she believed he would have been an excellent father to his own children, but her circumstances robbed them both. She laughed on the occasions the teenager got ahead of him in an argument. Because she knew firsthand, his niece earned the rare victory.

With Riley's book report due, the girl left to go to her room. April volunteered to clean up the dishes after they finished dinner. She cleared the table of dishes and ran water in the sink. Brock stayed at the table drinking coffee. The comfortable ease between them must have been why she reflected on the early revelation of how he appeared to be a good father. "It was selfless of you to assume responsibility for Riley. Most men wouldn't have wanted the disruption of their personal life." She slapped her hand over her mouth. The heat of a blush stained her cheeks. "Sorry, that's really not what I meant to say."

"I don't object too much to the few interruptions my niece has tried to set up in my personal life. This particular one I have grown fond of."

Brock walked up behind her at the counter and lowered his head to her neck. "You know you are the disturbance, don't you?" Then he kissed the side of her neck below her ear.

She groaned as he caressed the sensitive spot with his lips, and his arms pulled her back against his chest. She melted into his warm body. He then turned her around and searched her eyes. His head bent down, and his lips covered hers. She moaned, and her lips parted. He deepened the kiss before pulling back. She gasped for air. "Oh, what a sweet interruption you are," he stated.

April remembered the feel of his hands and wanted more. She stood, stared, panted, and prayed all at once for strength. With firm determination, she finished the dishes in the kitchen and mumbled, "I should go to my room."

Brock escorted her down the hall, caressed her lips once more, and said, "Good night."

April's body sizzled with pent-up passion leaning against the closed bedroom door and drew oxygen into her lungs. She put her hands on her stomach and questioned her ability to control the inner fire. Like the night before, she went to the window seat to think.

The cool windowpane against her forehead calmed her until a knock shattered the peace and brought back the warmth. She nervously opened the door, to be greeted by Riley and a comforting cup of tea, which eased her apprehension. "I didn't wake you up?"

"No, I just sat down to watch the snow falling. Did you need something?"

"No, just checking on you."

Riley stared at the floor, moved one foot, then the other before handing her the warm mug, but did not leave. She knew the girl well enough by now; there was a reason for the visit. "Come on, Riley, out with it. What do you want to know?"

"Okay, I'm curious. Why did you get your tattoo?"

"You saw my tattoo when?"

Riley once more lowered her head before she looked up and confessed, "I remembered seeing you at the shelter."

April touched the butterfly tattoo. "I wanted something to remind me you couldn't trust anyone apart from yourself to land where you wanted. Over time, though, you learn you can have faith in some people who truly want what is best for you."

"It is pretty. The butterfly looks like it is landing on a flower." Riley walked towards the door. "Good night."

"Wait, did you want to get one yourself?" The real reason for the late-night visit, April surmised.

"I might," the girl replied, then turned and hugged her.

"If you get something, you need to be satisfied with it the rest of your life."

Riley asked, with wisdom greater than her age. "Are you happy with yours?"

"Yes, now it signifies beauty and love to me with the freedom to give life and to change a path." She thought about the beautiful baby's future she enabled. Funny how suddenly the tattoo took on a totally different meaning. The conversation made her aware of certain facts, which gave her peace.

The snow stopped the next morning before April woke up. After breakfast, Brock informed her that the roads were clear, and he had already called for a tow truck to pull her car to the ranch to allow her to go home later in the day. No more close encounters with the man.

Life went back to normal. April continued to mentor Riley. Spending the afternoons together felt right. Between study sessions, they discussed how the teenager grew up with Julie and Cash. Brock being close by gave the young girl another perspective at the ranch. The appreciation of nature. Julie also insisted on the teen helping with the shelter and knowing what it stood for. Hope.

April wondered about her daughter. Would she be independent like Riley, after all *they* were about the same age? Hopefully, whoever raised her carried a caring heart to show her right from wrong.

Following a successful practice test and improved grades, April asked, "Do you want any more help?" The teen teared up at the subtle hint and became upset. She quickly changed the suggestion. "Don't panic; it was just a thought. You might tire of having me around."

"Never!" Riley sputtered.

"I didn't intend to imply we stopped being friends."

April left the ranch afterwards with a heavy heart and knew she needed to discuss the situation with Bonnie. When she got home, she picked up the phone. "You recall I have befriended Riley, been tutoring her, and we connected over stories Julie told me about the girl's youth? I'm wondering because she has been doing better in class, do I sever ties with her and risk her grades?"

Bonnie didn't hesitate. "What if she backslides? You like her, don't you?"

"Yes, she is a very smart, cute and likeable girl." April declared spontaneously.

"Then, keep assisting her in her studies and the therapeutic process."

April wished in a way Bonnie had taken sides with her to sever ties since Riley progressed. This way, she wouldn't have to risk being around Brock too much to have her secret discovered months later. Losing a possible reawakened relationship with him and with the friendship with Riley in jeopardy, both potentially included the power to destroy all of them. The fissure created if he ever found out exactly what she had done only grew wider, with no means of healing the rift.

As spring break at school neared, she welcomed the vacation from the everyday routine. This breather allowed her to rethink how to widen the gap between herself and Brock. Pulling apart from Riley wasn't possible.

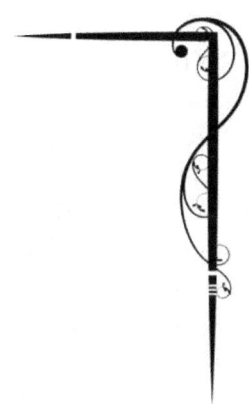

Chapter 14

Once the winter weather cleared, and the house went back to a normal routine, the paperwork sat on Brock's desk, untouched. He couldn't concentrate on the task. He stared out the window behind him. If he listened hard enough, he still heard April laughing during her stay there. She and Riley giggled and played together. It reminded him of how Julie and their mom used to interact.

He missed the random tiny glimpses while she cooked or just stood and gazed into the flames in the fireplace. The heated kisses they shared, although brief, awakened a serious longing in him for her. Being together during the snowstorm showed him the possibility of a different life.

Brock gave up on work, shut the door to his office and went to the kitchen for breakfast Mrs. Shefield placed on the table. Riley walked in and joined him. "Good morning, uncle."

"Good morning. Before I leave, I need to know something."

"Okay, what?"

"Your sixteenth birthday is coming up soon, and I wondered what you wanted for a present?"

Riley finished chewing the slice of bacon she took off the platter and leaned back in the chair with a solemn look on her face. After a few more minutes, she peered over at him and grabbed another slice of bacon. "It will be my first birthday without Mom and Dad and, as you pointed out, my sixteenth. I'm not sure I want to do anything. It doesn't feel right to celebrate without them."

"I know it is another milestone we have to face without them. Don't you think they want us to go on and try to be happy? Give them the respect they deserve by living a good life in the future," Brock stated.

"I'll let you know if I decide on something. Love you."

"Love you more, my favorite niece," he teased.

"You haven't called me your favorite lately."

"I know."

Spring break neared, and before Riley left on the school bus, she knocked and waited for him to invite her into his office. When she was young, he instructed her about an important rule. Never enter his office without his being present. "Come in, Riley."

"I have figured out what I want for my birthday present."

"Okay, tell me and I will arrange it."

Riley got quiet. He knew from experience she wanted something outrageous by the look on her face. The girl raised her head and shoulders and announced, "I want a tattoo."

"A tattoo, Riley. Why?" He closed his eyes in exasperation.

"Miss Palmer has one. It is very cute. I decided I want a small one."

"When did you see Miss Palmer's?"

"One day at the shelter, helping Mom, I kind of sneaked into the kitchen and caught sight of a pretty tattooed woman. I know now the tattoo belonged to Miss Palmer. We talked about my seeing hers during the snowstorm, and the purpose behind hers."

Brock asked, "Did she give you a reason for hers?"

"Something about life choices and misjudging people."

He shook his head, baffled at April's explanation, then replied. "Absolutely not until you are an adult."

Riley cut him off. "Please, you asked what I wanted?"

"What kind of tattoo do you have in mind?" Brock asked, though he already knew the answer.

"A butterfly similar to hers. You know, I have always liked them."

"A butterfly necklace was the very first gift I got you."

"I know. I still have it."

He lifted his finger and pointed. "It has to be small, and we will make sure the tattoo shop is safe. You can't take it back."

Riley jumped up and ran around to hug him. "Miss Palmer said the same thing. And I'm sure, Uncle Brock, thank you."

The gift request should have surprised him. His niece idolized April. He wondered if it had faded. His tongue watered instantly, thinking back of how he gently traced the outline of the butterfly, with her squirming. He moaned with sexual longing to see it again. Then he put the image out of his head and drove into the office.

Rather than wait until her birthday, Riley got her tattoo the first day Brock found the opportunity to take her. He saw a near-identical match to April's butterfly on the afternoon they left the tattoo studio. "Now, you have your present. Do you want a party?"

"I don't want anything over the top. Perhaps a picnic with Kadina and Miss Palmer."

"Are you sure?" he asked skeptically, since it was her sixteenth birthday.

"Yes, I am positive. I will ask Miss Palmer and call Kadina."

Forecasters predicted spring-like temperatures for the weekend of Riley's birthday party, which wasn't far from the school's two-week break. His stomach tightened with doubt about whether April continued to tutor Riley during her time off. He wasn't sure if the brief vacation apart benefited any of his plans to get closer to the beautiful woman. For the moment, Riley's brilliant plan enabled him to spend more time with her. He smiled eagerly when April pulled into the driveway, and both girls ran and gave her hugs.

Mrs. Shefield prepared salads and burgers with all the trimmings for their dinner, along with a chocolate cake for dessert. Brock set a table under the shade of a gigantic oak tree in the yard where the girls placed everything. A cool breeze drifted under the canopy of leaves. The intimate setting placed a tranquil mood over him. It didn't seem possible the girl had just turned sixteen. Losing his sister and Cash suddenly at a crucial stage in Riley's life made him appreciate April, an important person from his past, who stepped in to help the girl. Sadness threatened to put a dark cloud over the event, to dampen the party, but he refused to allow it.

They gobbled down the food, and later April brought the cake out from the house with two candles on it. The numbers one and six in pink stood out on top, and they sang Happy Birthday to Riley and gave her presents.

Brock leaned back in the Adirondack chair and watched April tease one girl, then the other. She hadn't played favorites, which he knew came from her profession. Often, their conversations pulled him into their no-nonsense arguments, frequently ending in laughter. It gave him pleasure to know Riley kept good friends to share the day with.

Both girls started into the barn to put up the new saddle blanket Kadina gifted Riley and teased each other about a boy they went to school with. He thought they had finished kidding each other until their tones of voice changed. Still seated in his chair and April at the table, they overheard the girls shouting at each other and both took off running towards the barn. The barnyard became completely silent as Brock halted by the building. Holding his breath, he watched a bucket of water seemingly in slow motion fly toward April. She stood gasping, with water dripping from the end of her nose, and he heard Riley shrieking in horror. "Oh, Miss Palmer, I am so sorry. I meant to hit Kadina." Neither girl dared blink. They just paused with their mouths open. After the initial shock, he bent over and laughed so hard tears ran down his face

April took a second to wipe the water from her eyes and looked at the two girls with a smirk on her face. The next moment, both girls, armed with full buckets of water, threw them at Brock. He spat and sputtered as the three of them cracked up with amusement at his expense. His face showed shock, then he grinned with mischief in his eyes.

"Run!" Riley yelled at the other two.

Brock couldn't catch the teenagers. They took off across the fields to escape him. He focused on April, an easy conquest, and saw her run into the barn. He remained outside the doorway for a minute to let her think she was safe. Her labored breathing revealed her location. He walked into the empty stall, cornering her with wickedness on his face. "I can't believe you conspired with them against me."

"On your side? Why should I be? You doubled over with delight when I got drenched?"

"I think you owe me an apology, and I intend to collect one from you," he said and sauntered closer. He leaned in toward her lips, not touching any other part of her body. The kiss went from zero to scorching hot in a matter of seconds. She melted against him, and the heat practically dried their clothes. He considered throwing her down in the straw. With her soft skin, he didn't want to cause irritation, and besides, the girls were right outside somewhere.

"Miss Palmer, Uncle Brock, where are you guys? We are both sorry." The two troublemakers came into the barn with no idea what they had interrupted.

Brock pulled away and hollered, "We are in here looking for two juvenile delinquent girls. Have you seen any?"

"No. We are pleading the Fifth."

Brock walked April back to her SUV at the end of the evening. "We need to finish the conversation we started in the barn."

"We weren't talking."

"I think we spoke the same language, though." He backed her up against the door, slid closer, and took her in his arms. They stared at each other before he parted her lips to explore her tongue. The kiss intensified and made them both lose track of their surroundings. He grasped her shoulders and deepened the pressure of his lips. The need for oxygen won out. He broke the seal and placed his forehead on hers. "I need to let you go home before…"

April took a deep breath and caressed his face. "Yeah, you do. Thank you for a very entertaining evening."

Brock stood in the circular drive by April's vehicle and waited until she finished the next afternoon's tutoring session. He grew increasingly excited with each of her visits to the ranch. If the birthday party and the mind-blowing kisses showed him anything, his tenacity was working. Even so, he wanted to ask her out on a proper date. Perhaps gentle blackmail became the key. They sparred well together. She might get mad, or would she take the dare? "April, may I have a word with you?"

Apprehension crossed her face. "Is there a problem?"

"Not if you say yes."

"Yes, to what?"

"Spend an evening with me."

April looked at him with suspicious eyes. "On an actual date! What is the catch?"

Brock realized she saw through him. With a spark of mischief in his eyes, he said, "Simple. Have dinner with me tomorrow night. However, if you refuse, then I am afraid you can no longer tutor Riley."

"Uh - huh, if I say no, then Riley suffers. You don't play fair."

"Remember, I **am** a lawyer. I haven't always played fair to get what I want," Brock said with implied intimidation beneath the surface.

"Be careful, counselor, of what you want and how you play the game," April warned.

"Oh, I think I know how to. Make no mistake." He saw her breath catch in her lungs. The silent risk loomed between them.

"I don't want Riley's studies to suffer. Therefore, I have no choice, do I?"

"I'm glad you have seen it my way. I'll pick you up at your place tomorrow at seven."

"Don't you want my address?"

"No, I already know where you live. I own the house."

She sputtered, disbelief in her voice. "Doesn't Mr. Tobias own it?"

"No, I pay him to manage the property for me. I thought you knew. Miss Burton called to see if I knew of any rentals available before you moved to town," he explained. "I recently gained the house in a trade for my services and offered to rent it."

"No, I didn't know."

"You have no reason to worry if you pay your rent promptly."

She rolled her eyes at the subtle challenge. "My best interest then is to honor my lease. "

He let out a sigh of satisfaction as she pulled away from the house.

The next day, he just needed to complete the drawn-out county regulation case before he went home to get ready. Instead of waiting until evening, he impulsively called April on the way home. "Hey, you haven't forgotten our date, have you?" He heard her suck in her breath at the reminder he roguishly tossed out.

A false sweetness dripped from her voice. "No, I haven't forgotten."

"Good, see you soon," he answered smugly and broke off the call when he pulled into the drive.

Brock walked to the barn and checked in with his manager before going into the house, showering and changing clothes. He stuck his head in the living room doorway, where Riley sat on the couch, watching television. She glanced over and her eyes perked up. "You look handsome tonight."

He dropped a kiss on her forehead. "I'm going on a date and won't be home until late."

"It's about time, Uncle Brock. Miss Palmer is very nice."

Brock teased. "Are you sure my date is with your teacher? What if it is another teacher or someone else entirely?"

"It better be," Riley threatened with a tentative laugh.

He let her off the hook. "Don't worry, it is."

"Good."

As April opened the door, his mouth suddenly felt parched. The woman he saw wasn't the young woman from his past. A mature, self-confident adult female faced him. She wore a cream-colored cashmere boat-neck dress. Tight without being too snug, just right to show off her curves, to his delight. She left her crimson hair down where it fell around her shoulders in waves. Her jewelry — gold knotted earrings, plain yet elegant.

Brock purposely wore a black buttoned down shirt with the collar open under a black twill suit jacket and crisp black chino slacks not to look like a cowboy tonight. He licked his lips before reaching for her hand. "Are you ready to go?"

"Where's your cowboy hat?"

"In the car if I need it tonight. Will I need it?"

"I don't object to this look."

"Good. I'm glad you approve." He saw the cushions on the porch swing, which made the setting cozy. "I see you have made yourself at home here. Exactly what I wanted for whoever rented the place."

"It is comfy, and I love to sit and relax in it."

Brock placed his hand on the small of her back and helped her into his silver Lexus. The urge to pull her tighter against him burned in his fingertips. However, he couldn't rush the intimacy he craved at this moment.

They drove to a stylish Italian restaurant on the outskirts of Tulsa. The hostess escorted them to a table secluded in a corner. They sat down, and he ordered a bottle of wine while they read the menu. Delicious aromas filled the air in the romantic atmosphere, yet his appetite for food diminished with the soft and dreamy music in the background. He took a sip of his drink, stood up and reached out his hand. "Please dance with me?" His confidence soared with the notion of her being back in his life on a more permanent level.

She rose from the table and placed her hand on his. He walked them to the dance floor and pulled her into his arms. His body fit perfectly with hers, and there was no coherent dialog on his part as they swayed to the music. Heat and yearnings exploded from him, hot as a Fourth of July firecracker. The scent of her vanilla perfume brought him a sigh of pleasure. A sexy moan escaped from her as he grasped her waist tighter.

During the next dance, Brock whispered into her ear, "Riley has a plan to get us together in case you hadn't noticed."

April snickered. "She has attempted to push us together more than once. What do you propose we do? Tell her no."

"Probably not. Look where we are now. Somehow I don't mind."

Before the dance ended, he gazed into her vivid blue eyes for a minute, searching for a welcoming sign. He didn't see a rejection, which gave him hope. Then they strolled hand in hand back to their seats, where he relaxed, and his hunger returned. The fettuccine Alfredo met the restaurant's high standards.

The conversation between them wasn't strained either. They discussed the shelters they both worked at in the past. The homeless population grew, with no foreseeable future of anything different. They caught themselves in more than one debate over the state of the nation or the economy. She intrigued him with her intelligence. No harsh words or wounded pride remained between them leaving the restaurant. The ultimate challenge he threw out to her for this date seemed unnecessary, since they agreed with each other on many topics. They both declined dessert and settled for coffee, and their truce stayed intact. They left the restaurant and drove back to Broken Arrow.

Brock escorted her back up the sidewalk where they stood on her front porch and faced each other. He hated to spoil the camaraderie between them by mentioning the challenge. Not being able to resist, a smug look on his face. "Now you can tutor Riley."

April hesitated for a brief second until relief slipped into her shoulders. "Okay, thanks."

No sooner than she moved to enter the house, he seized her shoulders, drew her to him, parted her lips and plunged his tongue into her mouth to wage a war until they both gasped for air. "One date will not be enough for us, and you know it," Brock admitted the second he broke from the smoldering kiss.

"You said one solitary date to fulfill the condition placed on our agreement."

"You don't get rid of me easily," Brock declared. "I'll call you in a day or two, and we'll go out again. Good night, April." He put his hands in his pockets and strolled to his car, started it, and left the driveway, and reflected on the evening driving home.

This kiss, hotter than the one shared in the barn at Riley's picnic, proved the fire grew larger. The few women he dated over the years didn't compare to her. A combination of smart, assertive, beautiful, arousing, yet with a hint of shyness about her. Or did she hide her true self? This newer version of the woman captivated him. Intrigued by the enigmatic April Palmer, his lack of understanding simply strengthened his resolve to solve the puzzle she presented.

He put the car in the garage and, to not to wake Riley, he sneaked into the house carrying his shoes. An inquiry about his date was the last thing he wanted. His past held far more memories than he realized, weaving through him, waiting to be analyzed. Tomorrow, he conceded soon enough to explore them and then fell asleep.

Brock slammed his fist on the clock when the alarm blared. Hadn't he just gotten to sleep? Lying on his back, his body ached from the passionate dream where he had made love to April over and over. Kissing her felt like heaven, something he wanted to repeat. He needed a cold shower.

While April continued to tutor Riley, he tantalized her with his presence often. Sometimes a brief wave to draw her attention. On other occasions, he interrupted by asking what they studied. Anything to show her, he remained serious in his pursuit of her.

The region enjoyed a pleasant period of warm weather, which gave him an idea of how to expand his endeavor. He stopped her before she left for the day. "I have a question. Do you remember how to ride a horse?"

"I haven't forgotten your lessons. Why?"

"I thought we could go for a ride in the morning if you have nothing to do."

"No, I don't have plans."

"Bring a sweater. It will be cool at first. I'll treat you to lunch later."

Brock was afraid he would have had trouble convincing Riley not to come along on the ride when he announced his intentions that evening after their dinner. However, she told him to go ahead without her the next morning since she needed to study some more. He feigned disappointment.

The chilly air lingered in the early dawn when Brock made his way to the barn, waiting for April to arrive. Clouds disappeared on the horizon, and the sun rose in the sky, promising another beautiful day. April parked her SUV, and he noticed she had taken his advice and was wearing a sweatshirt. He handed her a granola bar and orange juice. "It will hold you over until we eat later."

He walked with her to the corral, where Riley met them at the stable door. His plan to assist her onto the horse backfired and surprised him when she mounted Pepper by herself.

"Look at you, Miss Palmer, getting on all by yourself."

"I guess I'm off to a good start then." April laughed.

"You guys have fun, and I'll see you later. Goodbye."

"We will. Take a break from the books and get yourself some fresh air." Brock instructed.

"Goodbye, Riley. See you when we get back." April waved and rode out behind Brock.

Riley's comment reminded him of April's strength in overcoming her past. Brock couldn't hide the look of anticipation on his face. He mounted his own gigantic horse, Pegasus, and flexed his arms to release the tension. He couldn't seem overeager in his reaction to being alone with the woman.

With her here, he scanned the area and saw the landscape through her eyes. He loved the gorgeous trail. More outcrops of rock jutted out of the land. Rust-colored layers or white lines of limestone shown visible in the boulders. Gulleys cut across the landscape. Small trickles of water flowed from stone crevices and made them glisten in the sunshine. Morning sounds of birds accompanied their ride through the beams of sunlight, and the sight of an occasional rabbit or deer nibbling on the grass made him happy. These sights reminded him of how well she fit in and confirmed they made a good match.

While they rode through the meadows, Brock realized April had never told him about her early childhood. In fact, she never stated specific details at all, and the chance to talk freely arose. "Tell me more about how you grew up?"

"Why?" she asked.

"I know you said you grew up in the foster system, but why?"

"My mother wasn't a wonderful mom. She liked to drink and yell at me. I guess the pressures of trying to raise me got the better of her, and one day, well, I found my five-year-old self alone at a shelter. The people there searched for her. Soon afterwards, they called social services and placed me in my first foster home."

"How many homes?"

"Six or seven if you don't count the one I ran away from."

"You ran away? Why? Was it really terrible?"

"Worse. The foster mom brought strangers into our rooms at night, and then when we woke the next day, a roommate was missing. Learning that the girls had become prostitutes and drug addicts, I ran."

"It sounds like you've lived a really tough life; I'm sorry."

"It strengthened me."

Brock felt he had a better idea of where her power came from, and a new understanding settled in his heart. No wonder she did not trust anyone, including him. Now he had to work a little harder to gain her precious trust.

They continued crossing the pasture, letting the peaceful scenes set the tone while the morning dew dried on the grass. Soon the sun warmed the land. Brock observed April struggling to remove her pink sweatshirt. Attempting to keep her thin T-shirt in place, it got hung on the heavier clothing. He shook his head at her apparent modesty, couldn't resist, and moved closer to where she sat on Pepper. "Do you need help, or are you trying to work on your tan?"

She scowled, then rolled her eyes, which he noticed was a habit of hers when she became edgy. He reached out and stopped both horses, dismounted, and walked towards her. The blush bloomed on her cheeks. He grinned. "Hold still while I separate the two shirts." He held the T-shirt down over her back, covering it from temptation while she removed the heavier sweater. His fingers tingled with the overwhelming urge to explore her bare skin, and the tug of awareness strained at the zipper of his jeans. He willed the bulge to dissolve, got back on Pegasus, and rather than antagonize her further, he simply enjoyed the sights and sounds of nature. The old saying that time flies when you are having fun held true.

An hour later they finished the ride and unsaddled the horses; the same sense of contentment flowed through Brock. He laced his fingers over hers, and they walked to the house hand in hand. Riley joined them in the kitchen for the light lunch of club sandwiches. Comfortable quiet drifted around the table. Might this be a glimpse into his future? Answers visualized before his eyes of ways to make her see she truly belonged here. Brock let himself fantasize about the three of them together.

Chapter 15

April sat at her kitchen table with her hand around the back of her neck. She rubbed at the knots left from the emotional strain of being near Brock. She shouldn't let the man get any closer to her, no matter how the attraction hung on. Ironically, here she sat, coming home from the second date. Only the two of them rode across the pastures of his ranch. No buffers of teenage girls. This didn't even count the picnic for Riley's birthday party and the scene in the barn. Then, all three of them ate lunch as a family.

Her body throbbed, self-conscious of the sexual tension burning between them. He hadn't hidden his magnetic appeal. Although both danced around each other, maybe he would be content to become friends. Even now, they never talked about their mutual attraction.

A workable solution to her problem of attraction to him swiftly popped into her mind. Perhaps if she returned the money Maria owed him, he'd get the message that she owed him nothing and he needn't pursue her. She hurried to her writing desk and took out an envelope. With his name across the front, she placed a crisp twenty-dollar bill in it and sealed it.

On Monday afternoon, when her last class dismissed, she handed the envelope to Riley. "Please take this to your uncle for me."

"Sure, what is it?"

"Don't worry, he will know what it is for." She trusted he understood the meaning behind the message.

April got into her vehicle as school dismissed and drove to the grocery store. She wanted to fix a fresh salad and top it off with ice cream to celebrate her newfound liberation from a certain weight named Brock on her shoulders. However, on her arrival from the grocers, a familiar truck blocked her driveway. He must have been home before Riley got off the bus with the envelope and then raced back to town. To avoid an argument, she almost drove away, sensing the hot-blooded passion which radiated from the pickup. A showdown became inevitable. She stayed.

April blew the horn, letting him know she wanted access to her house. Aggravation stemming from the imminent confrontation caused her to thump her knuckles on the steering wheel. She wrenched the car into her garage to escape quickly. He rushed her too fast, and she saw the raw heat in his eyes. "Tell me, what is the meaning of this?" He waved the twenty-dollar bill in her face.

"What does it look like? I told you I'd pay you back someday," she said in an upbeat voice, even though to her own ears it sounded lame. She opened the back door of her SUV and leaned in to get her groceries.

"Are you saying that if we're even, I'll want nothing else to do with you? I'm not buying such a lame excuse. Besides, I told you at the ranch you will always have the upper hand over me."

He towered in front of her. She stood up with her bags and blinked. One gaze at his much too close face, with eyes flashing daggers, and all hope silently evaporated from her resolve. Oh, Lord, the word handsome didn't cover his looks even in fury. Her rapidly beating heart betrayed her, and she didn't have the will to resist. "We never talked about those nights, and I wanted to make sure I didn't owe you."

"I don't give a damn about the money. Don't you know I want you?"

She gulped at the certainty of his statement. "As a friend?" she mumbled. Rationally, she wanted him to say yes, though she longed for him to say no.

Brock took a deep breath, rubbed his hand over his face and said something she never in her wildest dreams imagined. "I propose we start over. Make a clean sweep of our past. Pretend we just met. Go on a date with me and let's find out what we want out of this relationship."

"Defining it as a relationship is a big assumption, isn't it?"

"We won't know until we try."

Her resistance shattered with one glance at his puppy-dog eyes and the sexy smile. "Fine, one more."

"Great, I'll call you." He brushed her lips, waved, and left her garage.

After April put the groceries in the refrigerator, she walked onto the front porch. His behavior baffled her once more. The swaying motion of the swing where she sat did nothing for the turmoil in her body. She thought she possessed willpower strong enough to resist him, except one brief encounter erased all the bravado regarding him.

The birds sang in the trees while the last ray of sunlight faded on the horizon. Darkness settled on April in more ways than one. Even though they discussed his manners at the shelter, neither of them broached the subject of their temptation to each other back then or now. Starting over with a fresh slate was alright for him, although she knew her history with him could never be totally spotless. A redheaded girl somewhere existed as living proof.

Rather than wait for warmer weather, April spent each afternoon in the yard searching for spring bulbs pushing through the soil. She used any excuse to avoid thinking about Brock manipulating her and then ignoring her afterward. He must have only wanted to prove she would be open to another date, since it had been a week without hearing from him.

Her phone started ringing on the front porch. Grumbling at the interruption and short of breath, she grabbed it and snapped out an aggravated, "Hello?"

She heard concern in his tone. "Are you okay?"

"I'm fine. You caught me in the yard."

"Why outside? It's not warm yet."

She explained, "I assumed you planted the area with future flowers."

"On the lawn, uh? Well, okay then. I'm calling to see if you will go to dinner with me tonight. Somewhere casual."

April paused briefly before responding in a nonchalant tone. "I suppose it's quite possible." Secretly, she hid the eagerness and locked her growing feelings of attraction for him in her heart. The ones she kept trying to ignore.

"I'll pick you up at six. See you then."

She finished working in the yard until she finally found a few bulbs just beginning to break the ground. Satisfied with her feat, she showered and put on an outfit she deemed casual. And waited for her date. When Brock knocked on her door, he carried a bouquet. "Future flowers aren't blooming yet. I brought you ones, which are."

April buried her nose in the cluster, smelling its perfume. Then, she thanked him and placed them in a vase of water. She smoothed out her blouse and asked, "Is this casual enough?" She wore jeans and a peasant-style blouse, which dropped off of her shoulders, in a bright shade of turquoise. The color made her dark red hair pop. His glance up and down her body pleased her.

"Anything you wear I approve of." Brock helped her into the truck and started driving towards Tulsa. She had spent the entire afternoon in the backyard in the bright light, whereas at the moment, wispy clouds played peek-a-boo with the sun. "I see you didn't wear any sunblock today. Your nose is bright pink. "

"Pinkish." She commented boldly, then touched her nose with one finger and realized it was tender.

"Don't worry, it looks cute on you." He reached over and tweaked the tip.

"Where are we going?"

"To dinner, and a new movie came out I want to see."

"Nothing scary, please. I need to sleep tonight."

"Action only movie, no ghosts or aliens."

"Good."

To April's satisfaction, the casual dinner of burgers and fries with chocolate shakes hit the spot. The movie theater stood down the sidewalk from the small diner, which made it convenient to walk the short distance with him holding her hand. Possibly, this simple gesture became an acceptance of her own part in their new beginning. He led her to a row of seats in the middle of the screen area. "I don't suppose you saw too many movies growing up?" Brock asked as they waited for the feature to start.

"No, not too many. It was kind of hard to sneak into one. Once in a while, though, I got lucky."

Brock grinned. "You're telling me you can be sneaky?"

In the backwash of grasping what she admitted to April, blushed slightly. "Hey, a girl needed some entertainment. Uh, I didn't mean entertaining pertaining to…" Her red cheeks grew brighter.

"I know what you meant," he acknowledged.

She noted the remorse in his voice. "Hey, don't beat yourself up. I wasn't completely innocent. I had kissed a boy before." Then lowered her voice and admitted, "Just not a man like you."

"Hope I didn't disappoint?"

She stuttered, then, surprisingly, laughed out loud. "No, you didn't."

This easy banter and light flirting set the tone for their night. April relaxed as Brock's arm slid around her shoulders and drew her closer. She leaned her head on his broad shoulder and breathed in the tantalizing scent, all man. The lights dimmed, and the movie started. During the movie, they snuggled into each other, whispered occasionally about portions of the show, and she felt absolutely content. Enjoying a carefree night developed into something she wasn't used to, especially around him.

When the lights came back up and the movie ended, April speculated about how long this peaceful truce between them lasted. Plagued with constantly having to worry about their closeness and her secret, she acknowledged that a confession would destroy the man she was getting to know better. The price, likely too high.

Brock pulled the truck into her driveway and turned the engine off. Anticipation temporarily robbed her voice. Would he kiss her again? Did she allow it, or prove her reluctance of a relationship with him or expose her building attraction?

A strong woman emerged partially from his actions, and no matter how much she wished to change the past, it wasn't possible. Inhaling air into her lungs, she extended an olive branch. "Would you like to come in?" Then she slowly exhaled.

"Are you certain?"

They got out and walked to the house. She unlocked the door and ushered him in. "How about a cup of coffee?"

"I don't want to be any trouble."

"No bother." She fibbed. "Come on in." Her pulse jumped another notch when he followed her to the kitchen.

His eyes were on her movements, and she tried not to let her hand tremble while she prepared the coffee. Although her idea — inviting him in — the need to make unpretentious conversation abruptly filled the silence. She leaned against the counter and chose what she thought to be a safe subject. "The movie was pretty good. You have excellent taste."

A smoothness in his tone. oozed from his voice. "Yes, I do."

Not being able to resist, she smothered a sigh of pleasure at his apparent double meaning. Pouring their coffee, she nodded. "Why don't we go to the living room?"

"Wherever you want to go."

She may have been overreacting slightly. Everything he said held a sexual meaning.

Before sitting down, Brock walked to the fireplace and flipped the automatic flames on. "Now, isn't this cozy?"

Not answering him, she swallowed hard, knowing what the invitation encompassed. She couldn't stop the thrill coursing through her body. Gripping her cup while sitting on the couch, she watched each move. The eye-pleasing sight of broad shoulders made her mouth water.

Next, he left the hearth and sat on the couch close enough for her to once again smell the sandalwood cologne he wore. She nervously took a sip of the drink and then exhaled a deep breath.

In slow motion, he placed their cups on the side table and stared for a minute before tilting towards her. Her heartbeat ran rampant in her chest. He took her face between his hands and rained tiny kisses along her nose. Moving to her lips, he tugged until she opened her mouth and granted him access. Heat rushed across her stomach, hotter than the flames in the fireplace. The hint of a smile on his face did her in.

She unbuttoned his shirt with shaky fingers to reach the sexy, hair-covered chest she remembered. Her fingers teased his nipples, then she caressed his skin with her lips. He moved his hands over the neckline of her blouse. Tugging the sleeves down further gave him a clear path. Moaning, she leaned her head back against the couch, savoring the tenderness he gave her on now exposed breasts. Their bodies fit together again perfectly. Soft sighs rose in her throat until he reached for the zipper of her jeans. Placing her hands on top of his, she squeezed his fingers. The movement brought them both back to reality. Panting rapidly, "No, Brock, we can't do this. It's too soon."

He backed off and straightened, rubbing his hand through his hair. "I know. You're right. I'm sorry, April. We need to slow down. Damn, woman, you are tempting!"

She stood and pulled the sleeves of her blouse back into place, took a deep breath thinking about how she knew exactly how it hurt to put the brakes on. Slowly, reluctantly, she walked to the door with Brock. Raising up on her tiptoes, she gently kissed his lips, then promptly backed away. She couldn't risk igniting the passion again.

He touched her lips with his fingers and strolled out the door. The smugness of victory on his face worried her sense of independence.

Sitting on the swing, she once again relished the pleasure of his kisses. In the next moment, she berated herself for responding to those mind-blowing embraces, which left her breathless and disoriented and, regrettably, wanting more. With understanding came the realization of his power to shatter her world. Should she permit it? One minute, they debated her teaching methods or discussed current events; the next, they found themselves wrapped in each other's arms.

This new version of Brock seemed to be more of a mystery. Maturity seemed to have replaced the guy who insisted she change her future. In the past, he hadn't gotten to know her well enough to give her the chance to explain what she desired. She had been willing to go along; however, he never followed through with the help she really needed.

She risked her heart and lost. The old version of herself grew up and fought for and realized her own dreams. Could she go back to being the same girl from their past? No longer a charity case, life taught her to be stronger, and the sooner he realized it, the better off they were. Her ache for the love she lost by giving up her baby caused her to gain the strength to fight for herself.

The question rambling through her mind caused a blinding surge of panic. Suppose she acted on Brock's suggestion and started a relationship with him? Her inner voice assured her that their sexual chemistry was never a problem. How did she continue growing close with the untold truth she held silently between them? His obvious devotion to his niece showed her he had matured. He would hate her and never forgive her for the actions in the past. Finding the courage to confess wasn't in her right now, if ever. Yet, learning life sometimes threw you a curveball gave her hope.

April woke up the next morning with no answers. She went to the park for a hike to clear her mind of complicated life problems along a trail off the beaten path, which she often took. Although not completely deserted, the place let her be alone with her thoughts. Walking a few yards, she came across one of her fellow teachers. They met for dinner with a group of coworkers when she first moved here. "Hi Chloe, how are you?"

"I'm alright, April. How are you and what are you doing here by yourself?"

"I needed some fresh air and exercise. You know, being in the classroom doesn't afford us much."

"Yeah, I seldom find enough for myself. Between grading papers and making lesson plans," Chloe replied.

"Do you want to get a coffee with me? We can talk about anything you want or nothing at all."

"Sure, I'm finished with my walk. A cup will hit the spot."

"There's a new cafe nearby. Let's try it out."

April met Chloe at the nearby shop, and they went inside and chose a table. Both women ordered a cappuccino along with a croissant. She appreciated the friendly gesture. Being always around other teachers, they'd never chatted alone. Aside from Julie, Riley's mother, she rarely experienced equal treatment from women over the years. She found the pull of friendship pleasant.

At first, typical small talk ruled the conversation until Chloe asked, "Have you been going on any dates or is the subject too personal to ask about?"

"I have sort of been seeing someone."

"Just not anything serious, then?"

"No, not really. He wants to get serious. I'm not sure if I can." Luckily, Chloe hadn't asked for more details. They finished their drinks and agreed to meet again soon. Her phone rang the minute she got back to her car and pulled out. "Hello, Bonnie, what are you doing?"

"Finishing work at the shelter. What are you doing?"

"Going home from a walk. I felt the need for some fresh air. Is there something you needed?"

"No, I'm just checking in."

A twinge of guilt pushed forward. "Why don't I come up this next weekend and spend it with you and go shopping?"

"If you aren't busy. I don't want to take you away from anything or anyone."

April swallowed the sudden lump in her throat. She assumed Bonnie had put two and two together and come up with the correct answer long ago. The unquestioning trust earned respect. Did the woman know about Brock? Then she remembered the camping outing and the comment he made. "I'll arrive early Saturday. Have your walking shoes on. I need some pretty clothes," she teased.

In a rush, April got home, cleaned the house, did laundry and graded papers, before she threw together an overnight bag. She placed her hand on the doorknob to leave the next morning as the bell rang. Brock looked down at the case clutched to her side. "Did I catch you at a bad time?"

"Sort of. I'm on my way to see Bonnie. We are going shopping. Is something wrong?"

"No, go enjoy being with her. We can talk later."

She gently caressed his cheek. "Thanks, I knew you'd understand."

The trip to the city provided the perfect escape from her problems. Bonnie didn't pry into her personal life, which suited her fine. She cleared her head of the anguish from trying to decide what to do about Brock. Whether to continue dating him and build a relationship or to keep it casual. Her intuition told her he wouldn't go along with the latter scenario at all.

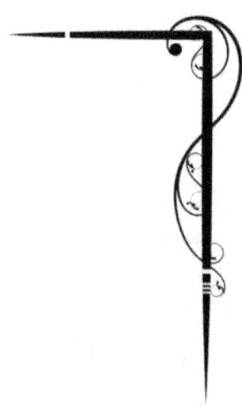

Chapter 16

Brock's unannounced visit to see April and discuss their future turned out to be a risky move and didn't pay off because she had already made plans. A shudder rippled through him in frustration as he headed to the office to close a case for a client. He wanted her, determined to make their future work somehow.

One week later, Brock couldn't get her off his mind. If she hadn't pulled back on their last encounter, he'd have wrapped his arms around her body and taken her then. Understanding why she stopped didn't lessen his cravings.

The softness of her lips amazed him, and the thrill of being with her once again intrigued him. Nothing else compared to the thirst he held for her. His desire for another date stemmed from her being the perfect woman for him. He dialed her number. "Be ready tonight at seven."

"Well, hello to you, too. Are you positive I will go out with you again?"

"Yes, I am. I suspect I have been in your thoughts like you've been racing through mine," he replied.

"Confident, aren't you?" April snickered. "Fine, I accept your invitation."

"Wait until this evening and trust me, you will see confidence." She giggled again at the brazen comment before hanging up the phone.

He arrived right at seven on the dot, knocking on her door. She opened it and taunted him. "At least you weren't late, considering how little time you left for me to get ready."

"Oh, I didn't want to waste a single second on our evening." Brock put his hand around her waist and escorted her to the car. He admired the blue sundress, the exact shade of her eyes, she wore and said, "You look beautiful."

"Are you saying I looked attractive, even soaking wet? You recollect the day in question, don't you?"

"Oh, I remember, and yes, you were gorgeous even then," he admitted. She blushed at the compliment.

He took her to a local restaurant known for its delicious seafood. Brock couldn't keep his eyes off her. His attention ought to have been on the menu, trying to decide what to order. The sight across from him felt right. The casual manners he used to experience with a woman reminded him this wasn't a schoolboy crush either. It marked the potential of being very serious.

April brought up the subject of Riley's plans to be a lawyer. "What will she have to study in college? Tell me the particular courses she will need, ones I need to address in her tutoring."

He struggled to concentrate on what she said and answered vaguely. "Basic courses and then some political science, history and maybe criminal justice classes." Then prayed, the response he gave was correct. He took a sip of wine, oblivious to the server pouring it.

"Okay, those will help me lead her in the right direction. Thank you."

No sooner than their server placed their dinner on the table, he played with the steak and shrimp, pushing the food around aimlessly on his plate. He glanced over at April, saw her doing the exact same thing, and laughed. "Aren't you hungry?"

"I could ask you the same question?" He nearly buckled at the sight of the starvation etched in her eyes.

When they last met, she stood at her front door, bag packed to see Bonnie, leaving him to postpone the talk until she came back from her visit. The intensity of lovemaking on her couch reminded him of their first night together. He acknowledged and accepted the undeniable truth of something emerging between them and knew a confession about said attraction posed a problem.

Brock tried to keep his composure, which proved extremely difficult. He swallowed the last bite of food and told himself to slow down, then signaled the server for the check.

Perhaps he required fresh air to clear his head or at the very least cool the craving. His decision to forgo a tie became fortunate; otherwise, it would have choked him.

After he settled the bill, he remembered a nearby park with a walking trail and suggested they take a stroll around the area. They laughed at the ducks in a small pond chasing bugs for their own dinners. The night breeze made the area feel cool and deserted. He drew her into a tender embrace and kissed her intimately. Thank goodness, the place was empty.

She moved away from him, went to the play area, sat, and swung. Brock observed the pure joy on her face. Her face lit up like a little kid. She went higher, as though she didn't have a care in the world. He watched in awe, leaning against the frame of the playground swing.

Within a few minutes, April stopped and stared at him. Brock walked over, tugged her up into his arms, and devoured her with a smoldering passion barely below the surface. She stepped back from him, breaking the intense touch, and gazed up into his eyes. He searched her face for any clue or visible sign to warrant putting the brakes on and didn't see any, so he held out his hand. She placed her hand in his, and they went back to the car. He stole glances of opportunity while he took them to her house and parked the vehicle. Before either of them opened the car doors, he turned to her. "We need to discuss this. I don't want to make the same mistakes again." He heard her take a deep breath.

April nodded, got out of the car, and started towards the house. She didn't stop until she had unlocked the door. He followed her like a lost puppy.

Brock walked into the living room and waited for her to turn on the lamp beside the couch. Light gave the room a golden glow. He sat on the couch and discovered this self-assured side of the woman when she stated, "Okay, let's talk."

"It may be too late, but I sincerely want to know about your dreams in the past. I pushed my opinions on you without giving you enough space to think about what you really wanted out of life, and then I didn't follow through."

"True, you did. Until I met you, I wasn't sure if anything good existed in my life, and you didn't stick around to find out. My wishes were few. I wanted pretty clothes." She blushed at the flippant remark, then whispered. "Not to be invisible."

"I regret abandoning you. Do you trust me? Because I see someone worth the world to me?"

"Yes, I do."

"Do you know what you want at this very moment?"

"Forget slow and steady; we've proven the concept is impossible," she chuckled. "This demands our attention; let's move to the next phase."

"I think we'll enjoy this step." Brock pulled her to him, kissing her again and again. Her lips parted and granted his tongue access. Then he scooted back further on the sofa. Not breaking contact, he put her on his lap. His hands stroked her back down to her hips, and his lips put a string of feather kisses down her neck.

He licked her tender skin with the tip of his tongue, not wanting to give her body a chance of retreating from the onslaught of pleasure, which similarly ran rampant through him. Her arms tugged him closer, and she kneaded his shoulders and smoothed his upper body. He trembled at the first touch when she played with the rigid muscles on his chest and ran her fingernails down his arms. He shuddered, nearly losing control. Yanking his shirt out of his jeans, she undid the buttons and raked her nails down his hair-covered muscular chest.

Brock inhaled, then exhaled and drew back from her shaking body and whispered, "Let me stay, April, and make love to you?"

He gazed into her eyes, ones that smoldered with the same passion and desire sizzling in his. She stopped and drew back from his face. The painful hardness pressing against her stomach indicated his insatiable hunger. He moved her to the side and stood up. Then he reached for her hands, removing her from the couch, and led the way down the hallway to her bedroom.

His body melted slowly into molten liquid. He turned on the bedside lamp. She reached to turn it off. He stopped her. "No, I want to see every inch of you." He bent down and took off her shoes, where she sat on the edge of the bed and watched. Bit by bit, he started slipping her clothes off and kissed her soft skin. He pushed her onto her back, leaned over, and separated her legs, with his head between her thighs, lingering by her soft core. First with his lips and then his tongue, he entered the wet slickness of her body.

She moaned, which caused his desire to rage unheeded. Grasping his shoulders to jerk him closer, she raked her nails down his back as his mouth continued assaulting her womanhood. He then wound his way back to her stomach and took off her bra, giving him total access.

He hesitated momentarily, seeing the tattoo. She held her breath until his eyes left the butterfly and moved to her taut breasts. Aching to touch them, he cupped one and then sucked each rosy petal.

April took off his shirt before they ever made it to the bedroom, so Brock hastily stripped off the rest of his clothes. Watching her with half-closed eyes, he let the fire take over. An enduring hunger replaced all sane thoughts with the same unending sensations which rocked his world years before. Distant visions of those nights came back real enough now to be an all-out consuming inferno. Cravings, unbridled longings, and enthusiasm flew through him all at once.

He stood before her, naked. With his manhood rigid, he gazed down at her. She reached up and dragged him down to join her. They kissed, and he entered her in one quick thrust. Allowing her body to adjust before he moved. She wrapped her legs around his taut hips to pull him in deeper. His constant thrusts gave all the pent-up pressure of being with her again an escape route with each movement. Thrusting in and out caused his mind to go out of control until they fell over the edge of ecstasy. He saw stars twinkling in her eyes, giving himself an insight into the intensity she felt with his lovemaking. This response upped the euphoria, which raced through his own body.

When they regained their breath, they continued to kiss and cuddle each other until they reached the peak of pleasure once more. They nurtured and intensified their need, allowing it to flourish with increased passion.

April snuggled into his chest and slept. Lying quietly, he watched her. Having his suspicions answered, this was Maria of his past and April of his future wrapped into one glorious woman. Kissing her temple with a whisper, "Good night." He dressed silently, locked the door, and then left.

Brock drove back to the ranch, where he pulled into the garage and just sat and remembered the spectacular night. April, beautiful, like a siren from mythology with long, lush red hair, those bright blue eyes and the butterfly tattoo on her chest.

Tonight, all those years melted away, with her under him like the first time. The difference now, his mind perfectly clear. The idea of being able to stay buried once more in her should have lessened the aching for her. All the curves weren't noticeable before; however, the intense thirst remained the same. He craved her more than ever before.

His fingers sizzled with a blistering fire as he touched her body tonight. The slightest touch caused her to moan, and his desire for her came back intensely. He recalled the moment he offered to stop, having realized she was inexperienced. Later, sated, he dozed off into a deep sleep.

Noiselessly, Brock walked into the house. And even though a weekend; he didn't want to wake Riley up to question his actions. The satisfied state of his body should have enabled him to fall asleep immediately. It didn't!

Instead of lying wide awake, he got back up and walked to his office. He poured a glass of bourbon and stared out the window behind his desk. They reached a height of ecstasy tonight he truly believed hotter than before. The physical side alone wouldn't be enough for him. To convince April that they stood a good chance of a future together and to make sure she stayed in town was feasibly a challenge. Besides, Riley would be upset if by some chance his actions caused her teacher to leave.

Brock went back to his room and lay on the bed. He groaned; replaying the evening caused him to harden again with desire. He pushed one of his pillows into his chest, wishing for a certain warm, sexy body instead of a polyester-filled substitute, and willed his body to calm down. Soon, he hoped the other side of his bed held a partner to share it with him. Making love half the nights and then waking up beside her in the mornings would be heavenly.

When he opened his eyes wide the next morning, sunshine streamed through his window. Someone knocked loudly on his bedroom door. Grumbling to himself about the inability to sleep in, he hollered, "Who is it and what do you want?"

"Uh, it's me, Uncle Brock. Are you okay?"

"Yeah, I'm fine." He glanced at the bedside clock and groaned. Almost noon. He never slept late. Then, the memories of the night before came crashing back. April!

"I'll be out in a few minutes."

He heard her walk back to the kitchen and speak. "He's fine, Mrs. Shefield. I woke him up."

The smell of coffee wafted down the hall. Getting dressed hastily, he strolled into the kitchen and poured a cup and asked, "What is your rush this morning, Riley?"

"I'm not in a hurry. You seldom sleep this late. I became worried."

"Uh, I got home late." He hoped the explanation satisfied her.

"I hope your date went well."

"Yes, it did. Now we need to get to the barn and help the boys clean the stalls out. You know it is always nice to have reliable help, and I'm sure they'd appreciate an extra hand." He grabbed another cup of coffee, and they walked to the barn.

Riley continued to talk and wanted to know details of his date with her teacher, which became a challenge.

Specifics he wasn't willing to share. Although they mucked out stalls in relative quiet, he couldn't prevent his own mind from replaying the date.

Brock decided he needed a better distraction to keep her from asking personal questions, and what better way than a horseback ride? However, an everyday sight drew him back to the weekends April spent out at the ranch. Whether the glimpse of a hawk in a tree or a deer crossing the pasture undeterred by the cattle, his memories always came back to her. He vowed last night to himself not to rush her. Being over-opinionated without following through in the past drove her away. Unless she reached out to him first, he must give her some space.

Following their ride, his head ached, and then his stomach growled. Waking up late, trying to fend off Riley's inquisitive mind, he realized he'd missed breakfast. Going into the kitchen, he raided the frig, warmed up some leftovers and took the food to his office, going over paperwork. With work never in short supply, he scanned the details of two more cases, which took up the rest of his day. A rap on the door interrupted his work. He looked out the window and noticed the sun lowering in the western sky and leaving a rosy glow on the horizon. "Come in."

"Hi, Uncle. Do you have any plans for this evening?"

"No, not really. I think I'll stay home and go to bed early. What about you?"

"Why couldn't we build a fire in the pit and roast some marshmallows?"

"Sure.

"Good. I'll gather the supplies and meet you in the backyard."

Brock groaned, then put a fake smile on his face, sucked it up, and went along. He shook his head because whenever he tried to put space between them, April intruded somehow. The gratitude for getting his sweet Riley back rushed into his heart. Even if the two of them couldn't get past problems from their history, he knew deep down the woman would stay in Riley's future somehow.

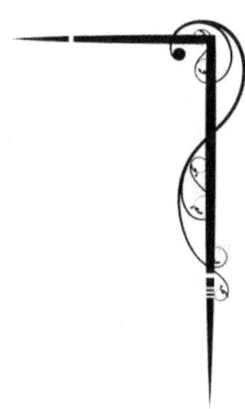

Chapter 17

L ight poured into April's bedroom window, and she stretched her legs like a cat waking from a nap, practically purred and turned over slowly. The cold sheets told her Brock wasn't there. Getting up, she showered, dressed and fixed coffee, then walked out to the porch to watch the world wake up, trying to center her thoughts. She knew she would be alone; he couldn't have left Riley overnight by herself.

While at the park the night before, she sat on the swing and gazed up into his eyes. Her sanity had disappeared, replaced by an overwhelming need. On their first encounter together, he took charge with gentleness. In his dorm bed, he kissed and caressed her body, taking her to a different level of fire and more excitement. Last night, in her own bed, his calloused hands roamed with impatience all over her body and made it impossible to concentrate on anything except what those lethal weapons were doing. She reasoned that their separation for years explained the reaction. Deep down, intuition said something special took place, which left her feeling adored and cherished.

The comment he made about not wanting to repeat the same mistakes haunted her. She knew he meant the ones about his failure to stay and help her, then the rejection. How little he knew. If only she possessed the courage to confess. However, she didn't, not yet. By any chance, if he ever found out her secret, the cost became too steep for her.

April finished her coffee and tried to decide what to do for the rest of her day when her phone rang. Surprised at the prompt morning call, she checked the screen. "Good morning, you are up early, Bonnie."

"Uh, April, this is Molly. Bonnie's assistant."

"Oh, I'm sorry. Is something wrong?" April's heart skipped a beat, and dread filled her suddenly.

"Bonnie is in the hospital, and you need to get here."

"Why is she in the hospital? Did she fall?" April's imagination began running rampant.

Molly said in a quiet, steady voice, "No, she didn't fall. She is very sick, and the doctors suggested I call you."

"I'm on my way."

April tried not to panic. If the doctors wanted her there, it couldn't be good. Fear caused too many scenarios to race through her mind. Surely modern medicine worked miracles these days.

Quickly, April packed an overnight bag, stopped long enough to gas up her SUV and grabbed another cup of coffee. Lucky for her, the traffic on the freeway moved at a rapid speed, and it didn't take long to reach Oklahoma City and Bonnie.

She arrived at the hospital parking lot and found a convenient spot near the entrance. Before she got out of the vehicle, her phone rang. With a quick glance at the screen, she let the call go to voicemail. The sun's heat warmed the pavement as she hurried into the structure. Out of the bright sunshine, she paused in the lobby momentarily to regain her vision, spotted the information desk and walked to the attendant. "Where will I find a patient named Bonnie Burton?"

The volunteer asked. "Are you family?"

Without hesitating, April said, "Yes, I'm her daughter."

The woman told her which floor and the room number, and she raced towards the elevator. As she got off the elevator, she looked around and noticed a woman in the hallway. "Are you Molly?"

"Yes, you must be April."

"What happened? I talked to her last weekend, and she never hinted at any sickness."

"She hid her illness from you and wouldn't allow me to contact you. Said she didn't want to be a bother. The doctors won't give me the specifics. I'm not family. However, all you have to do is inform the attendant at the desk."

"Molly, thank you then for being here for her. I appreciate it." April walked to the counter and informed the nurse of her arrival and wanted to meet Bonnie's doctors. The woman assured her that the doctors would be with her soon. Swallowing the fear creeping into her stomach, she opened the door, frightened by what she faced.

Bonnie lay in the sterile-looking hospital bed and looked too pale, small and frail. April clutched her hands tightly together and couldn't keep the tears from filling her eyes. She took a deep breath, placed a cheery smile on, tiptoed to the bed, and stood looking down at the kind friend, much like a mother to her for years. It made her wonder why the woman remained quiet about being sick. Peacefulness lingered on Bonnie's face. Unfathomable now, to believe how the years had slipped by, particularly the minute you've faced the prospect of losing someone you deeply cared for.

April sneaked back out of the room, not wanting to disturb Bonnie. Sleep helped heal. She needed to speak with her doctors anyhow and checked in at the nurse's desk again. Then she sat in the waiting room until they arrived. "How long has she been ill, Molly?"

"Long before you moved to Tulsa. It started getting worse about a month ago. I tried to convince her to call. I don't have to tell you how stubborn the woman is."

"Believe me, I understand she's very selective about what she says." Experience taught April how well Bonnie kept secrets.

Two men, one older than the other, dressed in white coats, approached before any more dialogue took place. The older man, Bonnie's longtime physician, Dr. Waddel, introduced himself and the other man as the heart specialist, Dr. Roberts. They greeted April with a handshake and ushered her into a conference room. "Miss Palmer, we understand you are Bonnie's daughter?"

"Yes, I live in Broken Arrow. What can you tell me about her condition?"

"It's a terminal heart condition. Bonnie didn't want anyone to know, and there's not much time left for goodbyes." Both men appeared compassionate in their explanations of the disease taking its toll on her body. "We will make her comfortable." The tears fell gently from April's eyes.

The younger doctor said, "Bonnie can remain in the hospital where we will take good care of her. Be here for her."

"Thank you for doing this for us. I'm sure Bonnie is grateful, and I know I am."

Dr. Waddel patted her hand with sympathy. "No problem, Miss Palmer. Bonnie is very special to the city, and we will help her any way we can."

April thanked both men again and then made her way back to Bonnie's room. Sitting in the chair by her dear friend's bed, watching her sleep, she berated herself for being wrapped up in her own life. They talked often, though April knew it wasn't the same. Grief-stricken and lost in thought, she jumped when Bonnie whispered, "April, you're here."

"Yes, where else would I be after Molly called?"

"She shouldn't have called. Don't feel guilty."

A grin spread across April's face. "You're reading my mind, aren't you? How?"

"Perhaps since I've known you for many years. Even before we met, you were strong; now you are even stronger. You have become an independent woman. Keep being who you are — a beautiful, modern lady, and don't mourn for me."

"You are not going anywhere."

"April, I know my life is ending. Please don't be too sad."

"I can't help myself. You have taught me so much and provided me with a home. Now I have to face a future without you, and it hurts." April's tears fell unheeded. Bonnie squeezed her hands before drifting back to sleep.

She sat in attendance for several more minutes, wishing she possessed the power to stop the inevitable. Instead, she called the school and took a leave of absence to stay until the end. When evening visiting hours ended, the nursing staff insisted April leave to rest. They promised to call if her return became necessary.

April drove to Bonnie's house, which felt strange and heartbreaking, even though it had been her own home for years. Entering her old bedroom, the familiar surroundings offered her little comfort because she herself had become a different person and knew it wasn't her home anymore.

Consequently, April spent days at the hospital, from morning till dinner, sitting with a more responsive Bonnie. Sometimes, she strolled through the grounds in between the woman's naps, or they talked for hours about past celebrations, pleased to go down memory lane. She came back into the room after a break and noticed Bonnie was awake. Her memory of a special excursion the two of them embarked on surfaced during her recent excursion around the gardens. "Do you remember the trip we took to Branson, Missouri? We ate too much, saw at least three of the shows and then window-shopped until both of us collapsed. "

Bonnie smiled and said, "Yes, we enjoyed a great weekend."

"I'll never forget your response to my questions about your stretch away from the shelter."

"It still rings true. Life is too short to miss out on the things that make you happy. Please don't forget."

April contemplated the wise words and took another walk. The lushness of the flowers and the sounds of the fountains reminded her of the ranch, filling her with peacefulness. Could she be content with Riley and Brock? She didn't know. Her own past never allowed the luxury of faithful love.

The memories of her mother were vague, although one nightmare plagued her often growing up. The woman stood, pointing her finger and yelled, 'It's your fault,' shaking with fury. Because she herself had dropped a glass full of what April now knew held beer. Similar episodes happened frequently until one day they went to a shelter, and her mom merely disappeared. She knew Brock gave his niece unconditional love, which made her happy.

Earlier in the day, Bonnie fretted about the wellbeing of the shelter, so April promised she'd check on the building and the people operating it. "Of course I'll look in on them. I found you there, and it will always be a special place for me. Don't worry."

Bonnie said, "I can't help myself."

April reassured her that if anything appeared amiss, they would fix it. She waited until Bonnie fell asleep before leaving and kept her word by stopping at the shelter before going home. Astonished, she walked in and saw all the homeless people in need, more now than in the past. The place must operate with the same compassion after Bonnie's death!

Molly rushed to her side asking, "Is everything alright?" The woman explained, while they waited in the hospital for the doctors, how Bonnie had put her in charge of the everyday operations of the shelter.

"Yes, Bonnie is holding on for now. I promised to stop by and check in on everyone. You know she worries about this place and all of its people."

"She trained us well and will be irreplaceable."

"Well, it seems you have everything under control, so I won't worry." They chatted about everyday problems for a few more minutes. April surmised nothing seemed too urgent for immediate attention. "I won't keep you from your work, then. Call me if you need anything, please." Molly reached out and embraced her. With the hug from a virtual stranger, her first instincts were correct. The shelter remained safe.

As she parked her SUV in the driveway and walked into the living room, her cell phone rang. Looking down, she almost didn't answer it until Bonnie's words echoed in her ears. "Hello, Brock."

"Hey April, are you okay? Riley has been driving me nuts worrying about you. I guess you missed a call from her. The substitute teacher won't give her any answers."

"I'm well. Bonnie's not though. I've been to the hospital. I'm afraid she won't be with us much longer."

"Do you need me to do anything for her?" He hesitated. "Or for you?"

She faltered at his response. "No, keep us in your thoughts, please. Tell Riley hi for me."

"Are you sure you don't want me to come to the city?"

April took a leap of faith. "I want. However, now is not the time." She hoped he got the subtle message.

A heavy silence filled the air. She thought he had hung up the phone until he whispered. "Well, I'll call back."

Okay, he left the door open. Maybe Bonnie's wisdom rang true? "I need to take care of some things at the house before tomorrow gets here. Thank you for checking in with us. Good night, Brock."

His sudden interest in her welfare comforted her and, using the guise of Riley's concern to call her, warmed her heart.

Sometimes he enraged her with his actions. In the next moment, she barely allowed herself to breathe around him. They got along well at the ranch, both laughed and played, and she hoped in the future they got to know each other. Perhaps they stood a chance. He said he wanted to prove himself trustworthy.

She put her phone in her purse and went to the kitchen, where Mae, Bonnie's longtime housekeeper, waited for an update. "Bonnie remained in good spirits today. Worrying about the shelter. I stopped on my way home, and they're fine."

"Okay, Miss April, if it is all right, I will go on home. If you need me, call."

April sat in the living room sipping a glass of wine and eating the meal Mae left for her. She recalled the phone call with Brock and how pleased he sounded glad to hear her voice. He mentioned Riley missed her, not him. Possibly, she could return to Broken Arrow and find answers to her doubts. Her heart sang at being close to him. The sensations meant something, didn't they? Whatever they were, it wasn't right to explore those emotions now.

Optimistically, Bonnie seemed more alert than in the past few days. She bordered on exhaustion and needed to get some sleep before returning to the hospital. However, the decision not to go wasn't an option. Faithful duty to care for Bonnie rested with her. She shut the bedside lamp off and pulled the sheet over her shoulders and fell asleep.

The ringing of the phone startled her. She fumbled with the lamp, half asleep, looked at the clock, then dread sank deeply into her soul. Nothing good ever came from middle-of-the-night calls. She looked at the screen and saw the hospital's number. "Hello, this is April."

"I'm sorry to disturb you. Dr. Waddel is here with Bonnie, and he asked me to call. You need to return to the hospital."

"Okay, I'll be back in a few minutes." April hung up the call. Sitting on the bed, she wiped the sleep from her eyes and tried to breathe normally. Petrified, she faced another serious challenge, for the feared outcome approached.

The thought crossed her mind to call Brock, then immediately vetoed the idea. Getting dressed hurriedly, she got into her vehicle and drove to the hospital.

April slipped into Bonnie's room and gently took her hand. Her breathing slowed. She lowered herself into the bedside chair. One second she sat holding Bonnie's hand, and the next she was once again an overwhelmed teenager who had recently found out she carried a life inside her. This woman gave her hope, vowed to help her and then made good on the commitment. Tears streamed down her cheeks. She hadn't faced this much sorrow since giving up her baby. Mourning all they shared. Bonnie insisted she didn't want anyone to grieve. Impossible. For a long time, the woman acted in more capacities than a friend. She wept at Miss Bonnie Burton's generosity and compassion.

April held her hand as Bonnie sighed and whispered one word and drew her last breath. Erin. She slapped her hand over her mouth to keep from screaming. The modest woman wouldn't want her falling apart, and she intended to abide by her wishes.

Going to the nurses' station, she quietly told them Bonnie passed.

With the hospital arrangements completed, the light in the east brightened at dawn. April returned to the house in a daze. She showered, made coffee, and summoned the strength to continue. She first called Mae, then Molly, and passed on the bad news.

"What about a funeral?" Molly asked.

"Bonnie didn't want anyone fussing and didn't want any formal services."

April realized they hadn't discussed her wishes except for what pertained to a funeral. Walking into the office, she didn't know where to look for answers. At last, in searching through the desk drawers, she found a file. It contained the name of Bonnie's lawyer, a Mr. Baxter, the executor of her last will and estate.

She dialed the number and waited for an answer. When the receptionist asked her the nature of her call, she murmured, "I believe Mr. Baxter is the person I need to tell about Bonnie Burton's death."

"Sorry. Yes, I will put you through."

"Mr. Baxter, I am April Palmer. Sir, I'm not sure how to proceed with taking care of Bonnie's wishes. Do you have her information?"

"Yes, Miss Palmer, I do. We are very sorry to hear of her passing. Her last will is here at my office. We can set up an appointment to go over everything. I will get in contact with the people who need to be here for you. My assistant will call any charity heads or benefactors to be to hear her last wishes. You will not have to worry about anything. It will take us a few days."

"Thank you, sir."

Relief washed over April. The phone call enabled her to concentrate on packing Bonnie's belongings. April called Mae about Bonnie. The woman insisted on coming to work to help pack the house and its contents. She assured Mae that they would start tomorrow. For now, she wanted to grieve and then to rest. The next few days weren't going to be easy.

Coming into the kitchen the next morning, Mae made breakfast for them before they started the painful task of removing Bonnie's possessions. She donated most of the things to shelters, making it easier to deal with. Besides a few mementos, April would cherish her memories of Bonnie in her heart. The housekeeper listened while April told her stories about meeting Bonnie. Not the circumstances, but only the good times they enjoyed getting to know each other. Both women cried for their loss. Reliving those days helped April get past her grief to a point. The ache lingered. A feeling not new to her.

She knew she needed to get in touch with Mrs. Kelley about her job. "Hi, April, how are doing? I heard about Bonnie and am very sorry."

"I'm trying to organize everything. The lawyers are handling all the legal stuff. I have a lot of packing to do here. I'm almost finished, and then I will return."

"There is no rush."

April practically laughed out loud at the speculation about her future. She knew exhaustion ruled her brain and told herself not to make any rash decisions. Finish with Bonnie's estate, then worry about the next steps.

Brock implied he wanted to be around for her. If the truth came out, the consequences would be earth-shattering. Could she survive? Probably not very well. Don't return to Broken Arrow — another option.

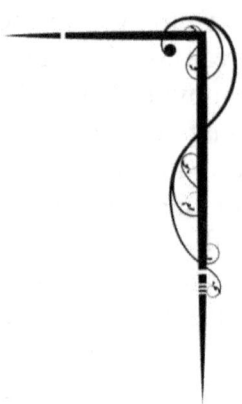

Chapter 18

Brock unsaddled Pegasus, leaving him in the corral to cool off. Earlier, he trotted across the field to inspect a new colt purchased the week before. Clay, his manager, upon his request, acquired a beautiful palomino for a fair price. He hoped someday April claimed it for herself, if everything worked out the way he wanted. While he waited for Riley to come home from school, he spent a few minutes discussing the young foal with Clay in the barn.

When the bus pulled away and left the driveway, he went towards the house, where Riley sat on the front porch, waiting for him. The look on his niece's face warned him. "What's wrong?"

"Everything!"

"Calm down and tell me what's bothering you."

"Miss Palmer hasn't come back to school, and the substitute said she will be gone for weeks. And I tried calling her again. She didn't pick up."

"I told you that Miss Burton is sick. She has her hands full, I'm sure," he reminded her.

"I know you did. There's also another problem. One of my classmates, Ada, has a blood disease and needs a bone marrow transplant. The school asked everyone to get tested for the possibility of making a donation. Will you take me to the doctor?"

"Why don't we both get tested to see if either of us is a match for Ada?" It made him proud. Riley wanted to help a friend. The lessons from Julie and April's reminders taught her the importance of caring.

"They suggested the students, not the guardians. Thank you, Uncle Brock." She hugged him.

"Why not me? I have bone marrow too."

Brock called the doctor the next day and waited for the receptionist to make the appointment. He remembered what else Riley had informed him of. April is possibly gone for weeks! He meant to give her space after they'd spent the night together. How much leeway and for how long? The last roundabout conversation with her presented him with hope. She gave the impression of wanting something more between them. The simple statement from her of 'I want' made his heart a little lighter.

Rather than wait, the doctor's office made room for them the following morning. With the blood samples drawn and his niece at school, he went on to the office. Work kept him occupied and prevented his anxiety level from rising too high over the prospect of a future with April. One night wouldn't be nearly enough for him.

Brock's latest case, crucial with water rights for their fields, hung in the balance. Therefore, he assigned Pete, his longtime private investigator, to find out any details. "Let me know when you have something about the other lawyer. His reputation isn't very reliable, and it ought to work to our advantage." He trusted the man to find what he needed to make the judge rule in their favor. It wasn't all about winning, given he sometimes lost, but this one benefited the community. No one man or ranch owned the right to withhold a vital natural resource from the area.

"I'll call you the second I know more."

"Thanks Pete. I appreciate you."

His receptionist rang through with a call right before lunch, and he hoped it was Pete with news, since this speedy result would assist in his case, wrapping up with the outcome he expected. The nurse from the doctor's office called instead. "The test results are in from this morning, and Dr. Melbourne wants you to come by to talk to him."

Maybe one of them was a match for the young classmate of Riley's. "I can come in on my lunch break at twelve thirty."

"Okay, we'll see you then."

Apprehension rushed through Brock's chest suddenly because the results came back awfully fast. He went back to scanning the papers on his desk, trying to put the upcoming meeting in the back of his mind. And then finished writing the proposal before driving to the doctor's office.

When he arrived, the nurse greeted him and ushered him into the office. The physician walked in and over to his desk, where Brock sat and waited on the other side. Confused, he asked, "Is one of us a match for Ada, since you wanted to talk to me personally? Or is something else wrong?"

Dr. Melbourne leaned back in the chair with a serious look on his face. "No, neither of you is a match, I'm afraid. There is a slight problem. Not anything serious, although I'm puzzled. Maybe you can straighten it out."

Brock breathed a sigh of relief. Their tests were okay, but the man acted strangely. Curiosity took the place of sudden worry. "How am I able to solve this mystery?"

"The day you gave me Riley's medical records, didn't you mention some of your family adopted her?"

"Yes, my sister and her husband did when she was three years old." Uncertainty once again clouded Brock's mind.

"Why do you and she have the same blood type, then? Did you father her with a surrogate and then give her to them to raise?"

"No, I did not," Brock answered sharply.

"Could it be possible you donated to a sperm bank?"

Something more than curiosity raced through his mind before he asked the next question. "What are you trying to say?"

"What I'm attempting to say is, you are Riley's biological father. After the lab tech reported an anomaly, I ran the test again myself."

Brock's mouth gaped open. "I don't understand."

"Riley is your daughter."

"How did this happen?"

Dr. Melbourne stood and patted him on the back. "I think you know how. Let me know what you find out."

Rattled, he shook his head to clear the escalating roar. He must have misheard. Riley, his flesh and blood!

The doctor took another look at him and said, "Why don't you sit here for a few moments to get your thoughts together? I don't need the room. Stop at the front desk and get a copy of the blood results before you leave."

He needed more than his bearings. The entire conversation sounded preposterous. Why would a woman he'd had sex with years ago have hidden the pregnancy from him? His mind jumped to one conclusion: Maria. Red hair, blue eyes, just like Riley! Why didn't she ask for his help? Never hiding the fact of his family being well off, he would have gladly claimed the baby or at least provided financial assistance.

Brock remained in the room for another few minutes to get a grip on the situation. The nurse handed him some papers, and he blindly accepted them before he practically stumbled out the door. Once his focus resumed, he stood in front of his office and didn't remember getting out of his truck, much less driving. Numb with anguish, he couldn't wrap his head around it. He entered his door and informed the staff not to disturb him unless the building was on fire.

Brock sat down at his desk with the papers the doctor left for him twisted in his fist. Right there in black and white. The once very adorable little girl, now the beautiful, almost grown young woman, his child. Surely Julie hadn't known. It hadn't been in her DNA to keep this kind of secret and allow them to go through life thinking Riley wasn't any blood relation.

Perhaps the answers he sought were at the ranch, with all the important papers Julie and Cash saved. Riley's birth certificate offered the fastest way to discover the truth. He told his secretary where he would be and then left town to get home before Riley got out of school. Not wanting to be disturbed, he immediately went to his office and locked the door behind him. In truth, he couldn't see her right now without possibly shattering from the too-fresh jolt.

Too many questions plagued him, and he needed answers right away. More confident in his belief that Maria proved likely Riley's mother, he needed a full investigation of her past before confronting her. Then, if it wasn't her, he needed to find out who had become pregnant with his child and why they hadn't come forward? His gut told him his first guess was the correct one.

Pete answered his call right away. "Hi boss, did you forget to tell me something else? We talked this morning."

"Yeah, I know. This is about something different. Do you remember the young girl I hired you to search for in my college years?"

"Wow, that was a long time ago. Maria, right? I couldn't find her. Why?"

"I need you to run a check on another name, April Palmer? Find out about her past. Expect to find some familiar results from the first search. Focus, especially from her age of seventeen until now. Everything — medical, place of birth and past residences — and get back to me ASAP."

"Do you mean this Maria from your past and April Palmer are the same?"

"Yes, exactly." Brock hung up the phone. Having faith in Pete's effective handling of many inquiries proved his capabilities at work.

He searched through the legal papers Julie and Cash saved about the adoption and didn't find the original birth certificate. It wasn't inside. He scanned the stack again and discovered a letter, which sealed the adoption documents notarized by the court. Miss Burton must have written it herself.

Brock called a good friend, Mitch Anders, a judge in Oklahoma City. He partially explained the dilemma to him, not going into details about the child in question. Mitch assured him he would start unsealing the records.

He didn't know how he was going to keep his sanity around Riley until he found out what he needed. The facts were undeniable, looking at her picture on his desk. He saw bits of himself in her features. This gorgeous child, from his own flesh and blood, made those signs very clear to him, and sadly bittersweet. The next several days promised to be the longest he'd ever spent. If the girl caught him staring constantly, her curiosity willed her to ask questions, but he couldn't seem to stop

To think his own sister raised his daughter. He watched her grow up at the ranch, put band-aids on her knees when she fell down and hugged her when she cried. It ripped his heart apart to think about her calling him daddy instead of uncle. This couldn't be Julie's fault. She would have changed the outcome and not wanted to deprive him of his own child. Maybe the birth certificate held the answers he sought.

He poured himself a drink and laughed at the irony before he turned the glass up and drained it. If April proved to be Riley's mother, alcohol helped with this whole mess. Well, liquor and his bruised ego.

Riley came home from school and found him still at his desk. Fortunately, he placed the papers face down before she entered the office. The blood tests were the first thing she asked about. Brock nearly choked on his own saliva before he grasped the girl meant the results for her friend. "No match, kiddo, sorry."

"Alright. We tried."

Time crawled by for him, and the anxiety pushed his patience to the limit. He couldn't say anything until he knew all the information. Everything depended on the outcome of Pete's search and the adoption papers. The position to give April more space shortened, with a different outcome on the horizon.

Later, they ate their dinner and then moved to the front porch and watched the sunset in the west on the swing. Ribbons of gold and red unfurled across the sky. His heart swelled with pride at how compassionate Riley seemed to be now. If it hadn't been April reminding her to be a kind and giving person, this wouldn't have happened. Even if the woman wasn't Riley's birth mother, he would always be grateful.

"Are you okay, Uncle? You seem sad."

To hide his true feelings, he forced a cheerfulness into his voice and said, "Yeah, I'm fine."

"We have been through a lot of changes lately. Perhaps you've grown older and forgotten your wild younger days?"

The outrageous comment from her reminded him of the young girl who often teased him in the past, and he laughed out loud. "What do you know about my wild years?"

"Mom told me you were ornery back then. For instance, you once tried to put her in the dryer just to get her clothes dried."

"Okay, maybe a little mischievous, not too reckless."

Riley snorted and patted him on the shoulder. "If you say so." Her eyes grew wide. "Wait, did you really do it to Mom?"

"Yeah, your mom 'accidentally' fell into a puddle, and I wanted to get her dry before your grandma came home and I got into trouble." Riley scoffed. "Don't worry, she rescued her before I turned the machine on." Fine, if he thought back, maybe he possessed a crazy streak. Other careless things from his youth, thankfully, hadn't lasted too long. Sadly, though, the pranks he pulled on his little sister were no more.

Because time stood still at the office and with no word from Pete or Mitch, Brock took the next two days off. He couldn't concentrate on important cases, which wasn't the best way to conduct business. People depended on his moral judgment, and right now he didn't have it. Nonetheless, being home didn't help either. A restlessness settled in his soul. He grabbed his cell phone, walked to the stables, saddled Pegasus, and rode across the field. Nature's sounds calmed him slightly, yet his many questions remained unanswered.

What if April turned out to be Riley's mother? Too many coincidences existed not to mention their past. Could the three of them become a family of some sort? Sudden excitement washed over him at the possibility of having April and Riley in his life together. Before the idea grew, another question punched him squarely in the gut. Did she know all along about Riley? To keep something this huge hidden, right in front of him, if true, unforgiveable. How did he look at her again? His jumbled thoughts flitted wildly from one outcome to another. Too many decisions hinged on the reports he waited for.

Brock began the trip back to the barn. Before he unsaddled the horse at the stables, his phone rang. He glanced at the screen and rubbed his neck with his hand to ease the sudden tension and dreading the answers. Eager to hear what Pete said, he connected the call.

"Sir. I started back further into her life. She's clean, with no record. Mother abandoned her, and she lived in foster care under the name April Palmer from the age of five until she ran away at seventeen. I couldn't find any records of a Maria Palmer anywhere, just as before. I found no accounts, medical or otherwise, of either name anywhere for a year after she ran away until she graduated from high school using GED services in Oklahoma City. Then she entered college and graduated top of her class. She taught for 10 years in Oklahoma City until she moved to Broken Arrow. No other immediate family either. That's all I found. Sorry."

"Okay, thanks for your help," Brock said and hung up. Perhaps Bonnie hid more than he knew. What was the correct explanation if no records of April or Maria having given birth existed? With pent-up frustration, he slammed the phone back into his pocket and shook his head. Nothing appeared to be giving him the responses he craved. With only one more chance, perhaps Mitch brought the solution.

While Brock brushed Pegasus and gave him a rubdown, his anxiety rose again as his cell phone rang. His secretary informed him that a pressing matter required his immediate attention, leading to settling another case. He needed to come back to town to handle the matter.

With the task completed at the office, he grabbed some lunch and headed back home. Brock heard over the car radio on the local news about Bonnie passing away. It saddened him to hear about the woman, a close friend to his parents, who introduced Riley to the family and comforted her when Julie and Cash died and, of course, April's 'mom'. She played a huge part in his past. News reports revealed how far her community influence reached. Homeless shelters and clinics for the needy. The woman wielded a lot of authority in the city and in the state. This power, he acknowledged, probably affected his life more than he could've imagined before.

Now he waited on the front porch for Riley to get off the bus and dreaded telling her. "Miss Palmer may not be back. Miss Burton passed away. They announced it on my way home from work. A lot of things will have to be settled on her estate."

"Yes, I understand," the girl said. "I remember how Miss Burton comforted me when Mom and Dad died. I am sorry for her loss. This doesn't mean my teacher won't be back. I'm positive she'll return to town."

"I know the two of you became good friends. She will have a lot of responsibilities to take care of in the city. Don't get your hopes up too high, is all I'm saying." He admired Riley's faith in April. Could he find the same belief? Well, maybe...

A few days later, the judge's office in Oklahoma City called Brock, informing him the adoption papers were unsealed, but they couldn't give him the results over the phone, forcing him to take a trip to the city. With everything squared away at the office, Brock arranged for Mrs. Shefield to stay overnight with Riley.

"Uncle, I don't need a babysitter. I am sixteen now."

"Oh, I'm aware of how old you are. However, I'd feel better if you weren't alone. Humor me, please?" He hugged her. "Behave while I'm gone."

She laughed. "Goodbye, and you be good too."

Brock's trip to the city passed without incident. He parked alongside the downtown courthouse, and Mitch met him at the front desk. "I suppose you heard about Bonnie Burton passing?"

"Yeah, I heard. I'm not sure whether you examined the findings I asked for. She is the main reason I am here."

"I didn't read them. But if she did something, it must have been for a just cause."

"My parents' trust in her stayed until their deaths. I haven't objected to her until now," Brock shared with a heavy tone edged in his voice.

"Good luck, Brock. If you need anything else, let me know and I'll try to help you."

The judge's clerk ushered him into an outer office to review the papers in private. He entered, paused, and pondered the document's potential revelations. Answers to the questions agitated his mind and his heart. *Only one way to resolve the mystery. Open the paperwork.*

Riley Hope. He kept reading. Mother's name, Maria Palmer. Father, unknown. He read the word again. Unknown. It stung to see the empty word.

Brock gripped the paper and stared at the words, which provided clues about Riley's birth mother, Maria Palmer. It did not identify him as the birth father. For some reason, the shrewd lawyer sealed the records of Riley's birth. *Why would the counselor have gone to the trouble of concealing April's baby's father's identity? A girl she knew nothing about.*

A sudden recollection shot through him. Seeing Miss Burton in the college dorm's lobby on the night, April helped him back to his room. Of course, she had known him. His parents and the woman were business partners and remained close friends. Hell, the woman babysat him and Julie. She acknowledged him and probably recalled April being with him. Bonnie must have intervened to rescue the teen from street life. The name signed on all the legal documents, plus the note about the twenty dollars, Maria.

The next question weighing heavily on his mind resulted in more pain. Could his whole family have known all along that Riley was his daughter? Maybe that was the reason behind the secrecy. To prevent his finding out the truth. He couldn't believe April spiteful enough to withhold Riley's parentage from him. His gut told him she didn't know the whole truth any more than he did.

Before Brock left the judge's office, his phone rang. Mr. Baxter, the executor of Miss Burton's estate, said they needed him to be present for the reading of Bonnie's will. He made a call to Mrs. Shefield and told her he needed to stay in the city for another day. Knowing April grieved, he couldn't bring himself to add to her worries right now. It killed him to wait for answers, but he would.

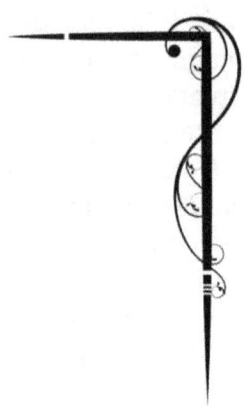

Chapter 19

Helping Bonnie's staff at the college pack her belongings kept April busy. Only a few more days encompassed getting accustomed to her drastically changed life. Once again, she'd be by herself. The law firm that handled the estate scheduled the will reading for the first thing next week.

Lack of quality sleep at the house pushed April's nerves to their limit and left her exhausted. City lights shone brighter than the small streetlights in Broken Arrow. She quickly recalled the high noise levels in town. Much louder than back home. When this meeting concluded, she would be glad to get back to her job and her own bed, provided she kept either by then. She knew that the confessions facing her needed to be made and couldn't avoid them any longer. Their prospective relationship, along with her future teaching career, depended on Brock's reaction.

The rest of the week sped by. She, with the help of Mae, boxed everything at the house and arranged for delivery to the shelter. They always welcomed donations.

With a heavy heart, April drove to the lawyer's office. Mr. Baxter said there shouldn't be any conflicts to resolve. Attending this meeting made everything final. Reading Bonnie's wishes closed a big chapter of her life. Her memory of the kind woman stayed with her. To put it simply, she was sad.

Brock entered the room, and April tentatively smiled. He did not. She assumed his profession had brought him here. He sat down at the opposite end of the table and glanced at her. Coldness was clear in his facial expression. The hostile encounters between them in the past hadn't been pleasant. He pressed the issue, and she held her own. Now, a chilling air, like an iceberg's icy breath, seemed to separate them. Why the cold shoulder? With Bonnie's death, between packing up the house and the college office, there hadn't been an opportunity to call him. Besides, it wasn't like her passing wasn't on the news.

Mr. Baxter shook her hand in greeting and handed her a copy of the will. He explained the process to her since she was not a lawyer. "Everyone is here, allowing us to begin." His assistant nodded and passed a paper around. For him to continue, he needed it signed, which documented their presence.

The will stunned, then humbled April. Bonnie named her the primary benefactor of her estate. She inherited the main house, along with a few rentals in the area. The shelter and clinics received large amounts of donations to keep them up and running for years with the help of Mr. Baxter's firm and April's recommendations. The lawyer then listed the additional charities to benefit from Bonnie's generous donations

As the executor finished, the attorneys, along with the trustees, filed out of the room. Meanwhile, Brock also rose to leave but quizzed Mr. Baxter. "Did you make some kind of mistake? I don't know why I am here."

The attorney shook his head and replied, "No, I didn't overlook you. If you wait, I'll explain the reason to you."

He shrugged his shoulders and sat down again. "Fine, as you wish."

April got up to leave, but Mr. Baxter stopped her. "Miss Palmer, will you remain in the room too?"

"Aren't we finished?" April looked at Brock for guidance. His cold eyes met hers with a blank expression. Therefore, she sat back down.

The older man closed the door behind them and spoke. "Now, Mr. Ruggle, thank you and Miss Palmer for remaining in the room. This way we can finish. There is one more matter to be handled, which involves you both."

April's breath caught, absolutely terrified. She glanced at Brock. His eyes widened, and he looked confused, then irritated. Whatever the lawyer was going to reveal, he didn't have a clue any more than she did. A disastrous notion abruptly arose and paralyzed her. What if Bonnie revealed her secret? Vivid scenes played out in her imagination of the man lashing out at her and then telling her to leave town. She almost screamed to halt the next words from the lawyer. Instead, she bit her bottom lip to keep quiet.

"I'm still not sure why I need to be here?" Brock asked Mr. Baxter again.

"If you will remain in your seats. I'll be right back with the paperwork, and it will explain the reason for your presence."

The attorney returned, and he handed them each a letter. "These are for the two of you. They are identical, and I hope they will clear up some confusion and give you both peace of mind." He then left the room.

April stared at Brock again. Neither one said a word to each other before they both opened the sealed letters. With shaking hands, she took her letter out and unfolded it with fear pitted in her stomach.

"Dear Brock and April, please keep an open mind while you read this letter. A child needs love growing up. You, Brock, were much loved by your parents, as I witnessed, but April was not. That is why she did what she did, and I did what I did."

"Brock, I owed your parents so much. I let my heart rule in this decision to give them the opportunity to love their grandchild. Trust me, they never knew the truth. April knew neither, so please don't blame her. She came to the clinic pregnant. I recognized her from the night you were at the college dorm, and that inspired me to care for her and the baby. She decided on her own to put the infant up for adoption, aware of her own circumstances. She concluded she could never be a good parent and provide care for the child. Therefore, I prearranged to have the baby cared for. I kept Riley safe and out of foster care for either you or Julie to raise her. When Julie got married, I gave the sweet little girl to your sister."

"Once again, I have meddled in your lives with my heart. I know April will now become a wonderful mother. Brock, I have put her back in your life and also in Riley's. Hopefully, the two of you will forgive an old woman's interference and love your child together. Finish raising her to become the very loving young woman I know she will be."

Bonnie Burton

April's tears, streaming unheeded down her face, blurred the words of the letter in her hands. Not sure if what she read was correct, she perused it again, then dared to look over at Brock. Water ran down his face too. "I didn't know she did any of this. Did you Brock? And Riley is the baby I carried all those years ago." A whisper, barely audible, escaped April's tear-choked throat. "Our baby!"

Somehow, he found his voice. "I found out last week."

"Only last week? Are you sure?"

"Yes, I'm sure."

"Bonnie said in the letter she knew your parents and was thankful to them. What did they do, Brock, to make her grateful enough to help keep a grandchild in their lives, telling no one about her?"

"I don't know of any motive. Bonnie visited my parents at the house often after they became partners in the law firm until something happened in her life. She sold the firm to them and disappeared for months. Then, one day, she began operating the shelter, where my mom volunteered."

"Wait, was your mom's name Kayla?" April blinked her eyes, trying to make sense of things.

"Yes, why?"

April's breath caught. "Bonnie told me she had adopted a baby with Kayla's encouragement and was grateful to the woman. The red-haired baby died of SIDS and would have been about my age. Your mom must have been with her through the grief, and this must have been why she helped me and kept Riley in your family." April's heart went out once again for the pain Bonnie endured from losing Erin.

"Yesterday, until I unsealed her birth certificate, I wasn't sure. You signed her birth certificate, Maria."

"Why did you decide to unseal her birth records?"

Brock explained to her about the blood tests. "I needed to know for sure. Bonnie locked the birth certificate. A friend who is a judge opened it. What about the note you signed? Why April? Why the confusion?" He pleaded. "I need answers only you can provide."

"As I told you months ago, April is my first name and Maria is my middle name. Everyone on the streets knew me as April. Street people didn't trust strangers, as I found to be true." She apologized. "I'm sorry!" Realizing how sharp the words escaped, before she carried on with the conversation. "Giving you my middle name seemed right and safe. When I delivered the baby, Bonnie suggested I sign the birth certificate Maria. Maybe because she planned this all along, she believed it somehow hid my identity from you or Julie. I don't think she knew I used my middle name the first time we met. From the start, I believed she knew you fathered my child. To come right out and ask, she never pried."

April now knew why Bonnie had pushed for her to live, and teach, in Broken Arrow. To get her closer to her daughter and maybe closer to Brock. The woman followed her baby's life and looked out for her. She sat astonished, with her head down and her hands clasped together until her knuckles turned white. "Please, you can't say anything to Riley yet. I need to process this," she pled.

"I won't for now, but we can't keep this from her."

From the tone of his voice, she knew he wouldn't give her much leeway. Her eyes darted around the room in panic. Finally, putting her hand over her chest, she took a deep breath and willed her pulse rate to slow.

Brock moved over to a chair closer to her. He placed one of his hands on top of hers and the other under her chin and raised her head. Then he looked into her eyes and promised, "We'll tell her together. Don't worry."

"Don't worry!" April exclaimed and jerked her hand from under his. "I just found out she is my daughter. The baby I gave up sixteen years ago, whom I have always loved. Now I have known her for almost a year. What if she doesn't believe it or, worse, what if she doesn't want me in her life?" Her voice cracked with sudden terror at the thought.

Brock said in a gentle voice, "Riley is a very reasonable young woman who already cares for you. I know you care for her. She will understand and accept both of us, since we just found out."

"I hope you are right," she whispered. Before they left, she turned to him once more. "Please, Brock, I'm begging you, permit me to adjust to the fact of her being my daughter."

They both walked out of the lawyer's office together. April tried to make sense of what took place. Her mind refused, and she stared into space and blindly strode to the parking lot beside Brock. He offered to escort her home. "No, I have to be by myself to make sense of this."

April went back to Bonnie's home in a daze. She walked into the near-barren house and went to the office, where she sat at the desk in the dark. Quiet remained except for memories. She shed many tears over her life choices again, and they came flooding back. Right here in this empty room she used for studying, where she tried to mend her broken heart and put her life back together. Instantly, her heart broke again.

Her mind became filled with a million and one thoughts, leaving her in a state of bewilderment. Brock hinted before he wanted her in his life. What about now, though? Did he still want her? What if Riley hated her? What if he took their daughter away? How did she live without her now? Fight him or surrender and slink away with a crushing remorse much more severe than the guilt sixteen years ago?

The answers became scarier than the questions. Riley might not want her. Brock might object to her being in his daughter's life, since he remained her legal guardian. For a brief second, an idea crossed her mind. Leave? No, unless Riley wanted her to go. The idea became more painful than giving away the baby at birth. He said they would tell her together if he didn't change his mind.

April attempted to suppress her memories of the infant she'd briefly held. To avoid pain, she tried not to imagine what her grown daughter looked like. It turned out to be impossible. Would she be a kind and generous person? The wondering, a thing of the past.

Riley, her and Brock's daughter. She should have known, *shouldn't she*? The red hair and those bright blue eyes. Then the dimples, his definitely. She knew a lot of her personality traits came from him from being around him more often.

Then another thought went through her tortured mind. Did they all know who Riley belonged to before allowing Julie and Cash to raise her and leaving Brock free of his responsibilities? How did she find out the answer? What if the confession regarding her baby's birth discovery proved truthful, or a fabrication to mask the reality? If a coverup, the thought outraged her. Surely, he couldn't have been so emotionless.

Anger at all the distinct possibilities spurred April to rise from the desk and take control of a situation she possessed the power to complete. Extensive work to complete all preparations and list the house and other properties for sale faced her. She got in touch with Mr. Baxter again and hired the lawyer to file the proper paperwork, which allowed her to put most of the proceeds in a trust for Riley, even if the girl wanted nothing to do with her birth mother.

The big dilemma facing her was how she handled being near her daughter. Until they told her the truth, she required all of her willpower to remain silent. The words Bonnie said on her deathbed gave her courage. 'You are a strong woman.'

Rather than put off the decision to return any longer, the distraction of her job should help her heal from the loss of Bonnie. She picked up the phone and called her employer. "Mrs. Kelley, I wanted to let you know I will be back at work next week to finish the school year."

"April, we were very sorry to hear about Miss Burton."

"Yes, we already miss her. At least she is at peace and not in pain."

"Do you know whether you will continue teaching here next year?"

"I can't make those kinds of decisions right now. The only thing I'm positive about is that I'll finish out this year. I will see you Monday morning."

"April, we look forward to seeing you."

She left the city on Friday afternoon, needing the weekend to settle and to prepare for the rest of the school year. Panic hit her the closer she came to Broken Arrow. She hadn't informed Brock of her return. The nerves ate at her stomach, not knowing how much more space he gave her.

By being absent for a month, with nothing fresh in the refrigerator, her stopping at the grocery store on her way in became a necessity. April stored the food and then opened the windows to rid the house of stale air. As she carried the boxes of mementos of Bonnie's into the house, desolation filled her. Instead of reliving the past, she went to the familiar porch swing to seek comfort.

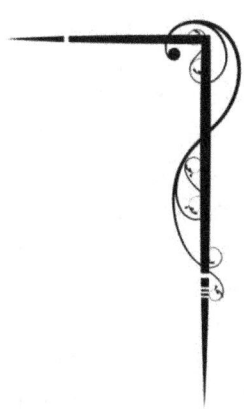

Chapter 20

Brock had assured April everything would work out and left her sitting in her car. She hadn't rejected him, just a ride home. It was apparent the situation blindsided her more than him. And honestly, he needed to process all of it himself. The first wave of anger subsided before he came to Oklahoma City. His job demanded incredible patience, especially in dealing with uncontrollable situations; but if things became personal, they were much harder. He reflected on the discoveries from the day before and then focused on the present circumstances. Clearly, solving this together, an option.

The devastation on April's face proved her reaction authentic. The look of anguish the moment she comprehended Bonnie's deed was like witnessing her soul being carved into pieces by a knife. Initially, the deception infuriated him, and he felt betrayed. He knew he needed to forgive the older woman and then reassure April he didn't blame her for anything.

The elaborate plan Bonnie instigated weighed heavily on him. The events, which floated around like pieces of a jigsaw puzzle, all fell into place. First, she called him about a rental house after convincing April to move here. Second, it wouldn't surprise him if the woman communicated with Mrs. Target and insisted she put Riley in April's class or at least got the two of them in contact with each other. Had the woman been clever or just hoped things worked out best for them all?

Waves crashed none too gently into his chest with a need to look at pictures before Riley came home from school and asked questions. Why had he been late coming back from the city, and why did he have her baby pictures out?

Brock didn't hear any noise upon entering the house. Mrs. Shefield must have left for the day, which left him alone to look at the books with no interruptions. From the living room bookcase, he retrieved the family photo albums. The ones he brought home from Julie's. With them in his lap on the couch, he inhaled deeply before slowly opening the first one. Riley's photos, from the adoption day to a year ago, stared back at him. Blissful family memories of happy times.

He studied the pictures closely of Riley, now being roughly the same age as April when they met. Touching the precious photos eased his pain to a point. Her red hair and blue eyes had haunted him immediately. The dimples were identical to his, and then the fact of how her personality matched his. Incredible to think of just how Bonnie's confessing to his parents might have changed everything. Speculation would have arisen from his doubt about the child's mother's identity. Then again, perhaps not. They all knew his previous lifestyle.

While Brock wiped the moisture from his face, he temporarily closed the image of love, and put the albums away before Riley came home. He knew to clamp down on his emotions, because telling Riley too soon might scar her emotionally and ruin his relationship with her. The past stared at him in the pictures, and the future held the unknown. Maybe one day they'll add new family snapshots. Besides, he promised April.

If he jumped the gun by saying something too fast, he risked losing any chance of the family he sought. He hoped she reached out to him soon to go to their daughter together. *Their daughter.* Wow, those words sounded strange in his mind, though not in his heart. So, he would wait!

With April, he felt utterly powerless, and an intense hunger for her totally overwhelmed him. Every minute of the day, he thought of her. Of how he wanted to hold her in his arms and protect her. He knew she wouldn't have been receptive to him because of the shock, though he nearly confessed to her in the law office.

Brock took the birth certificate and letter from Miss Burton, along with the other papers, to his office and placed them on his desk. They were secure there and gave April the period she requested.

Riley arrived home, all smiles. He hesitated on the porch and questioned his sanity as she ran to him. "Uncle, I have missed you."

"I have missed you too, my sweet girl," he said and hugged her a little tighter than usual. Tears threatened to overcome him as he observed Riley in a new light. Hiding the emotions was hard, because he needed to hold on to the secret. He blinked the moistness in his eyes away. "Have you kept up with your studies? I hope you haven't given Mrs. Shefield any trouble?"

"I was the perfect angel. Did they have a funeral for Miss Burton in the city, and did you see Miss Palmer anywhere?"

"No, Miss Burton didn't want any funeral services. The college honored her with an assembly and a prayer. I saw Miss Palmer. She will be okay and return to work soon."

He spoke presumptuously, hoping his assumption that the teacher would return to school soon was right. He hugged her once more and told her, "I love you. Never forget."

They went into the house, where supper waited in the kitchen. The smell of Mrs. Shefield's meatloaf, one of his favorites warming in the oven, didn't entice him. Stress understandably caused his loss of appetite. He picked at it to act normally.

On account of April's request, Brock's life at the ranch became tormented. The week following the bombshell passed slowly. Riley's eagerness for her tutor to come back to school became a constant reminder of the events in Oklahoma City. Both past and present.

With his anger long gone, all he wanted to know was why April hadn't told him about the pregnancy. She bonded with Riley and the ranch as though she belonged. She wasn't afraid of him and proved it by not backing down in arguments. Brock, not being able to get April out of his mind, kept replaying how she felt in his arms and how right he felt holding her again. Sure, the first time pure physical attraction ruled, but the next... way more than lust. He missed everything about her. Her smell, her look, the way she smiled at him. No other conclusion. He was in love with April Maria Palmer.

They needed to talk about their daughter. Both of them needed to be present to tell her the truth. Then, with those confessions settled, he wanted to talk to April about their future.

Patience, Brock discovered, wasn't a virtue for him. Waiting for news from April kept him on edge, and the mere mention of her name caused a ripple effect of tightness in his chest and in his jeans.

He couldn't find any peace, and Riley constantly brought the conversation around to her teacher. After the last round of questions, he tried to escape to the barn for a horseback ride; however, his niece followed him. "Are you okay, Uncle?"

"Of course, I'm fine. Why wouldn't I be?"

"If I mention Miss Palmer, you shut down. And the next thing I see is you walking away, like you are doing now. Did she do something?"

Squaring his shoulders, he remarked. "No. I'm the one with difficulties."

The half-truth placated her. "Alright, I'm going to go back to the house and study some more. Have a pleasant ride."

He mounted Pegasus and rode across the pastures, attempting to relieve his frustrations before returning well after dark. His neck ached from the tension the ride hadn't eased. Instead of going into the house, he sat on the front porch with April still on his mind.

Riley came outside and sat down beside him on the steps. "Are you coming in tonight, Uncle, or are you still angry at Miss Palmer?"

"I told you I wasn't mad."

"Yeah, if you say so," Riley commented.

A diversion seemed in order along with the denial. "I said I wasn't upset. Isn't it past your bedtime? You know school is in session tomorrow."

"Yeah, yeah, I'm going. I love you, Uncle."

"Sweetheart, I love you too. Good night." Even if Riley didn't understand the reason for his irritation, it remained his responsibility to safeguard her future now more than ever. Brock let out a deep breath and followed her into the house. The girl wasn't blind, and if he didn't put his fears of the future aside, she'd become suspicious about his odd behavior. Although with each passing day, he became more uneasy about April's call.

To him, Riley seemed to grow more distant towards him after questioning him about being upset with April. Rather than having her on guard about his reactions, maybe a distraction with an invitation for Kadina to spend the weekend with them at the lake was the answer to taking the pressure off him. He sighed with relief as Riley accepted the impromptu invitation for her best friend with a cheerful face. Kadina's dad dropped her at the ranch on Friday afternoon, and the two girls ran to the barn to their horses, saddled them, and took off across the pasture, huddled together in conversation. His scheme appeared to have worked.

Brock proposed a camping trip, thinking it'd be less effort than entertaining at home. Saturday morning, they met at the barn, where three saddled horses waited. They left, heading toward the lake by way of the old trail. With all the recent rain from the spring rains, the land came to life with a patch of wildflowers blooming, making a colorful carpet of color across the pasture.

As the horses walked, wind-blown grass brushed their legs. The familiar path welcomed them back with the hints of more summer days to be enjoyed on the ranch again. Brock didn't pay attention to the beauty with too much on his mind while he searched for answers to give him peace of mind. An impossible task.

The girls rode ahead of him. When they took a break, the two walked off together, whispering. Both seemed upset to Brock. Hey, they were teenagers, and he became used to the teen's mood swings. Rather than confront her attitude, he ignored it.

They arrived at the lake, and all the memories of being at the lake with April flooded back. How her face glowed in the sunshine, the way she opened up to him, and then the reverence she displayed at a simple sight of Mother Nature's wonder. Her spirit was everywhere.

As before, Brock prepared their evening meal, and later they roasted marshmallows over the campfire. Though both girls helped with supper, they had little to say to him. To break the silence around the camp; he attempted to make conversation. "Hey, do you girls recall first coming to the lake? We explored the boundaries and pretended the Indians might find us."

Riley grunted, "Yeah, we remember, Uncle. "

Brock raised his eyebrows at the way she said his name. Almost like an accusation. They showed no interest in reminiscing. He stayed quiet, watching the sunset in the sky and leaving a golden cast on the horizon. While the air cooled for the evening, he lingered by the bonfire, staring into the flames in his private world.

Riley stood and spoke. "I have a headache. If you don't mind, we're going to bed early. Good night, Uncle. I'll see you in the morning."

"Alright girls, sleep well, and Riley, I hope you feel better soon."

Both girls crawled into their tent and zipped the door tight. Overhead, the stars glowed in the dark night sky. Clouds hid the moonlight. The sound of the distant creek bubbling into the lake always gave him the peace to relax. Brock unrolled his sleeping bag and lay with his hands behind his head and stared up at the twinkling fairy lights in the sky.

Instead of falling asleep right away, old memories invaded his peace of mind. Weekends spent here with April and many others, like tonight, with his daughter. The girl's lantern burned into the night, and he heard crying. He kept quiet and decided that if something important arose, then he'd hear about it, eventually.

He finally drifted asleep only to dream of making love to a teenage April and then a mature woman. His body recalled being excited and aroused more than with any other woman in his life. Tiny details of the vision gnawed at his insides and left an enormous appetite.

The darkness lightened with streaks of clouds behind his eyelids, giving the sky a soft rainbow of pastel colors. He stretched, opened his eyes and groaned, being more tired this morning than the night before. Okay, maybe the trip hadn't been such a good idea. Determined to get through, he swallowed the ache, arose and built a fire. While he drank a cup of coffee and viewed the sun rise higher in the sky, the sight hinted that a beautiful day lay ahead of him.

When the girls climbed out of their tent, rubbing the sleep from their eyes, he couldn't help himself and grinned at them. Kadina smiled back at him. Riley looked worried, stood and stared at the calm waters of the lake for a few minutes. Brock glanced from one girl to the other, waiting to hear an explanation of the tension in the air. Something upset her, he knew for sure. Whatever had reared its head the night before passed, and suddenly Riley was in a better mood. They ate a couple of granola bars and finished the coffee. Then he put out the campfire.

Being more optimistic, Brock went out on a limb and asked, "What do you girls want to do today?"

Riley's face lit up with excitement. "Maybe go for a hike up to the outcrops?"

"Are you certain? It'll be very warm today, and the rocks are quite distant."

"We are up for it if you are, old man?" She teased.

He pretended to be offended, then grabbed his backpack, filled it with a couple of bottles of water, and challenged, "Let's see if you can keep up with me."

Both teenagers laughed, then grabbed their own packs and followed him down the well-worn trail, which led to the small mountains. He watched his daughter play in typical teen behavior with Kadina. Then they chuckled over a baby deer who hurried along and tried to keep up with its mama.

It struck him hard exactly how much he had missed out on in her life, and he became angry once more. He should, no, he needed to put it in the past and enjoy the future. Life slipped away too fast, and it wouldn't be long before she left for college.

The sun warmed the air fast, just as predicted. They hiked for an hour amidst the red rocks without incident until Riley started whining. "I'm hot. Can't we turn around? We have come far enough."

"No, this was your idea," he pointed out. "Listen up. Here is a lesson for the two of you. You must finish the journey to maintain your self-worth. That's life."

"You're mean." Riley replied.

"I know, but you love me anyhow." Brock laughed.

The rest of the hike passed with little backtalk from the girls. All three of them sweltered in the heat before they got back to the lake and campsite. Riley and Kadina took off their shoes and waded into the shallow, cool water. Brock sat down on the log and pulled his own boots and socks off, letting his toes dangle in the water. Riley splashed him with water, then ran away laughing. The water hit his chest and ran down, leaving a wet streak on his shirt. Despite the warmth of his body, the water felt icy and made him gasp. He glared at her teasingly. "You will pay for this. It is a promise."

"Uncle, I tried to cool you off faster. Nothing else, I swear. Did it help?"

"Oh, yeah, I feel energized again enough to walk back to the ranch instead of riding."

Both girls yelled, "No!"

Despite his threat of making them leave on foot, they rode back to the ranch after breaking camp. Brock washed the dust and dried sweat from his body. His mind automatically fantasized. *What if April joined him in the shower?* His stomach muscles tightened at the thought. Sighing with frustration, he dressed and left his bedroom.

Brock entered his office before he checked on the girls' plans for the rest of the weekend. A fresh case awaited him on Monday, and he wanted to go over the details. Scanning his desk, he noticed the paperwork scattered around. All the records about Riley and even the letter from Bonnie lay on top of the pile. Well, with his melancholy mood and the pending camping trip, perhaps he forgot to put them up. He corrected the mistake and locked his desk drawer. It wasn't wise for anyone to see them.

Mrs. Shefield cooked dinner for them, and it awaited on the stovetop. The girls helped Brock warm up the casserole and fixed a salad. Despite a few too-close memories, like the pure joy on April's face, tasting the roasted hot dogs, or the proud look when she mastered riding, the rest of the weekend passed uneventfully. He enjoyed spending time with his daughter. Thankfully, no one mentioned April during the weekend. The fact now struck him as strange. If only the girl's mother called, his future could potentially look brighter.

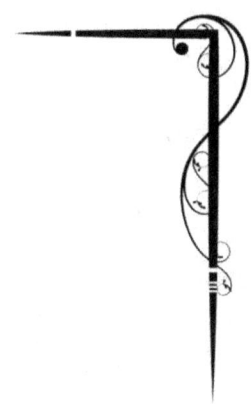

Chapter 21

April returned to work on Monday. Most of her students and co-workers expressed their sympathy. Right now, she needed to focus on her pupils, not reminders. The last class loomed, and she watched the clock with trepidation. If she burst into sudden tears the minute she saw her daughter, it wouldn't be easy to explain.

Of course, the girl walked into the classroom, ran straight to her, and hugged her before April pulled back. "Welcome back. I missed you."

At first, she hesitated and then, taking a deep breath, she returned the gesture and said, "I missed you too." Tears stung her eyes, then she blinked them away.

Riley waited at her desk when class finished. "How are you? Uncle told me about Miss Burton, and I am sorry."

"I appreciate it, and I'll be okay."

"I understand you just returned, but will you resume tutoring me in the future?" The girl asked with puppy-dog eyes, much like Brock's.

Throughout class, she tried her best to refrain from constantly gazing at Riley, but here, facing her alone, it proved impossible. She at last pried her eyes away and broke the captivating spell of simply looking at her beautiful daughter. How did she actually carry on normally with turmoil running through her body? "Will you give me a week to get settled in?" She used paperwork as an excuse to sort out her feelings.

Riley replied, "Yes, I can wait. Knowing you are home is enough for now."

"Thank you." April gulped and wondered about the strange comment. Enough for now. What did the girl mean?

Uncertainty about Brock's presence admittedly plagued April the first afternoon back at the ranch, and she felt tempted to cancel as her nerves threatened to overcome her. However, it might set a precedent for him to keep her away when the truth came out. She kept a close eye on his whereabouts, but he only watched from afar.

Eventually, he started strolling into the room and stood by the table where she and Riley studied. He didn't argue with her anymore. On rare occasions he spoke; their sedate discussions of the pre-college courses disappointed her. Disagreements between them became commonplace ever since she moved to Broken Arrow, not this passive reaction. Ultimately, this behavior stumped her. Was it to lessen the pressure on her, or did a different motive entice him?

She sensed a basic anger in him. One he seemed to hold in check. They didn't discuss details in the lawyer's office, though he told her he wanted an explanation of everything

He remained on her mind constantly, more than ever. Whether by reliving the past or replaying their recent dates.

Movies, dinners or a simple walk in the park were part of her attraction for him. He also showed her respect and a willingness to make her happy, even before they knew about their child. Did she trust his previous statements of his wanting to reconcile or clean the slate?

Mother instinct kicked in when she thought about Riley. Loving her daughter, a smart, loving, and gorgeous young woman, became easy, and the laughter between her and Riley became comfortable. She caught herself staring endlessly in the classroom or at the ranch and hoped Riley didn't notice. She reminded herself not to be biased while grading a school assignment, since the girl should learn some things for herself if she wanted to succeed in law school.

Now she understood how Brock must have felt when crashing into her classroom about her teaching methods. He wanted to protect his charge. She understood the new feeling. Riley came first. Brock would always be there for his daughter. Whether she would be, she didn't know.

The beautiful girl was simple to love. Unlike her father. *Wait, what had she just said?*

———————————

Before April left to take care of Bonnie, she formed a friendship with Chloe. With her return, the two co-workers walked into the teacher's lounge for their lunch break together, chatting about lessons for their students. Sitting down with a sigh, April stretched her arms over her head. Chloe watched her for a minute. "Are you okay?"

"I think it is probably strain and delayed reactions to the past few weeks. I haven't slept very well, and it is getting to me."

"Perhaps go to the doctor and get checked out. Stress can wreck your body if you don't take care of it."

"Oh, I know. A few years ago, I almost quit school until Bonnie…" Tears threatened to spill before she blinked them back and took a cleansing breath. "Anyhow, anxiety compromised my courses until she talked me down off the ledge. Now with her gone, I sometimes get overwhelmed."

"Hey, you are not alone. I have told you before, if you need to talk, I'm here."

Acting on impulse, April reached over and squeezed Chloe's hand and said, "Thank you. Do you want to have dinner with me one night?"

"How about tonight? I'm free and hungry."

"Alright, me too. Meet you at the diner at six."

Being optimistic about actually having a reliable friend, April rushed home from school, quickly graded her papers and set the lesson for the next day. While she was changing clothes, her phone rang. Without glancing at the screen, she said, "Hello."

"Hello, yourself. How are you?"

Her heart skipped a beat. "Hi, Brock. I'm fine. What about you?"

"If you are fine, how about us meeting to talk?"

"I promise we will soon. Besides, I have already made plans tonight." She heard him take a deep breath. The sound told her he was becoming impatient with her. "I swear, Brock, it won't be long."

After another deep sigh, "Exactly what are your plans?"

By the tone of his question, she wondered, could he be jealous? "If you must know, I'm having dinner with my friend Chloe from school," she explained, with a prick of annoyance. He hung up. She stood perplexed, staring at the silent phone in her hand.

The question of when, not if, he confronted her before she properly formed the words to express herself, slowly expired. To ease the sudden tension, she rubbed her neck, then finished dressing and quickly left.

The diner the two teachers agreed to meet at looked similar to a throwback to the old-fashioned cafes. Red-checkered curtains and tablecloths adorned the room close to Route sixty-six. April parked, got out of her vehicle, and walked towards the door, where Chloe joined her. The other woman said. "The same idea crossed your mind. Get here early."

"Yeah, I told you I was hungry." In truth, she wanted to be gone in case Brock showed up anyhow. They settled into the booth and ordered club sandwiches and iced tea from the server. April remarked after they got their drinks, "Except for the brief encounter at the park months ago and then coffee, we haven't had a chance for the two of us to really talk in a while." Their previous conversations in the cafeteria or hallways were always brief.

"True. Why don't you tell me a little about your past? Where did you teach before?"

"I'm from Oklahoma City and went to school at the university in the city. Got my first job there. What about you?"

"I have spent my entire career living and teaching in this town."

Impressed, April replied, "Wow, how admirable."

Chloe revealed, "I didn't want to go anywhere else. Broken Arrow is perfect. Not too big and not too small."

"Perfect." April repeated the word and weighed the other woman's comment. "Yes, you're right. The area has grown on me. I hope I can stay."

"Why do you have to leave?"

The server brought their dinners to them, permitting April to determine how much to explain. "You remember I told you about seeing someone?"

"Yes, you hinted, not being certain of the relationship, if I recall."

"There are some issues in my personal life I need resolved before I decide about staying."

"I take it this guy is the issue. Is he giving you trouble? I'll take care of him for you," Chloe offered. Both women burst out laughing.

Being with a person who wanted friendship felt great. The idea of a simple bond between two colleagues appealed to her. April didn't feel comfortable enough to trust Chloe with all the details. Her concerns pressed the clamp down tighter on her chest and kept her mouth closed. She simply winced in silence, not wanting to betray Riley and Brock

Before she took the first bite of her meal, a wave of nausea rose into her throat. Putting the pre-cut section of sandwich back down, she grabbed her glass of tea and took a small sip. Surely, thinking about Brock didn't make her sick to her stomach. "I must have picked up a bug going around at school." The nausea subsided, and April took another sip of her drink. The tea settled her stomach, which enabled her to eat a small portion of her dinner.

Chloe looked at her with eagle eyes and asked, "Did you make an appointment with a doctor?"

"No, I didn't get a chance this afternoon. Before I left the house — well, he called, and I wanted to get away on the chance he showed up."

"Are you afraid of him? Or are you afraid of what he has to say?"

"No, I'm not afraid of him."

"I see you didn't address the second part of my question."

April grimaced. "I'm uncertain of what I want to say to him, if this makes any sense."

"Okay, I understand. Take my advice though and call the doctor, please."

"I promise." Although April's queasy stomach didn't completely pass, she managed to eat enough to keep Chloe from saying more about her lack of appetite. "Thank you for listening." The server placed the rest of her dinner in a doggy bag. Her stomach completely settled once she left the diner. To her relief, she enjoyed the rest of the evening without phone calls or visitors before bed.

Later though, she awoke in bed drenched in perspiration and panting. It seemed to be when she thought of Brock and or Riley that her sleep became interrupted. The chat with Chloe tonight skirted around them. In her nightmare, Brock and Riley stood over and laughed at her. They said they'd never forgive her and wanted her to disappear. She trembled and sobbed violently. Why did her life have to be complicated?

April got out of bed and went to the bathroom, where she wiped her face with a cold washcloth. Two more days of school this week. She groaned. Never in her entire career, no matter the problem, had she ever dreaded a day's class.

Taking the advice given freely out of concern from Chloe, she scheduled an appointment for the next day with a primary physician at the local facility. She reckoned all the stress of Bonnie's death and finding out about Riley being the root of her problems. Better check anyhow.

Everyone at the clinic seemed to be nice and concerned about her symptoms. The doctor gave her a thorough exam and told her to go to his office to meet with him. Despite likely wasting his expertise, she sat on the other side of his desk on the edge of her chair and tensely waited for an explanation.

The doctor entered, sat down behind his desk and asked her, "Miss Palmer, did you have any problems with your first pregnancy?"

She automatically said, "No."

"Good, then you shouldn't have any problems with this one," the doctor said.

April's face paled to the color of a white bedsheet. She gripped the arms of the chair, and the room dimmed for an instant. With her mouth gaping open, she tried to process what he said. Her ears started functioning again, and she heard him already making another appointment for her to return and see an obstetrician. She mumbled, "Did you say six weeks pregnant?"

"Yes, I did. You're not pleased with the diagnosis? If you aren't, there are other options," he replied, noticing the ashen color of her face.

Outrage boiled up, and her face reddened before she controlled it. "Believe me, I know all about options. I have paid a heavy price for one for years. And I'm still paying."

"I'm sorry. It is my job to offer."

"No, I'm the one who should apologize, not you."

"I don't want you to make the same mistake again, if the first one was an error."

A light bulb went off as she considered what the doctor said and replied, "The first one was a chance of a new life for all concerned. Not a wrong decision. Thank you, doctor, for all your help." Her sound judgment in the past, in doing the correct thing, primarily guided the conclusion. A gift for all their futures.

Before leaving, April stopped at the reception desk to get her next appointment confirmed. She walked out of the clinic in a fog. Driving home in a fuzzy state of mind wasn't the safest move. What other choice did she have? She punched the opener to close the garage behind her and stumbled into the kitchen. Slamming the inside door shut, she slid her body down the wall, crumpled to the floor, and hugged her knees. Rocking back and forth, she squeezed her hands together and wept. *Not again.* Panic threatened to take over, which made it hard to catch her breath.

April replayed the words the doctor said and tried to make sense of them before her focus shut down. Possibly later, sanity returned. At this moment, all she dwelled on was that both times she slept with Brock Ruggle, she ended up pregnant.

She eventually pulled herself off the cold tile and made a cup of tea. Taking it to her bedroom, she placed it on the dresser and stripped out of her clothes. Looking at her body in the mirror, she placed a hand over her stomach. Would she be raising this one by herself?

She stepped into the shower after the water warmed up, and once more found herself on her butt, sobbing nonstop. Water cascaded down her back, mixing with the tears. The emotion of being vulnerable and miserable, with no transparent solutions, didn't go away. Lost, the only word she came up with. She leaned her head back against the shower wall and tried to stop crying. Her life was a mess. Nothing in her past prepared her for the forlorn sensations washing over her.

Rather than go to bed, April went to the porch swing and let it sway gently, gazing at the dusky sky. Moments like these were when she missed Bonnie and the advice. Since they never discussed the parentage of her first baby, the two of them would have faced a heart to heart talk this time. She rested her hand in the middle of her chest to calm the rising anxiety before her life exploded.

Neither she nor Brock thought about the chance of pregnancy. Okay, maybe they rushed sixteen years ago because of the foolishness of their youth. Even though they were older and supposedly more responsible, they'd let passion overrule common sense again. April would pay the price once more, only now the amount was nonnegotiable!

She'd had her heart ripped out once before. Not again. The memory of her first baby never faded away. Was this new precious life she carried a gift? Yes, a second opportunity to be the mother of the child she carried. Blessed in a way made possible by how Bonnie provided for her. With determination, the decision to keep this child became the easiest ever made. Whether Brock supported her and this baby didn't matter. If she lost Riley and Brock, at least she wouldn't be alone, even if she needed to go back to Oklahoma City, away from him. Her baby, her choice again.

April finished the homework for the next day of classes and warmed up a bowl of soup. The doctor advised her to eat light until the morning sickness passed. She relived her first pregnancy. Eating crackers, drinking ginger ale, and sleeping more, including daytime naps, became common practice then. Now once more she followed the helpful hints.

The next day, she confirmed the appointment with the obstetrician. With a few weeks left of the school year, the short length could work to her advantage. Once she got past the morning nausea, her condition would become easier. Summer break provided a convenient cover for her pregnancy.

Because she wasn't due until November, she delayed her decision about returning to work. Besides, she really wanted to savor the pleasure of being a mother and raising her baby. Thanks to Bonnie's generous help, she no longer worried about providing for herself or her child. She went to bed and put everything out of her mind. Seeing rest was vital for her health and her baby.

The next morning, she ate the crackers happily until she remembered what hurdle still faced her. To be honest with her first child. If Riley desired, she vowed to remain in contact. The peaceful resolve melted away.

Chloe met her in the hallway later in the day. "Did you see the doctor?"

April stuttered, "Yeah, I did."

"Okay, was it a bug or something else?"

"Why do you need to ask?"

"I want to help if I can."

Tears quickly formed in her eyes, and she blinked to clear them. "Thank you. I may take you up on the offer if the need arises."

Chloe hugged her. "I'm here for you."

Chloe left to go to her own classroom, and April's resolve approximately faded the second Riley walked into the hallway. It'd break her heart if he forced her to leave the school, making this week her last.

Maybe it was her imagination or paranoia, but something strange was going on with Riley, especially lately. It appeared the girl fumbled with the right words to say around her.

April got through the rest of Thursday with her secret. Calling Brock late on Friday morning would ensure he didn't rush over before work and demand answers. Her chance of staying in their lives depended on admitting everything to Brock. When he first arrived at the lawyer's office, she detected anger. His negative feelings towards her likely stemmed from her past choices. Before they left the building, he seemed patient. Today she knew time was up for her, because he deserved the whole truth. What Riley thought of her caused her pulse to race with fear more than facing Brock. Whether her daughter's choice was love, acceptance, or even hatred, it encompassed staying strong and accepting whatever judgment came her way.

On her lunch break on Friday, she picked up her phone. She swallowed the fear and dialed his number. "Hi, Brock. Are you free to come over this evening? We need to discuss some things." He exhaled into the phone, and she wasn't sure whether it sounded like anticipation or anxiety or relief. Her nerve faltered.

"Is six o'clock okay with you?"

"Yes, six will be fine."

Hanging up, she also sighed, then inhaled and exhaled a deep breath to release the tension to get through the rest of her day. April changed and nibbled on a cracker after she arrived home. No one and nothing would put her second chance at risk.

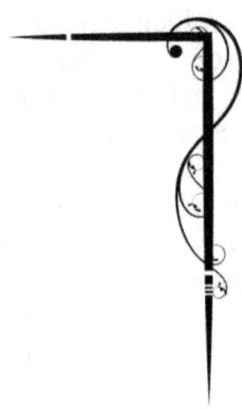

Chapter 22

Brock almost lost all patience with April well before her phone call. He was stunned that she wanted to talk at her house and not at the ranch with Riley. Understandably, he didn't want Riley to be alone and asked his housekeeper if she'd stay because he might get home late. Between the discussion about to happen and the uncertain future with April, his anxiety stayed elevated.

With a deep breath, he knocked on her door, eager for the meeting to go well. April responded the minute he withdrew his hand and ushered him in. He forced a smile onto his face. "Hi, I am glad you called." He noticed the dark circles under her eyes and saw her nervousness. A sign of little sleep and a lot of stress.

She lowered her head and started through the living room. "We can talk in the kitchen."

Left without a choice, he followed her into the room, where they stood and faced each other with apprehension. Time appeared to stop while he waited for her to speak

She finally broke the silence. "How about a cup of coffee? I'm afraid all I have is decaf. "

"Sure, decaf is fine." He pulled a chair out and sat down.

April stayed glued to the counter until the coffee brewed, then sat down when they both held a cup in their hands. She gripped her cup with white knuckles. "I need to start at the beginning, don't I?"

Sensitive of her situation, Brock chose his words carefully. "I've found that starting at the beginning is best. Bonnie's letter left out some crucial details, didn't it?" To this day, he knew she hid parts of her life from him.

"Yes, it did."

"Just tell me how everything started."

"I'm still trying to understand what drew me to you. A defenseless girl on the street shouldn't have walked off with a total stranger," April admitted with shyness and then a hint of bewilderment.

Brock reeled at the revelation. "You intrigued and then completely mesmerized me from the beginning."

"The evening, running out of the shelter, I'll admit I hid from you. Initially, betrayal and anger consumed me, then pain replaced those emotions. Most of the street people knew me by my first name, and it wasn't difficult to fade away back into the invisible street urchin. I convinced myself you were like other people who wanted to ease their guilt for having more. To treat me as a charity case. I hadn't trusted you enough to tell you about my dreams, which read more like fantasies."

Brock interrupted. "My search for you ended when it became clear you preferred to remain hidden."

"I know and am sorry. I didn't think I fit into your world. Then your apparent rejection made it worse."

"I have told you I'm sorry for the whole thing of turning my back on you."

"You explained your reasons, and I understand and accept them."

Brock looked over at her clinging to the cup like a lifeline. He wanted to draw her to him and make the pain go away, but he needed to hear the rest of her story for his own peace of mind. "How did Bonnie find you?"

"She didn't. I went to the clinic down the street from the shelter. The nurse then suggested I go to the shelter Bonnie oversaw. She carried the reputation of helping young girls in trouble and just kind of stepped in and offered me help. She told me later about the baby she lost years ago, who might have lived with better care. The one with red hair like mine." April rose and poured more coffee to regain her courage. "The first night we were together, I hadn't thought to look in your wallet for any identification. I opened it to take the money for food. I didn't think any reason existed for me to know your entire name or where you lived."

"What I can't comprehend is why you didn't explain all this to me months ago," Brock said in frustration.

"I feared if you discovered I gave away our baby, you would take away my new life. A fresh beginning, which I loved. Then blame me for denying you the chance to have loved a child of your own. Honestly, the baby's identity was unknown to me."

"Riley's birth certificate listed you as her mother, and I became quite angry. I think what hurt the most was the part about father unknown."

"Bonnie knew you and put two and two together. I didn't know the woman, and your parents knew each other and, well, you know the rest."

"Yes, she fostered Riley from birth until Julie got married."

"Please, Brock, believe me. I assumed a family adopted the infant right after her birth. She never told me any details except, my baby would go to a loving home."

"I met and fell in love with Riley when she was three years old." Brock's eyes filled with unshed tears. "She loved butterflies, and the first gift I bought was a necklace with one on it. You must have imprinted butterflies on her somehow." He smirked slyly. "I know I liked the one I saw."

April blushed. "Yes, she admitted having seen mine at the shelter, slipping in to get cookies. I stayed in the kitchen away from the little kids and didn't see her. It caused too much pain." She wiped more liquid from her face and raised her head, then asked. "What's our next step?"

"I don't have all the answers. We have to tell her together, though. She's acting weird around me," Brock answered.

"You noticed this strange behavior, too?"

Lost in his own suppositions, he gripped his cup of coffee. Once again, it proved his turn to sit in nerve-wracking silence while he wondered how to proceed. He eventually found his voice after another bout of quietness, and asked, "When do you want to do this?"

"The sooner the better." April paused. "Before I..." Then she bowed her head with a torrent of tears streaming down her face.

Brock reached over the table and took her hands in his and squeezed them. "Before you do what, exactly? And please don't tell me you are running again." He asked tentatively with his anger beginning to simmer.

She wept, barely audible, "Before showing... you know... the baby bump?"

Brock's breath stopped; his heart melted on the spot. He repeated, "Our baby bump." Then he swallowed the sudden lump in his throat.

"Yes, I'm not giving this baby away, even if I have to raise him or her by myself." April declared with her eyes flashing a brighter shade of blue than he had ever seen, and her head raised higher.

"I wouldn't have wanted you to give the first one away," he said with regret and tenderness.

"You really didn't know? Bonnie hadn't told you?"

When he first discovered the truth, he speculated whether she had known all along through Bonnie, who Riley belonged to now. He read her mind and, to ease the doubts they both experienced, said, "No, neither of us knew, sweetheart."

April looked up because he called her by the endearment. "You want this one too?" she asked in a whisper.

The raspiness in his own words hinted at the depth of his feelings. "Oh, hell yes, I want our baby. And if you will have me, I want you too. I have loved you for so long."

She responded with a softness he noticed right away. "I have always loved you and will forever." The barrier between his heart and hers crumbled like a too-dry cookie. The absence of the protective shield around their hearts exposed their love for each other.

They both cried over the baby. With a promise to raise the next one together, his heart soared.

Overwhelmed with love, he almost didn't hear, "When do we tell Riley?"

She started towards the sink with her empty cup, but he reached for her and gently pulled her onto his lap. He cradled her face in his hands and with his thumbs wiped her face, then kissed her eyes before moving to her lips. His mouth brushed over hers with intense passion. They gasped for air and tried to recapture the losses. He broke away from her momentarily and said, "We will go home in the morning and tell her. I warned Mrs. Shefield she might have to spend the night, optimistically hopeful our talk worked out. It has; I want you for myself."

April kissed him with passion and breathed, "I want to make love to you, and I know I'm selfish, because I don't want to share you tonight with anyone, not even our daughter."

Brock stood up with her in his arms and walked to her bedroom. With tender care, he placed her on the bed. Leaning over, he allowed the longings suppressed for years to escape and kissed her again before he raised back up and stared at her with anticipation clear in his eyes, along with apprehension.

She asked, "Why the serious look?"

"Has there been anyone, you know…?"

"No, not a soul."

"Although I went on dates, I felt guilty and unfaithful. Julie told me years ago after I met, then lost you, that I searched for something or someone. Now I know it was you." He splayed his fingers and held them on her stomach, which showed the slight bump of their second child. "I can't believe we get to raise this one together."

April stated, "I know. How blessed are we?" She placed her hands on top of his in a silent pledge.

Brock explored the recesses of her body. She moaned as he ran his fingers up her thigh, then gingerly touched her breast. "Are they sore?"

"Not yet," she replied. "Why don't you take advantage of them now?" She added, "I wouldn't object."

He obliged her willingly. Mesmerized by each breast, he took a nipple into his mouth and suckled. The likelihood of his child in the future nursing on them brought a wave of euphoria. He finally proceeded down her body with his mouth until he found the curly red mound between her legs. Before he replaced his lips with his hardness, he looked at her through awe and concern. "This is alright, isn't it? You know, with the baby?"

"You won't hurt either of us."

Brock sighed in relief and spoke from his heart. "I love you more now than ever before. You and our children are my life."

"I love you, too."

The moment she said the word love; he thrust into her waiting heat and savored. The movement gave more exquisite pleasure than he ever thought possible. Afterward, he cuddled her in his arms. She sighed, and he let the passion settle until they both fell asleep.

Brock woke up well before daylight. He looked lovingly down at the woman wrapped in his arms, asleep. She stirred enough to place her head on his chest. He stroked her hair to lull her back into the necessary rest she needed. He knew the past pregnancy explained the curvier curves, more luscious than before. His mind raced ahead to the shape of her body carrying their baby and fantasized about her glowing like a bright star. To actually be a witness to this every step of the way was going to be a dream come true.

Carefully, he slipped out of bed and made his way to the kitchen to make coffee. Having poured a full cup, he sat at the table with a huge grin permanently plastered on his face. His ego soared as he thought about April's response to him, resulting in two precious lives.

Brock poured her a cup and walked into the bedroom. She wasn't in bed. Then he heard her in the bathroom. Stepping in lightly, he asked, "What can I do?"

"Get me a glass of water, please?"

Handing her the liquid, he wet a washcloth and wiped her damp forehead. "I'm sorry."

"You should be. This is all your fault."

"I'm pretty sure you took part," he laughed.

When the nausea subsided, he helped her back to the bed. She noticed the cup he placed on the dresser. "Is this for me?"

"Only if you want it, or I can make you something else." A novel experience lay in wait, and he was a little at a loss about what to do.

"No, let me have a sip. The morning sickness has lessened over the last few days. Soon it will be gone."

Later, April secured a robe over her naked body, and they walked into the kitchen, where he poured more coffee. He brought up the other pressing matter they faced in the room. "We need to talk about Riley."

"I know I'm scared."

"Don't be. It is going to be fine," he reassured her.

"How can you be sure? What if she hates me?"

"She already loves you."

"Yeah, like her teacher. Will I be a good mother?"

Brock took her hands in his, rubbing one thumb over her knuckles. "You were a caring mother the minute you realized she needed more than you could give her. She's a reasonable kid. Once we explain the circumstances, she'll understand."

She brushed her lips over his thumb. "Oh, Brock, you have to be right."

"Trust me, I am."

They sat at the table for a few more minutes and sipped their coffee. He waited patiently for a reply. With what seemed like a lifetime to him, she answered, "Okay, I trust you. We will go to her and explain everything."

"Good. But first, my stomach is grumbling. You remember we didn't have any dinner last night? You seduced me instead."

"I did no such thing," she squeaked. "Like this baby on the way. All your fault."

"Alright, I'll take the blame for both. Except don't tell anyone I caved."

"I promise I won't. What do you want for breakfast? I have eggs and sausage links."

"Are you sure you can handle it?"

"Yeah, once it subsides, I'm okay."

Brock watched her put the links in a skillet, and then she grated some cheese for their eggs. Her movements were precise; she didn't waste any motion between putting the bread in the toaster and turning the sausage. Curious, he said, "Don't take offense. I wonder how you learned to cook growing up the way you did?"

"No offense taken. While in college, as an added distraction, Bonnie convinced me to volunteer in the kitchen. Connie, an older woman at the shelter, worked in restaurants. She took me under her wing and taught me how."

He stared at April once more. "You amaze me."

"Why? Because I can cook."

"Yes, but there's more. By the way, others forced you to begin your life and how you have overcome obstacles and excelled."

"I suppose I grew stronger than even I thought possible."

Brock laughed. "Not very many young girls have the nerve to rescue a drunken stranger off the streets and then go with him to his dorm room."

April looked at him with love in her eyes. "Perhaps I saw something worthwhile, even back then."

"I'm glad you saw value in me then. And I hope you will let me prove the cost was worth the price." Brock sauntered towards her and gave her a passionate kiss where she stood, wrapping her body tightly in his arms. A different hunger replaced all thoughts of food.

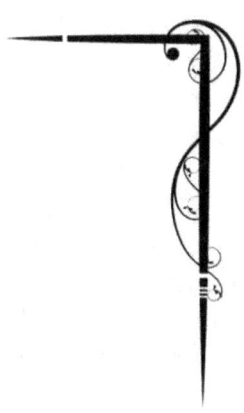

Chapter 23

After the mind-blowing kiss, April's reasoning resumed. "What did you tell Riley about not being home last night?"

"I said nothing about a date to her. Left that chore to Mrs. Sheffield."

"You didn't tell her whom?"

"No, for one thing, it wasn't any business of my housekeeper's knowing who I was with, and I wasn't sure about our talk."

"Terrific, Riley will be upset before we even get to the ranch."

"Then, seeing you will be a surprise for her."

"I sincerely hope it will be an agreeable revelation."

"It will be fine. I promise."

They finished their breakfast and cleaned up the dishes. Brock called Mrs. Shefield and told her they were on their way to the ranch. April went to the bedroom to get dressed. He followed her in to find his shoes and shirt. Fire stirred in her stomach at the view of him naked to the waist. Not being able to drag her eyes away, she encircled his hard chest and gave him a fiery kiss with the same intensity as the one he gave her in the kitchen. With hunger-filled eyes, she took his hand and led him to the shower.

While the water warmed, she ran her hands down his muscular chest. Those sexy tufts of hair tickled her fingers. She didn't break eye contact with him and unzipped his jeans. Brock tried to pull her hands away to finish taking his jeans off. She slapped his hand. Assuming control empowered her. She gripped his rigid length through his boxers, and watched, enthralled, as he growled. April gasped for breath before she removed his boxers.

Her own courage amazed her. Was this the version she kept hidden all her life? A brave and bold woman. She enjoyed every single minute with a joyful heart and investigated the new power.

The drive to the ranch sped by. Her heart raced in anticipation as she clung to his hand for the entire ride. Brock's words of encouragement gave her hope for the strength needed to face her daughter.

When they entered the house, silence greeted them. She wasn't sure if the quiet welcomed or cursed her. Brock kissed her cheek for reassurance and said, "I'll see if Riley is in her room. Will you be alright here until I get back?"

"Yes, go ahead. I'll sit on the couch and wait." April looked around the room. Pictures of Riley sat on the fireplace mantel. Before looking at them, they were merely photographs of her student. One frame held an array of photos — pre-school, kindergarten, and on through her present year. Little changed in her looks over the years. Tapping her hand to her heart, she tried to keep the pain under control and fought to keep herself together.

She stepped away from the mantelpiece as Brock walked into the room, knowing her face exposed her thoughts. He stepped closer and put an arm over her shoulder. "Riley wasn't in her room. After we talk to her, there are albums Julie made of her life. You can look at them all you want."

April pulled a tissue out of her pocket. Tears threatened to fall. She softly touched his chest and said, "Yes, I want to look at them."

"Come with me and we'll find Mrs. Shefield."

They walked into the kitchen; the housekeeper stood at the sink washing dishes. She turned and smiled at their interlocked hands.

"Where is Riley?" Brock asked.

Mrs. Shefield shook her head at them. "I told her you called and were bringing a guest home. She said she didn't want to see your new friend. Then she left a few minutes ago on her horse."

"Which way?" he asked.

"Toward the lake," she told him.

Brock looked at April. "Do you feel like a ride?"

"We don't have a choice," April replied.

He called down to the barn and asked one of the ranch hands to saddle their horses. Brock helped her onto Pepper and then got on Pegasus. They set off across the field together to find their daughter, riding on the same path taken before. April twisted her head around and looked at the trees, which seemed taller. The grasses leaned farther over onto the ground and swayed in the breeze. "Why does the land look different to me?"

"You know you are home."

Skeptically, she replied, "Only if she accepts me."

Brock answered, "She will."

Seeing Brock didn't reveal his date's identity; a potential problem exacerbated the situation. Meanwhile, April prayed that if they explained everything, she would accept them as her parents. They kept riding towards their daughter.

Brock pointed towards the lake, where Riley sat on a rock beside the water. They tied their horses to the tree alongside Riley's mount. April nodded and took a deep breath. With their hands entwined, they walked closer to the edge. He squeezed her hands, giving her strength.

Speaking, Riley did not turn towards them. "Is it true?"

Brock spoke, "What?"

"Are you my father?"

"Yes."

"And I am your mother, Riley." April's apprehension vanished the exact minute she spoke the words out loud.

The sound of April's voice caused Riley to turn her head towards them. It took all of her resolve not to run and embrace her when she saw the girl's tear-stained face. Instead, she squared her shoulders and held back. Truth required them to explain and let their daughter make up her own mind and hopefully accept them.

Brock sat down on one side of Riley, and April took the other side. He asked, "Will you listen to us?"

The teen reached into her pocket and took out her phone, opened it up and handed it to him. "Yes, I think you two have a lot of explaining to do."

He flipped through the pictures. "How did you find these?"

"They were on your desk. I knew something happened. I snuck into your office looking for answers."

"Despite knowing you shouldn't be in there." Brock handed the phone to April.

She handed the phone back to Riley after scanning the pictures of the documents. Brock disciplined Riley even at this precarious time, proving him to be a good father. She took a deep breath and asked, "Okay, now you know the basic facts. Did you want the entire story?"

"Yes, I want the whole truth. Tell me everything." Riley cried.

"On the evening Brock and I met; we knew nothing about each other except our first names." Riley was old enough not to need sugar-coated facts, and April chose not to. "Our instant attraction led to your conception."

She looked over at him with a deeper, safer knowledge of those feelings, which shone deeply in her eyes. His look mirrored hers. Before she spoke again, he reached over for her hand and embraced it with encouragement. They left their entwined hands on Riley's lap. "You know I lived in foster care and then was a runaway. Once I found out I was pregnant, I chose a better life for you. Hear this and believe me, Riley. I always loved you and still do. I prefer to stay in your life if you will allow me to." She held her breath, watched, and asked warily, "Do you hate me?"

April and Brock previously discussed how to approach Riley and decided she'd handle most of the explanations. He stayed quiet. The girl looked at one and then the other. Silence fell over the lake while they waited for an answer.

Brock prompted. "What do you think? Will you allow April to stay and make me a lucky man? And us a family," His face glowed with emotion.

Riley stood up in front of them with a huge grin, tears running down her cheeks. "My heart won't permit me to hate either of you. I understand why you chose for me to have a chance at a good life and why you didn't tell Uncle." Her usual name for him outweighed the new one. "Now I have a second chance to have great parents again."

They stayed at the lake and talked well into the afternoon. April answered all the questions for Riley happily. She told her more details of how she and Brock met and in what way everything happened. The most important aspect she wanted to express was that neither of them was aware of her true identity.

When they finished their story, Riley sat up straighter and looked at them. "Now I want to say something."

Brock and April both said with apprehension, "Okay."

"Don't let all of Miss Burton's hard work and planning go to waste. Finish raising me together like she wanted."

Overwhelmed with joy, April cried uncontrollably. Riley approached her with open arms, reaching out to be hugged. Her arms instinctively tightened, not wanting to let go.

Brock wiped his own eyes and said, "See, I told you our daughter was smart and reasonable."

April laughed, then sobered when Riley spoke again. "It'll take some time until we get to know each other in this way."

"We both love you and want you to understand we always will. We love each other also and want to become a family." Tears flowed freely down April's face.

They rode back to the ranch, and April insisted she should go home. It wasn't like she wanted to leave, but her instincts kicked in and told her Brock needed to spend some moments alone with Riley. Truth be told, she needed to be by herself. So much transpired in less than twenty-four hours. Her head spun like a top.

Brock and Riley both accepted her without judgment. Though they hadn't worked out any specifics about the future, she pinched herself to make sure everything wasn't a dream anymore.

He called her at least twice in the evening, and she assured him she was fine and needed to adjust.

"Please don't change your mind, April."

"Why? I have everything I ever dreamed of. Good night, my love."

"I love you too. We will talk in the morning."

Sunday morning dawned brightly. Perhaps the feeling of acceptance made the sunlight look extra dazzling. Riley's

"Good morning" pleasantly surprised her when she answered her phone.

She stuttered, "Good morning yourself."

"I wanted to make sure you were okay."

"Don't worry about me. I'm fine. How are you doing?"

"I still can't believe everything. This doesn't mean I'm not happy, because I am."

"Sounds good." The joy in Riley's voice mirrored April's own. Before ending the call, she spent a few minutes talking to Brock, confirming she was fine, and that she loved him.

April went back to her job on Monday, beaming. Chloe stopped her in the hallway. "You are glowing. The weekend and your issues with a certain person must have worked out."

"Better than I ever thought possible."

"Good, you deserve it."

With school almost out, April stopped tutoring Riley. Instead, the two spent the days looking at family photo albums and got to know each other in a different light. They teased each other, laughed and shed tears frequently. Truth and affection flowed between them, thrilling her with Riley's acceptance. She loved every second. Brock often came home early, whether from the law office or from work at the stables, and joined them. She appreciated the fact that he had afforded them space to be alone together.

Two weeks passed swiftly. She pinched herself again and again at the prospect of a genuine family. The three settled into a comfortable routine. Neither she nor Brock discussed the future and what it potentially held, even though they professed their love for each other every day. Did he expect her to move in and live with them, or did he want them to co-parent Riley and the baby living apart?

She tried not to dwell on it too much. Indecision wasn't healthy for the baby.

At the end of the last week of school, Riley bounced into the living room on Friday after she completed her homework. "What about a family camping trip?"

April looked up and asked, "When?"

"How about this weekend? The weather is supposed to be nice."

"It sounds good to me. Have you talked to Brock?"

"Oh, I already asked Dad, and he said yes."

April's legs turned to jelly from Riley's statement; grateful she hadn't gotten up from the table yet. Her daughter called Brock Dad. While pleased for him, slight envy lingered within her. She pushed down her discomfort at the lack of "Mom" and asked. "How can I argue with the two of you? Let's go to the lake." Riley squealed.

Two tents greeted them on the gravel pad. April laughed. She glanced at the familiar ground by the lake and raised her eyebrows at Brock. "Are you going to sleep in here with me?"

"Yeah. Perhaps in the future, join me under the stars and night sky."

"You could have saved whoever set this tent up if you had asked me where I wanted to sleep," she boldly stated.

"Are you implying you'll give up your tent for my sleeping bag?"

"If you say please?"

"Oh, I can say please."

Their lighthearted banter showed her a more relaxed side of the man she loved from the old Brock. She liked this one better.

The sunset in the evening glowed spectacularly. Reds, oranges, and dark blue streaked across the horizon. She sat beside Riley as they once again roasted hot dogs along with the cowboy beans Brock warmed up. Her heart swelled with delight and with the logic of perfection. How foolish of her to assume the two people she cared for most would abandon her.

While Brock placed more wood on the fire, she totally enjoyed the view of his broad and strong back, amazed at how he kept in shape by working on the ranch. Longing for the child she carried to be a son for him to pass on the knowledge and good morals to, she sighed. Then she realized it didn't matter whether their child was a boy or girl, they'd raise and love it the same.

April didn't complain that Riley went to bed after the fire died down to a soft glow. She and Brock sat by themselves. The evening air cooled, and they enjoyed the bright stars, which multiplied in abundance in the darkened sky. She shivered from the chill of the dying fire and snuggled closer to him. He pulled her tighter and whispered, "How's my baby tonight?"

"Which one? Me or the baby?"

"Both." She melted when he placed his hand on her barely noticeable bump.

April reached for Brock and tenderly nibbled on his lips. Running her hands down his back, she caressed the muscles she always admired. The touch made them ripple beneath the shirt. He growled and returned the kiss before he pushed her down on the sleeping bag. Her mind went blank, and he took her to a different world. A realm where the stars raced across the sky in a silver blaze. Not being able to do anything but moan, she let go and enjoyed the ride.

The next morning dawned without a cloud in sight. Some major decisions were ahead of them. April merely admired the sunrise from where she sat by the campfire to stay toasty. She strove for the calmness that seeped into her soul to last. While she sipped her coffee, Riley and Brock's giggling discussion caught her attention before the pair approached the fire, hand in hand, and sat down beside her.

A sudden wave of nausea hit her. She held her breath for a minute. "Oh no, I am going to get sick, Brock."

He jumped up and got her a bottle of water, ignoring Riley's curious look. "Take a sip and I'll get you a cracker."

"Okay, thanks."

Riley, with an intriguing gaze, asked, "What is going on? You don't seem surprised she is sick to her stomach."

Brock's face beamed with happiness as he looked at their daughter and then back at her. April knew it was time to confess their last secret. She swallowed the sudden rush of nerves and took the cracker from him. Her heart raced. "We are going to have a baby."

Riley opened her mouth, speechless. What if their daughter became upset? The idea of different parents was still new to her. April's eyes quickly focused on Brock with her breath paused. He didn't move a muscle either. The teen stood, turned around, and jumped up and down. "Oh, wow, a baby. A little sister."

"Well, perhaps a little brother," Brock said.

"It doesn't matter which, as long as we are all together."

Brock stood and pulled them both up and into his arms. "Since we are confessing, I have something very important to say. Riley, do you think you would be okay if I ask April to marry me?"

Riley asked, "She's pregnant and you haven't asked Mom yet?"

Brock shook his head. "No, not in a proper proposal."

April stared with enormous eyes. Mom! Her daughter just called her mom. Lost in the surge of even more love and talk of confessions, a marriage offer hadn't crossed her mind. She opened her eyes wide, looked at him and Riley. Her heart overflowed at the obvious sight of his love. No doubts lingering in her mind.

He stood up from the log and took two steps toward her. After he lowered to one knee, he pulled a box out of his pocket. Opening it, his hand shook. When she glanced at the beautifully cut diamond, he asked, "April Maria Palmer, will you marry me?"

She glanced at Riley, who bounced up and down on the log, not in the least bit surprised. "Is this what the two were whispering about?" Love touched her heart and soul. Her own hands trembled. "Yes, I would love to marry you."

The wedding took place at the lakeside after school ended for the summer. A few close friends attended the simple, elegant ceremony. After their guests left, just the two of them rode to the lake. The only difference this time, grilled steak and new potatoes replaced the hot dogs just this once. It was their honeymoon, after all.

Aaron Andrew Ruggle arrived in the world right before Thanksgiving. Brock and April put their arms around their daughter and newborn son. Hugging them tightly, April said, "Now we are a genuine family." Silently, she raised her eyes to thank the compassionate counselor who, with her own heart's decision, had made April's heart's desire come true.

About the Author

Jeanie Clayton is an award-winning author of contemporary romance stories. Retiring from the lifelong restaurant business and after reading countless romance novels, she discovered storylines of her own begging to be unlocked. She lives with Gracie, her Shih tzu in southwest Missouri and enjoys new traveling adventures with her family.

www.ingramcontent.com/pod-product-compliance
Lightning Source LLC
Chambersburg PA
CBHW051454170626
46811CB00002B/485